Like many authors, Lesley started  chequered beginning, including j crew and nightclub DJ, she fell in including *Business Matters*, *Which?*,

She progressed to short stories for the vibrant women's magazine market and, following a Master's degree where she met her publisher, she turned to her first literary love of traditional British mysteries. The Libby Sarjeant series is still going strong, and has been joined by The Alexandrians, an Edwardian mystery series.

Praise for Lesley Cookman:

'Nicely staged drama and memorable and strangely likeable characters'
Trisha Ashley

'With fascinating characters and an intriguing plot, this is a real page turner'
Katie Fforde

'Lesley Cookman is the Queen of Cosy Crime'
Paul Magrs

'Intrigue, romance and a touch of murder in a picturesque village setting'
Liz Young

'A compelling series where each book leaves you satisfied but also eagerly waiting for the next one'
Bernardine Kennedy

'A quaint, British cozy, complete with characters who are both likeable and quirky'
Rosalee Richland

MURDER IN AUTUMN

LESLEY COOKMAN

ACCENT

First published in 2023 by Headline Accent
An imprint of HEADLINE PUBLISHING GROUP

1

Cataloguing in Publication Data is available from the British Library

ISBN 978 1 0354 0566 4

Typeset in 10.5/13pt Bembo Std by Jouve (UK), Milton Keynes

Printed and bound in Great Britain by Clays Ltd, Elcograf S.p.A.

HEADLINE PUBLISHING GROUP
An Hachette UK Company
Carmelite House
50 Victoria Embankment
London
EC4Y 0DZ

www.headline.co.uk
www.hachette.co.uk

To the wonderful professionals in the NHS.
Thank you for all your help.

The village of
Steeple Martin

Allhallow's Lane

High Street

to Canterbury

Oast House
Theatre

Manor Drive

The Manor

The Pink
Geranium

Pub

Maltby Close

Steeple Farm

to Nethergate

S. Alison

Character List

Libby Sarjeant
Former actor and part-time artist, mother to Dominic, Belinda and Adam Sarjeant and owner of Sidney the cat. Resident of 17 All-hallow's Lane, Steeple Martin.

Fran Wolfe
Former actor and occasional psychic. Owner of Balzac the cat and resident of Coastguard Cottage, Nethergate.

Ben Wilde
Libby's significant other. Owner of the Manor and the Oast Theatre.

Guy Wolfe
Fran's husband and father to Sophie Wolfe. Artist and owner of a shop and gallery in Harbour Street, Nethergate.

Peter Parker
Freelance journalist, part owner of the Pink Geranium restaurant. Ben's cousin and Harry Price's partner.

Harry Price
Chef and co-owner of the Pink Geranium. Peter Parker's partner.

Hetty Wilde
Ben's mother. Lives at the Manor.

Flo Carpenter
Hetty's oldest friend

Lenny Fisher
Hetty's brother. Lives with Flo Carpenter.

DCI Ian Connell
Local policeman and friend.

Detective Sergeant Rachel Trent
Local police officer and friend.

Constable Mark Alleyn
Local police officer.

Philip Jacobs
Barrister.

Constance Matthews
Former professional colleague of Libby's.

Freddie Cannon
Member of Glover's Men theatre company

Oliver Marcus
Member of Glover's Men theatre company.

Lady Prudence (Pru) Howe
Chatelaine of the Howe Estate.

Miss Dorothy Barton
Lives in Temptation House.

Nora
Tenant in Temptation House, companion to Dorothy Barton.

Karen Butler
Tenant in Temptation House, friend to Nora.

Hannah Barton
Resident of Nethergate

Trevor Taylor
Estate agent.

Barney
A dog.

Ricky Short
Barney's owner.

Jim Butler
Local resident.

Jinny Mardle
Libby's next-door neighbour.

Judy Dale
Singer – stage name Sadie O'Day

Cyd Russell
Another singer, Judy's friend.

Chapter One

Libby Sarjeant eased her foot off the accelerator and pulled in to the side of the road. Her phone, resting on the passenger seat beside her, buzzed with an incoming message, which she ignored, instead bringing up the map she had found earlier.

This part of Kent, practically London, she thought, was unfamiliar. She consulted the map again and peered out of the windscreen. Yes – there was the sign: 'Ashbury'. She felt an unfamiliar sinking somewhere in her insides and sighed. Checking behind her, she put the car in gear and set off again. Ten minutes later, she was pulling up outside Pendlebury Lodge, a self-important-looking Victorian building. A bit like its owner.

'Constance! How lovely to see you.'

'Libby. You're late.' The short, grey-haired woman leaning on a silver-headed stick stepped back from Libby's attempted kiss. 'Come in and collect my bags.'

Libby rolled her eyes. 'No "hello, Libby, good of you to come and collect me?" or even a smile?'

The woman called Constance raised her eyebrows. 'Why? How else would I get to Steeple Martin?'

'Train, perhaps?' muttered Libby, following her down the dark hallway.

Constance Matthews indicated two suitcases and retrieved a coat and handbag from a chair. 'Come along then. Let's not waste any more time.'

Libby managed to lift the two cases. 'How long are you staying?' she grunted. 'I thought you were just coming down to see the performance?'

'All that way just for one night?' Constance led the way back to the front door. 'Of course not.'

'Where are you staying?' asked Libby, as they emerged into the daylight again.

'With you.' Constance looked surprised.

Libby dropped the suitcases. 'With me? But I don't have room!'

'What do you mean, you don't have room?' Constance's face assumed the icy expression Libby remembered of old.

'I only have two bedrooms, and my cottage is tiny,' she said.

'One for you and one for me.' Constance turned to the car.

'No, Constance. One for me and my partner, Ben, and one for friends who are also coming to the performance.' Libby stood back, hands on hips. 'We booked you a room – for *one* night – at our local pub.'

'*Pub*?' Now Constance's voice was glacial.

'It's a hotel, actually,' Libby hastened to correct herself. 'Very good food.'

'What are you talking about?' Constance tried to wrench open the car door. 'I am staying with you. I do not eat pub food.'

Libby sighed with exasperation. 'In that case, Constance, I've had a wasted journey.'

'What do you mean?' Constance was now looking less sure of herself.

'If, when you asked me if you could come and see *Much Ado About Nothing*, you had asked if you could stay with me, I would have said unfortunately not. And I would have saved myself a journey through Kent.' She picked up one of the cases and returned it to the doorstep.

'All right,' Constance snapped. 'You'll have to wait while I unpack a few things, then.' She marched back to the front door and unlocked it, not waiting for Libby, who, with a resigned sigh,

2

manoeuvred the cases back into the hall before returning to sit in her car. Blowed if she was going to heave the damn things back to wherever Constance wanted them.

She should have known, she reflected. Constance Matthews had always been the same, imperious and uncaring of anyone else's feelings. A bloody good director when Libby had been on the professional stage, though, but that had strengthened her power complex. And now she was coming back to the car carrying only her handbag and a small dressing case. She paused as if waiting for Libby to get out of the car and open the door for her, but, when she didn't, opened it for herself and made a petulant performance of climbing in.

'But why has she suddenly got in touch with you after all these years?' Ben had asked.

'The Glovers' Men,' Libby explained. 'She wants to see Shakespeare performed as it was originally, by men. And that's what the Glover's Men do, isn't it?'

'But why you? Why here? There are lots of other venues on their tour.'

'Somehow or other she's found out that I – or we – run the theatre and she wants a free ticket and access to the company. How she knew where I lived heaven only knows.'

So here they were in Libby's little car, driving back down the M2 to Steeple Martin.

'How did you find me?' Libby asked.

'Social media,' came the sharp reply.

'Really?' Libby was surprised. It was like the King admitting to using TikTok.

'Looked up tour dates in Kent and had a look at both venues. You were mentioned.'

'I see. And you got my number from directory enquiries?'

'Of course.'

Libby risked a quick look sideways. Constance was staring through the windscreen, her mouth set in a straight line.

'Suppose I'd said no?' Which I should have done, Libby thought.

'You didn't.' Constance turned her head to look out of the side window. Libby gave up.

It still didn't quite explain it, Libby thought. Would directory enquiries have a number for Libby Sarjeant, Steeple Martin? Without a street address? She could have understood it if the original contact had been via the Oast Theatre, but the call had come to Libby's landline. She scowled out at the road ahead.

'I gather the Glover's Men have performed at your theatre before?' Constance's clipped tones cut through her thoughts.

'Twice,' said Libby. '*Twelfth Night* and the *Dream*.'

'Are they good?'

Libby risked a surprised glance at her passenger. 'Of course they are! They're part of National Shakespeare.' She looked back at the road. 'And that is, after all, the foremost Shakespeare company in the country.'

Constance sniffed. 'No guarantee.'

Libby sighed. It was going to be a long journey.

Just over an hour later, Libby stopped the car outside the Coach and Horses in Steeple Martin's high street. As she clambered out, she spotted a familiar figure about to cross the road towards her.

'Libby!' The Reverend Beth Cole beamed at her. 'Looking forward to tonight?'

Libby made a face and jerked her head backwards. Beth's eyebrows rose.

'Yes, we're all looking forward to it,' Libby said out loud. 'I just have to see my friend into the . . . er – hotel.'

'Ah.' Beth stepped backwards as Libby walked round the car and opened the passenger door.

'About time,' muttered Constance as Libby retrieved the dressing case from the footwell and stood holding the door open.

'Can I help?' Beth's friendly face appeared behind Libby's shoulder.

4

Constance looked up. 'No thank you,' she said coldly.

Beth, unperturbed, stepped back. 'I'll see you later, then, Libby,' she said. 'Good luck.'

Libby glared at Constance, picked up the dressing case and went to open the door into the pub, leaving her passenger to climb out on her own. 'Bloody woman,' she said under her breath.

Tim, the Coach and Horses' landlord, appeared, smiling broadly. 'Welcome!' he said, as Constance pushed her way through the door and past Libby. He looked startled.

'This,' said Libby, preparing to follow, 'is Constance Matthews.' She made a face.

Tim grinned. 'May I take your bag, madam?' he said, and relieved Libby of the dressing case, parking it just inside the door.

Constance turned to face them from just inside the small bar.

'Where is my room?' she demanded.

'I'll show you,' said Tim, waving a hospitable hand. 'This way.'

'Libby can show me.' Constance stayed put. So did Libby.

'This is not my hotel, Constance,' she said, folding her arms. 'Tim is your host.'

'As you have palmed me off on someone else, the least you can do is show me where I am to sleep.' Constance glared at both Libby and Tim, then turned her back.

Libby gave Tim a helpless shrug. 'Stop behaving like a child, Connie Matthews,' she said. 'You aren't my director now – in fact you're not anyone's director now. I'll show you to your room and I'll be back later to take you up to the theatre – and meanwhile, keep a civil tongue in your head.'

Taking Constance by the arm, Libby marched her past an open-mouthed Tim and up the stairs. In silence, she opened the door to room three, which overlooked the pub garden and the green between it and the theatre.

'There,' she said. 'I hope you'll be comfortable, and that you enjoy your dinner.'

She gave a tight smile, turned and went back down the stairs.

5

'Well!' said Tim, as she reached the bottom. 'What a rude old cow!'

Libby giggled. 'Me or her?'

Tim guffawed.

'She thought she was coming to stay with me for a few days.' Libby sighed. 'She wasn't pleased to find that she wasn't.' She spotted the dressing case. 'I'd better take this up.'

'Leave it, I'll do it,' said Tim. 'Want a stiffener before you go?'

'I'd better not,' said Libby with a sigh. 'Lots to do before tonight.'

'Everything sorted up at the theatre? Got their stage rigged up and everything?'

The Glover's Men performed on a replica of an Elizabethan booth stage on the Oast Theatre's normal stage, which added another note of authenticity to their performances.

'Yes, and they're all settled in at the Manor, except for the two you've got here. How are they, by the way?'

Ben's mother Hetty still lived in his family home, the Manor, which had been converted into an upmarket bed and breakfast, and handily stood next to the theatre. The cast and technicians of the company were lodged there, while the director and his assistant were staying at the Coach and Horses.

'Oh, they're fine,' said Tim. 'I just hope they don't run up against Madam up there.'

'Gawd 'elp us!' groaned Libby and shook her head. 'Oh, well. I'd better get on. I'll see you later.'

Libby drove round the corner into Allhallow's Lane and parked opposite Number 17. As soon as she got inside, tripping over Sidney the silver tabby on her way, she pulled out her mobile and went to put the kettle on.

'And tomorrow I'll have to drive her back home again,' she concluded to her friend Fran Wolfe, 'and no doubt listen to complaints all the way there about the Coach, the production, the theatre . . .'

6

'Perhaps she'll want to stay on for a day or so – after all, she thought she was going to – and then you can plead previous engagements.'

'I can't see her wanting to stay on,' said Libby gloomily. 'Not after today's performance.'

'Well, at least you don't have to sit with her in the auditorium tonight,' said Fran. 'You haven't put her with us, have you?'

Fran and her husband Guy were coming to see tonight's performance, and, as Libby had told Constance, were to stay overnight at Number 17.

'No, of course not. She's end of row C, so she can make a quick getaway if she needs to.'

'Why would she need to? I know she had a bit of reputation as a tartar and she's obviously not mellowed, but would she walk out?'

'Quite possibly,' said Libby. 'I just hope she doesn't get into a row with the company. They're such nice lads.'

'Hark at you, Grandma!' Fran was laughing.

'Well, they are. And we're so proud to have them here. It's amazing that they keep coming back after that first time. And especially nice that Oliver Marcus is in the cast, too.'

In fact, it was the third time the Glover's Men had performed at the Oast Theatre. The first had been not long after the troupe's formation, with an acclaimed production of *Twelfth Night*, which had been somewhat marred by a murder. Oliver Marcus, who was playing Benedick in the new production, had first come to the theatre many years ago with a troubled production of *The Second Mrs Tanqueray*, which in fact hadn't gone ahead, and the second visit of the Glover's Men had brought *A Midsummer Night's Dream*, which had been happily unclouded. Libby hoped *Much Ado* would be similarly untroubled.

'They come back because they love the theatre and they love staying with Hetty,' said Fran. 'Now, go on and start getting yourself organised for tonight. We'll see you in the bar.'

Libby would be on duty tonight as house manager, looking after the audience, while Ben would be on hand backstage in case he, as resident stage manager, was needed. And Libby fervently hoped that neither of them would be needed for anything more than a spot of metaphorical hand-holding.

She sighed, put down her phone and went to start an early dinner.

Chapter Two

'Why didn't you tell me you were hoping to stay with me when you first called?' Libby held the pub door open for Constance, who had been waiting on a chair at the foot of the stairs.

'I didn't think I had to.' Constance wouldn't look at her. 'And why didn't you tell me you'd booked me into . . .' she floundered for a moment '. . . to this place?'

'Well, I hadn't then, had I?' said Libby, surprised. 'I assumed you wanted me to book you in somewhere, so I did. I'm sorry we were at cross purposes.'

'Hmm,' said Constance, still not looking at her. 'Food isn't bad, though,' she reluctantly admitted after a pause.

'I'll tell the chef,' said Libby, with a private grin.

They turned into the Manor's drive.

'So you and this Ben own the theatre?' Constance waved her stick in the air.

'Ben and his mother do. It was an oast house, and Ben had it converted. He's an architect – or was, until he retired. And he, his cousin Peter and I are now on the board of the Oast Theatre Trust.' Libby looked sideways at Constance. 'I'm still surprised that you knew about us.'

A small, almost sly smile flitted across the older woman's face, but she made no reply.

They were now approaching the forecourt of both the theatre and the Manor. Several cars were parked to the side of the theatre, and the big double doors stood open. Libby ushered Constance inside.

'I'll have to leave you now,' she said, pulling forward one of the white-painted wrought-iron chairs. 'I'm house manager tonight. Can I get you a drink?'

'A decent white,' said Constance, seating herself gingerly.

'Yes, ma'am,' muttered Libby.

The foyer began to fill up and Libby was kept busy greeting audience members. Fran and Guy arrived and tucked themselves away at the end of the bar, manned tonight by Ben's cousin Peter and another member of the Oast's semi-permanent company. Libby dutifully checked in with Constance every so often, and diplomatically pointed her towards the toilets before the five-minute bell sounded. No one had been allowed into the auditorium until then, to allow the full impact of the booth stage to burst upon the audience, who, as they had done on previous visits by the Glover's Men, erupted into spontaneous applause. Constance didn't.

Libby had watched the company in rehearsal the day before, and was therefore prepared for the surprise that was coming for the audience, and which had somehow been kept out of the press during the tour so far. From her seat just inside the auditorium door, she hugged herself in anticipation as Don Pedro asked Balthasar for 'a good song'. She almost held her breath as Balthasar self-deprecatingly replied that he was an 'ill singer' and then, accompanied by a lute-player, began to sing.

There was an audible collective gasp from the audience, as the actor, in a perfect, clear soprano, exhorted his audience to 'Sigh no more, ladies.'

By the end of the song the audience, on stage and off, was on its feet, and Libby didn't think she'd ever heard such a rapturous reception. Except for Constance.

'Who's the old lady who doesn't like it?' a voice whispered in Libby's ear. 'She came in with you, didn't she?'

Hereward Fisher, director of the Glover's Men, stood behind her.

'She's a retired director,' Libby whispered back. 'Very old school.'

'Pro?'

'Oh, yes! And don't you forget it!' Libby sent him a quick grin and returned her attention to the stage.

Libby was almost unsurprised when she didn't see Constance in the foyer bar during the interval, but wasted little time either wondering or searching for her. The rest of the audience members were full of praise for both Balthasar and the production as a whole and she was kept happily busy with them. She did notice that Constance was in her seat for the rest of the performance, and was very obviously waiting for her at the end, arms crossed firmly under her bust and a formidable expression on her face. Libby sighed and, once she'd made sure that the auditorium was empty, made her way across the foyer.

'I want to meet the director,' said Constance. 'One does not play around with Shakespeare like that.'

'Eh?' Libby frowned. 'But I thought you'd be impressed! It's as near as possible to how an original performance would have been.'

'With a woman in it? I thought it was supposed to be all male?'

Libby's mouth dropped open and the penny dropped.

'You mean Balthasar?' She couldn't help laughing. 'That's the very male Freddie Cannon – and he's a male soprano. Surely you could tell he was a man?'

Constance looked even more aggrieved and angry. 'No such thing,' she snapped.

Libby sighed. 'What about the castrati? Not quite the same thing, of course . . .'

'Cut his balls off, did they?' Constance was now glowering at the members of the audience who were watching in puzzlement as her voice had risen. Libby tried to take her by the arm.

'Come on,' she said. 'I'll see you back to the pub.'

'I want to make a complaint!' hissed Constance.

11

'Oh, stop being ridiculous,' said Libby, losing patience. 'I've registered your complaint, and quite frankly you're not welcome here.'

'Need a hand, Libby?' Fran and Guy appeared either side of Constance and Libby breathed a sigh of relief.

'I think Constance wants to go back to the Coach,' she said.

'We'll take her,' said Guy, giving Constance a smile.

'No thank you.' Constance's voice was icy. 'Libby will take me.'

Libby shook her head in defeat. 'I'd better,' she said. 'Can you tell Pete and Ben for me in case I'm not back before we lock up?'

Fran nodded and stepped back, head on one side. 'I think you're an extremely rude old woman,' she said to Constance. 'Come on, Guy.'

Grinning, Libby hurried her charge out of the building.

Constance's grumbles lasted all the way down the Manor drive, varying from 'I've never been so insulted,' to 'Amateurish, sensationalist rubbish,' and 'Uncomfortable seats.' By the time Libby deposited her inside the Coach and Horses, she'd fallen silent, merely offering Libby a grunt as she disappeared up the stairs.

'Didn't like it, eh?' Tim emerged from the bar, eyebrows raised.

'No,' said Libby. 'And the main reason I'm not going to tell you about, because you're coming to see it, aren't you?'

'Don't want to spoil the surprise?' said Tim, with a grin.

'What do you know about it?' asked Libby suspiciously.

'I've got young Hereward staying here, haven't I? Can't expect to keep it quiet.' Tim glanced up the stairs. 'But I wonder why she's being like that?'

'Actually, I feel a bit sorry for her,' said Libby. 'She's no longer a big noise in the theatre – not that she was ever *that* big, but she was quite well known – and the world has changed a lot. *Her* world has changed.' She paused. 'And it wouldn't surprise me if she wasn't in the early stages . . .'

'Of dementia?' supplied Tim.

Libby nodded. 'Oh, well. I'll pick her up tomorrow, Tim. I hope she's no trouble till then.'

Back at the theatre, the crowd had thinned considerably, but Fran and Guy were still at the bar talking to Peter and Ben, who had emerged from backstage. The cast were going straight back to the Manor, where Hetty had given them the use of the big sitting room.

Libby repeated her thoughts about Constance while Peter poured her a glass of Prosecco.

'Such a shame, though,' she said with a sigh. 'It's quite taken the shine off.'

'At least she didn't manage to upset the cast,' said Peter, lifting his own glass. 'Cheers.'

The following morning, however, Peter was proved wrong.

Fran and Guy had already left for Nethergate when Libby answered her mobile while drinking her second cup of tea at the kitchen table.

'Libby!' Hereward's voice exploded in her ear. 'That woman!'

Libby didn't need to ask what woman. 'What's she done?' she asked resignedly.

'Put it all over Twitter! That's what she's done!'

Libby's stomach lurched. Surely not? She stood up and went into the sitting room to open her laptop. And there it was. And, of course, it had spread, although it hadn't altogether gone viral.

'Can you sue her?' she asked doubtfully.

'Hardly worth it, is it? It's out there now.' Hereward sounded defeated.

They both fell silent.

'I'm so sorry, Hereward,' said Libby at last.

'It isn't your fault, Libby. She asked you to bring her, didn't she? She would have seen us somehow, even if you hadn't been kind

13

enough to drive her down.' Hereward sighed. 'Oh, well, you know what they say?'

'No publicity's bad publicity,' they chorused.

The truth of this hackneyed cliché was proven when Libby, Ben and Peter checked the online and phone messages for the theatre. The public were, it seemed, desperate to see the Glover's Men – and, in particular, Freddie Cannon.

The three of them sat in Ben's office at the Manor.

'Have we got to call all these people back?' said Libby, staring dolefully at the list in front of her.

'We can record a message,' said Peter. 'The answer's no to all of them, because we're already sold out.'

'And while we're at it, record a new message for the answer-phone,' said Ben, 'telling any new callers the same thing.'

'Is it still called "answerphone"?' wondered Libby. 'Shouldn't it be "voicemail" now?'

Ben gave her an old-fashioned look. 'It answers the phone,' he said. 'I don't care what it's called these days.'

'Children, children,' admonished Peter. 'We'd better tell young Hereward about this. He may want to put out some new publicity, or extend the tour.'

'He was going to put something out on social media,' said Libby, 'to try and counteract the Connie effect.'

'To be honest,' said Peter, leaning back in his chair and stretch-ing long legs in front of him, 'apart from spoiling the Balthasar surprise, it's done them a favour.'

'We said that,' agreed Libby. 'Ill wind, and all that.'

'Is the old bat still at the pub?' asked Ben, standing up. 'Aren't you supposed to be driving her home today?'

Libby made a face. 'Yes. I suppose I'd better call Tim and see if she's ready.' She reached out for the landline on Ben's desk.

'Sorry, Libby, but she's already gone,' said Tim when she asked for Constance. He sounded surprised.

'Gone? But I was supposed to take her home!' Peter and Ben, who had been leaving the room, stopped.

'I don't know about that,' said Tim, 'but she called down for a taxi just after she'd had her breakfast, about nine, it was.'

'To the station?'

'No – she said something about Nethergate. I thought she'd have told you. Sorry, Lib.'

'Don't worry, Tim. Saves me a journey, anyway. She did pay you, I suppose?'

'Oh, yes. No tips, though.'

'Doesn't surprise me,' said Libby. 'See you later.'

She relayed what Tim had said to Ben and Peter.

'So, much as I'd like to have nothing more to do with her, now I'm going to have to call her and find out what she's playing at. I wouldn't have thought she'd even have heard of Nethergate.' She stood up. 'Are we going to do these recordings for the phone now?'

Chapter Three

Libby found herself putting off her phone call to Constance. Part of her wondered why she should feel compelled to make it, and thought it would be a good idea to let well alone, but another part of her was just too nosy to forget about it. Eventually, back at home, after scavenging in the fridge for something for lunch, she sat down at the kitchen table and made the call.

'About time.' Constance sounded annoyed. Predictably.

'What is?' Libby wasn't going to make this easy.

'Your call. I could have been dead for all you knew.'

'No, Constance. You went off this morning in a taxi without bothering to let me know I wouldn't be required to drive you home, or even to say goodbye. That, I think, is the height of bad manners. I shouldn't be surprised, after your appalling display of rudeness last night, I suppose.'

Constance made no reply.

'Right, then,' said Libby. 'Have a good time in Nethergate. Goodbye.'

'Wait!' Now Constance was sharp. 'I might need a lift in a couple of days' time.'

'What?' Libby gasped. 'You've got a bloody cheek. Make your own way home.'

'But . . .' The voice became weaker. Looking for sympathy, thought Libby grimly. 'I don't know the area. I don't know how to get home.'

'You knew enough to want to go there this morning,' said Libby.

'Well . . . yes.' Constance paused. 'I liked the look of the place.'

'Nethergate?' Libby's voice rose in surprise.

'Yes.'

Silence fell.

'There's a station in Nethergate,' said Libby, eventually. 'At the top of the hill. I'm sure you'll be able to get home from there. And please, Constance, don't post any more vitriol on social media. It's very unkind – and untrue.' And she ended the call abruptly.

Perhaps surprisingly, Constance didn't call her back.

'Oh, well,' Libby said to Sidney, 'no loss there. Nasty old woman.' Sidney turned his back and stalked off into the sitting room. Libby stood up, stretched and followed him.

The weather was turning colder. Outside, leaves blew along Allhallow's Lane, and the sky was turning grey, reminding Libby of her newest preoccupation. Earlier in the year, she and Fran had been made forcibly aware of the plight of the homeless, not only nationally and in big cities but in their own local area. This, in turn, had brought home to Libby the desperate state of the rental housing market, leaving her feeling terribly guilty about her own part in causing it.

'It's not you, dear heart,' her friend Harry had said. 'It's Ben who's the bloated plutocrat, and, to be fair, he can hardly let out his mother's spare bedrooms as living accommodation, can he?'

'There's the Hoppers' Huts,' Libby had countered. These were tin-roofed huts originally provided for the hop pickers who used to come down from London for the hop harvest before mechanisation. Hetty herself had been one of them.

'For goodness' sake, you couldn't actually *live* in those!' scoffed Harry.

'Well, what about Steeple Farm?' Libby stuck out her chin. 'That's a proper rental property.'

'Yes, petal, but it belongs to my darling husband,' said Harry,

17

waving a careless arm towards the kitchen of the Pink Geranium vegetarian restaurant, where Peter, the said husband, was making tea. 'And before you say anything, the flat upstairs here is already let out to your precious son, if you remember.'

Libby had conceded all these facts, and realised that she was actually not taking the roof from over some deserving family's heads. Steeple Farm, although she and Ben managed it along with the Hoppers' Huts, actually belonged to Peter's mother Millicent, Hetty's younger sister, who currently resided in a very upmarket home for the bewildered. It was far too large and luxurious for the average small family, unless Peter and his brother James agreed to lower the rent drastically, and in any case the energy bills alone would cripple the average family financially.

But Libby's conscience had been pricked. She was aware that she was a middle-aged white female, living in her own home – albeit a small cottage – with no mortgage and enough of a small income to feed herself. She also had the cushion of Ben's comparative wealth, and wanted for nothing. But she had been made uncomfortably aware that there were thousands, possibly millions, of people who were nowhere near as lucky as she and her immediate circle were.

It was a newspaper report that finally prompted her to see if there was any way in which she could help. She was obviously aware of the rise in holiday rental properties; after all, she and Ben managed some, and the proliferation of little key safes by the front doors of cottages in Fran and Guy's, Harbour Street in Nethergate, spoke for themselves. But when Libby read of a teacher and her family who had been told to leave their rented house because it was to be made into a holiday let, and that this was only the tip of the iceberg, she was horrified. And then she had found Lady Prudence Howe.

Lady Howe, the 'relict', as she called herself, of Sir Percival Howe, was now in sole possession of the Howe Estate, comprising the main house – a Victorian monstrosity, in her own words – three cottages, stables, barns and a folly. It lay between the Tyne

Estate, of which now only the chapel remained, and Nethergate. Lady Howe was currently in the process of converting all the out-buildings into properties suitable for renting out, and the Victorian monstrosity into apartments. It had been Guy who introduced her to Libby. He had joined a protest group against a large holiday development during Fran and Libby's recent adventure and was rather enjoying himself. As a reasonably well-known artist he had been a feather in the cap of the protest group, and his gallery and shop the Wolfe Gallery, also on Harbour Street, had become an unofficial meeting place for its members, who, now their original aim had been accomplished, had turned their attention to other sorts of holiday development. One morning in summer Libby had been delivering one of her small paintings, which Guy sold to tourists, when Lady Howe came in, as orchestrated by Guy. They had hit it off immediately, while Guy stood by with a smug 'I knew they would' expression on his face.

It was Lady Howe who had told Libby of some of the worst examples of landlord greed, which had later been confirmed by Libby's London-dwelling children, Dominic and Belinda.

'Oh, yes, Mum,' Bel had said over the phone, sounding sur-prised. 'I know people who've had to turn down jobs or give up uni places because they can't find anywhere to live. If rental places haven't been converted to holiday lets, they've been turned into short-term accommodation. And the cost! You wouldn't believe it. Dom and I are lucky because Dad's girlfriend didn't need this house once she moved in with him.'

Libby had silently ground her teeth at this reminder. Not that she regretted her divorce from Derek – the pneumatic Marion was welcome to him – but she regretted the disruption to her children's lives. Although they hadn't seemed too distraught at the time – or since.

Now Libby stared out at the chilly afternoon and thought about her own plans. She had managed to persuade the Glover's Men – and Ben and Peter – to dedicate the takings of one performance of

Much Ado to charity – Lady Howe was a staunch supporter of the Crisis homelessness charity – with the help of Oliver Marcus, who had volunteered to make a short speech at the beginning of the play. His tales of friends and colleagues forced into homelessness in London had been truly heartbreaking.

Meanwhile, the Garden Hotel in Steeple Martin's high street had been turned into apartments by Colin Hardcastle, whose partner Gerry Hall had persuaded him to rent them out rather than selling them. One, the penthouse formerly occupied by Colin and Gerry, had already been sold, but the others had rather stuck on the market. Libby was keeping a weather eye on the prospective tenants; she was determined not to allow Colin to choose second-home owners over the more deserving.

Her mobile began chirruping.

'Libby, it's Oliver.'

'Oliver! Hello. What can I do for you?'

'Well . . .' Oliver was hesitant. 'It's that woman.'

Libby closed her eyes and sighed. 'Constance.'

'Yes.'

'What's she done now?'

'She's been tweeting again.' Oliver cleared his throat. 'Um – it's not very nice.'

'I'm sure it isn't.' Libby opened her laptop and began to search. 'Oh.'

'Yes. I don't suppose there's anything you can do?'

'I've already spoken to her today and I think I've made it worse,' said Libby, reading some appallingly homophobic tweets. 'I really can't understand her, you know. She wanted to see the production because it was as close as possible to how Shakespeare performed it. Or how his company performed it. How's Freddie taking it?'

'He's all right.' Oliver gave a subdued chuckle. 'He gets used to people thinking he's gay because of his voice, despite the fact that he's rampantly heterosexual. But it's the implication that the whole company is gay – not that any of us would care if it was. It's just the nastiness.'

'I know,' said Libby with a sigh. 'When did you say Sir Jasper was coming down?'

'Tonight – I told you. You said you'd be there to see him.'

It had been Sir Jasper Stone's ill-fated production of *The Second Mrs Tanqueray* that had brought both him and Oliver to the Oast Theatre, introduced by another of Libby's theatrical friends, Sir Andrew McColl.

'Oh, yes. And he's staying at Anderson Place again, isn't he?'

'Yes. He knows Sir Jonathan, that's why,' said Oliver. 'No reflection on your Coach and Horses, and there wasn't room for him at the Manor.'

'He wouldn't want to stay with the hoi polloi anyway,' said Libby. 'Oh, sorry! I meant the cast!'

Oliver laughed. 'He'd love it, actually. Since he and Miranda – or should I say Mary? – split up he doesn't have to lord it over everyone.'

Sir Jasper had been married to the once-famous actor Miranda Love – or Mary Bennett, as she was on her birth certificate.

'And when's Liz coming? Saturday night, isn't it?'

'She's coming down on Friday, but she'll be in the audience on Saturday, yes. Her mum's having the baby for the weekend.'

Oliver's wife Liz had also been part of the *Mrs Tanqueray* company.

'I'm looking forward to seeing her,' said Libby. 'And in the meantime, I'll have another go at asking Constance to cease and desist. Mind you . . .' She paused as a thought struck her. 'Sir Jasper might have more luck. She'd probably toady to him. Or even Sir Andrew.' Libby thought for a moment. 'Yes – I could ask Andrew to have a word.'

'But Sir Andrew's gay, isn't he? Out and proud. She'd bite chunks out of him.' It was Oliver's turn to sigh. 'What a problem these dinosaurs are.'

21

After Oliver had rung off, Libby decided to make herself a fortifying cup of tea before attempting to persuade Constance to play nicely once again. Before she could do so, however, the landline began ringing.

'Libby, my dear! How are you? Jasper Stone here.'

'Sir Jasper! How lovely! Oliver and I were just talking about you.'

'Ah, yes. I'm so looking forward to seeing his Benedick tonight,' said Sir Jasper. 'And that was why I was ringing, actually. Are you very tied up with your theatre duties? Only I've booked a pre-performance table at that lovely restaurant your friends run, and I wondered if you and Ben would join me?'

'We'd love to, if the company can spare us.' Libby tried to remember who they'd asked to be on duty this evening. 'Could I get back to you, Sir Jasper? I'll just have to check on our rota.'

'Of course, my dear. I do hope you can — Andrew's joining me, although I believe he's going to watch on Saturday night.'

'Andrew McColl? Yes, he's coming on Saturday and staying with a mutual friend. I'll ring you back in five minutes. And I might have a favour to ask you.'

Sure enough, both the bar and front of house at the theatre would be adequately manned for the evening.

'So we'd love to join you,' said Libby on the phone, five minutes later. 'What time?'

'Six o'clock, I'm afraid,' said Sir Jasper. 'Your friend — Harry, isn't it? — said he's booked all week with early diners. Now what was the favour?'

A little hesitantly, Libby explained about Constance, trying not to give the game away about Freddie Cannon's remarkable rendition of 'Sigh no more'. She needn't have worried.

'I wonder if it has anything to do with young Freddie Cannon?' said Sir Jasper when she wound down. 'Don't worry, Libby. I know all about him.'

'Yes, it is. She's been absolutely hateful.' Libby hesitated. 'I just wondered . . .'

'If I'd have a word?' Sir Jasper chuckled. 'Well, Libby, dear, I can try, but you obviously know what Connie's like. Luckily, I never had much to do with her professionally, although she always made it her business to criticise everything I did.'

'I can imagine,' said Libby. 'Jealous, was she?'

'She was.' Jasper was quiet for a moment. 'Still, give me her number and I'll have a go. And I'll see you at six at the restaurant.'

'Thank you so much, Sir Jasper.'

'Oh, for goodness' sake, drop the "Sir"!' said Sir Jasper.

Chapter Four

When Libby and Ben arrived at the Pink Geranium, both theatrical knights had been seated on the sofa in the left-hand window and had a bottle of red wine and four glasses on the coffee table in front of them.

'I'm sorry, Libby,' said Sir Jasper after greetings had been exchanged and wine poured, 'but Connie wasn't answering her phone. I tried two or three times, and left messages on her voicemail, but she hasn't come back to me. I should be saying sorry to the company, really, shouldn't I?'

'I'm not surprised she isn't answering,' said Sir Andrew. 'She's probably getting inundated with angry messages.'

'Well, thank you for trying,' said Libby.

'And it has increased interest in the production,' said Ben. 'We were actually wondering this morning if we could persuade them to do an extra night, there's been so much.'

'I wonder if they could take legal action against her?' mused Sir Jasper. 'Although I doubt if anything she's said is exactly actionable.'

'Exactly,' said Libby.

'She could hardly be sued for giving the game away about Balthasar's voice,' said Sir Andrew.

'Or calling the entire company gay,' said Ben. 'It's hardly a scurrilous insult.'

'To Connie, it is,' said Libby, and heaved a sigh. 'Still, let's forget her for now.' She lifted her glass. 'Lovely to see you both.'

Harry arrived at that moment, smiling flirtatiously, as he always did, at Sir Andrew.

'Dinner is served, your lordships,' he announced. 'And others.'

'You haven't taken our orders yet!' said Ben in surprise.

'Due to the early nature of your dining experience,' said Harry loftily, 'orders were placed over the phone. We took the liberty of choosing your usual.'

'Might not have wanted quesadillas,' grumbled Ben half-heartedly, while the others laughed.

As always, the food was delicious and the service, by Libby's younger son Adam, who lodged in the flat above the Pink Geranium, impeccable.

'Only sorry we couldn't have stayed longer,' said Sir Andrew as they walked up the Manor drive towards the theatre. 'Still, we can have a drink together later, can't we? Or are you two going to have a night off?'

'No, we'll be around,' said Ben. 'We'll keep the bar open. Or are you both driving?'

'No,' said Sir Jasper. 'The hotel's sending a car to pick me up.'

'And I'm staying with Edward,' said Sir Andrew, 'so I'm getting a taxi back.'

'But I thought you were coming on Saturday?' said Libby.

'And tonight,' said Sir Andrew. 'Can't get enough Shakespeare.'

Tonight, if anything, the applause for Balthasar was even greater. Libby, standing at the back with Hereward, whispered: 'No publicity!'

'Is bad publicity!' he whispered back, with a grin.

'Not a bad actor, either,' said Sir Andrew in the interval.

'Worth keeping an eye on,' agreed Sir Jasper. 'Going to introduce us afterwards, Libby?'

'If they come out,' said Libby, 'but they might sneak out the back way to the Manor.'

'I shall ask young Hereward to bring them out,' said Sir Andrew, getting to his feet. 'We'd like to congratulate them, and I'd like to see Oliver, anyway.'

'So would I.' Sir Jasper smiled over at Libby. 'I keep an eye on him and Liz, you know, Libby. I feel responsible for bringing them together.'

'Are they going to come and meet their public?' Libby asked Hereward before he went in for the second half.

He laughed. 'What do you think? Those two might both be old stagers, but they're still names to be reckoned with. Only a couple of the lads weren't impressed. Freddie was practically wetting himself!'

'Oh, I do hope not,' said Libby with a grin. 'Think of the costume cleaning bill.'

In fact, the entire company poured out into the foyer bar at the end of the performance, and were made much of by Sirs Andrew and Jasper and the audience en masse. Libby and Ben were kept busy behind the bar, having unwisely sent this evening's bar staff home.

Eventually the audience and cast had left the building and Libby and Ben were able to lock up and leave themselves.

'How about a drink at the Pocket?' Ben suggested, as they made their way down the Manor drive. 'I haven't seen Simon since Friday night.'

The Hop Pocket was the recently restored and reopened pub owned by Ben's family, and Simon was the new manager. Tucked down Cuckoo Lane, it was doing very well as a local pub, especially as vicar Beth had donated a redundant upright piano from the church hall, reviving a good many villagers' interest in their childhood piano lessons.

'OK,' said Libby, 'although we'll only just be in time.'

In fact, Simon had already rung the bell for last orders when they arrived, and one of the regular customers was playing a mournful rendition of 'Show Me The Way To Go Home' on the piano.

'I hear the play's going down a storm,' said Simon, handing over their drinks. 'Despite all that uproar on Twitter.'

'Oh, you saw that, did you?' said Libby. 'Bloody woman.'

'You know her?' Simon was surprised.

'I bloody well brought her down here, didn't I?' Libby growled. 'And now she's disappeared. Trying to avoid the fallout, I bet.'

'Well it didn't do any harm, from what I've heard,' said Simon, 'but she was saying some pretty nasty things, as well as giving the game away about the singer. Not that I understood quite what she was on about.'

Libby and Ben explained about Freddie Cannon and his amazing voice.

'Shame you weren't in earlier,' said Simon when they'd finished. 'We had one of Colin's new tenants in.'

'Oh, really?' Libby leant her elbows on the bar. 'What were they like?'

'Seemed a nice enough bloke.' Simon threw a tea towel over the beer pumps. 'Works in Canterbury. His wife's hoping to get taken on at the hospital, apparently. They couldn't get anywhere they could afford in the town.' He shook his head. 'Colin's charging too little for those flats, if you ask me.'

'No, Simon, he's charging the right price,' stated Libby firmly. 'People are getting priced out of accommodation everywhere.'

Ben made a face at Simon. 'She'd have me letting out the Hoppers' Huts for ten quid a week if she could.'

Libby dug him in the ribs. 'So did this new tenant say he was pleased with the flat?'

'Oh, delighted. And the kids have got into the school, and seem to be very happy despite having to leave friends behind.'

'That's good.' Libby sat back on her stool and smiled. 'I look forward to meeting them all.'

★

The following morning Libby was relieved to be returning to a more normal routine. The theatre was fully staffed for the rest of the week, although she would put in an appearance most evenings, and especially on the last night, when Oliver would give his speech. But, for now the day was her own.

But, she realised, she actually had nothing to do. The season was over, so Guy needed no more little views of Nethergate painted to sell to tourists in the Wolfe Gallery and shop, no one was asking to rent Steeple Farm (not surprising at the price they were charging, thought Libby gloomily) or the Hoppers' Huts and there was nothing to do yet for the Christmas pantomime. Libby had been persuaded to return to her panto-guru role after a couple of years off and had updated her script for *Cinderella*, as requested; auditions were due to be held the week after *Much Ado*. She was looking forward to it.

So Libby was at a loose end. She could, of course, set about some serious housework – an idea dismissed almost before it was formed – or she could stroll down to Ahmed and Ali's eight-till-late shop and Nella's farm shop, although there wasn't anything she really needed. Sighing, she opened her laptop and began scrolling through social media. Perhaps later she would go and see Harry and have lunch in the Pink Geranium.

And then the phone rang.

'Libby? It's Pru.'

'Pru! You're a life-saver! I'm bored to tears here. What can I do for you?' Libby got up and went into the kitchen. 'I shall make myself a nice cup of tea while we chat.'

Lady Howe snorted. Or at least, that's what it sounded like. 'Better make it a large brandy,' she said.

'Oh?' Libby switched on the kettle. 'That sounds ominous.'

'It is.' Prudence took an audible breath. 'I need your help.'

'Of course.' Libby frowned as she dropped a teabag into a mug. 'Anything.'

There was a short silence. Then: 'You know all about police investigations, don't you?'

Libby's hand stilled in the act of pouring boiling water. 'What have you done?' she asked nervously.

'Nothing.' Prudence sighed. 'But we've got a body.'

'A – a . . . *what*?'

'You heard. In the wood.'

'Oh, gawd! Not another one!' said Libby.

'Eh?'

'Just before we met you – remember? The homeless man who was found near Rogation House?'

'Oh, right. Well, this is much worse.'

'Really?' Libby raised her eyebrows at Sidney and shook her head. Naturally, everything would be worse if it related to Lady Howe.

'Yes! It's on my land!'

'And that makes it worse how?' asked Libby.

Prudence was once more silent. 'Well, no, of course not,' she said eventually. 'It's just . . .'

'I know. Too close to home,' said Libby. 'So how can I help?'

'They're coming to question me!' wailed Prudence. 'What do I do?'

'Oh, for goodness' sake, Pru! Just tell them the truth. They'll ask you if you knew the person, that's all. Who found it?'

'Someone walking a dog,' said Prudence. 'I don't know who. The woods aren't private.'

'Well, there you are then. You know nothing about it, and that's what you tell them. Have you seen any police yet?'

'Oh, yes! There are swarms of them all over the place.'

'I meant, has anyone come to speak to you yet?'

'Only a nice young uniformed copper. He said someone will be along.' Prudence paused. 'I wondered if you'd come down and help?'

'How? Hold your hand?' Libby laughed. 'Believe me, I would only make things worse – specially if it's a police person I know.'

'Oh.' Prudence sounded despondent. 'I thought it would make things better.'

'Quite the opposite.' Libby fished out the teabag and added a splash of milk. 'Look, you go and wait for your interrogation and ring me afterwards. And if I can find anything out, I will.'

Although quite how I do that, I've no idea, she thought after Prudence had reluctantly ended the call.

A quick trawl through the news sites on the internet provided no information and Fran's phone, unusually, went straight to voicemail. Frustrated, Libby finished her tea, collected her cape and basket and left the cottage. She would go down to the Howe Estate and see what was going on after all.

She had just opened her car door when the phone trilled from inside her basket. 'That was quick,' she muttered as she retrieved it.

'Libby?'

That wasn't Prudence. 'Yes?' she said warily.

'It's Rachel. Sorry to disturb you . . .'

Libby felt the first stirrings of alarm. This was Detective Sergeant Rachel Trent.

'Rachel – yes.' Libby cleared her throat. 'What can I do for you?'

'We-ell . . .' Rachel hesitated. 'I really shouldn't do this over the phone, and to be honest, I can't actually believe—'

'Believe what?' Libby was sharper than she'd intended.

Rachel sighed. 'That I'm actually having to talk to you again.'

'Go on.'

'A body's been found.' Rachel paused.

'Ah.' Libby made a resigned face. 'Would it be in the Howe woods, by any chance?'

'Yes!' Rachel sounded surprised. 'Er – how . . . ? Well, I mean . . .'

'Lady Howe called me earlier. I think she wanted me to hold her hand.'

'Oh, you know her? Did she say who the body was?'

'No, of course not! She doesn't know. Who is it? Do you know?'

'We think we might.' Rachel paused again. 'And according to

the phone found nearby,' she continued slowly, 'the victim was in touch with you only yesterday.'

'*What*?' Libby's heart rate shot up and she felt perspiration break out along her hairline.

'I'm sorry, Libby. Can you confirm you know a Constance Matthews?'

Chapter Five

Libby's breath came out in a whoosh and she felt almost light-headed.

'Er – yes.' It came out as a croak.

'Are you all right?' Rachel sounded concerned.

'Um – yes.' Libby cleared her throat again. 'Yes, Rachel – sorry. It was a shock.'

'Of course. I just wondered – well, a couple of things really. First – do you know who her next of kin is?'

'Golly.' Libby made her way back to her front door. 'I don't know. She isn't married, and there aren't any children, but whether she's got siblings, or . . . or, I don't know – cousins or anything, I've no idea.'

'Right. She isn't local, is she?'

'No, north Kent. Ashbury.'

'Do you know why she was down here? Was she visiting you?'

'Not exactly.' Libby let herself in. 'She was down here to see the production at the theatre.'

'Ah.' Rachel paused. 'Libby, I know it's a lot to ask, but . . .' she took a deep breath, 'would you be prepared to identify Ms Matthews?'

Libby stood still. In all the years she had been involved with the horrific business of murder investigations, this was the first time she had ever been asked to view the body.

'I suppose so,' she said slowly. 'If there isn't anybody else.' She thought wildly of suggesting either Sir Jasper or Sir Andrew, both of whom had known Constance, but dismissed the thought as unworthy.

'Thank you.' Rachel sounded relieved. 'I'll let you know when we can pick you up. She – er – she hasn't been taken to the mortuary yet.'

'Oh. Do I get taken?'

'Oh, yes. We wouldn't ask you to get yourself there.'

'And will I get to meet – what was his name? – oh, yes. Mr Taylor-Blake?'

Rachel laughed. 'Our Franklyn? Yes, I'm sure that can be arranged.' She ended the call.

Libby took off her cape, sat at the table and tried Fran's number again.

'Libby.' Fran sounded exasperated.

'Sorry – am I interrupting?'

'Yes!' Fran sighed and laughed. 'No. Sorry. We're in the middle of putting away all the summer stock ready for Christmas.'

'I guessed you were doing something important because your phone went to voicemail earlier,' said Libby, 'but this is important.'

'What is? Don't tell me Constance has been meddling again?'

'No, Fran. She's dead.'

There was a charged silence.

'Well, say something!' said Libby.

'I don't believe it. I just don't believe it.'

'It's true. Prudence called me—'

'*Prudence*?'

'Yes – listen. From the beginning.' Libby recounted this morning's two disturbing phone calls. 'And now I don't know what to do.'

'What do you mean, you don't know what to do?'

'Well, if Rachel's going to send someone to collect me I can't go anywhere, can I?'

33

'She said she'd let you know when they were coming, didn't she? And that the body hadn't been removed to the mortuary yet. I would say it isn't likely to be before tomorrow.'

'Oh.' Libby thought for a moment. 'I was wondering about going down to see Prudence as she asked.'

'You mean you're being nosy again.'

'No! I told you – she asked!'

Fran sighed. 'I think you should stay away. You'll only complicate matters.'

'How would I do that? Besides, I want to know why Constance was in Pru's woods.'

'Going for a walk? They aren't fenced off, are they?'

'A walk? Constance? You must be joking!'

'Well, she was probably dumped there, then, and nothing to do with Lady Pru.'

Libby scowled at her feet. 'It is something to do with her. I'm sure of it.'

'Oh, you're the psychic one now, are you?' said Fran. 'Takes the pressure off me, anyway!' Fran was known for having the odd 'moment', as her friends called them, when she became aware of things beyond her – or anybody else's – actual knowledge. She had on occasion been able to help the police solve murder cases, although she was uncomfortable with her unusual talent and played it down as much as possible.

'All right, all right,' Libby huffed. 'I'll leave it alone.' She stared out of the window for a long moment. 'It is odd, though. Coincidence.'

'I know. And we don't like coincidences, do we?' Fran's smile came through her voice. 'I'll ask Guy if he's heard anything on the grapevine and I'll let you know.'

Libby ended the call and stood for a moment of indecision. Then she found another number on her phone and called Harry.

'If you're wanting lunch you'd better hurry up,' he said. 'I'm closing the kitchen.'

'It's only' – Libby checked the clock on the mantel – 'oh. Nearly two.'

'So hurry up. I want to get home to put me feet up.'

So Libby hurried.

The last couple of customers were finishing their coffee as Libby pushed open the door of the Pink Geranium.

'Coffee, soup or wine?' asked Harry, coming forward to give her a kiss. 'Or all three?'

'A sandwich?' asked Libby hopefully.

'You're no fun.' Harry sniffed and retreated to the kitchen while Libby made herself comfortable on the sofa in the window. He returned almost immediately with a large plate full of sandwiches.

'Help yourself,' he said. 'They won't keep.' He left her to attend to the customers who were preparing to leave. When they had been ushered off the premises, the door locked and the 'Open' sign turned to 'Closed', he fetched a cafetière and two mugs.

'I take it you want to talk,' he said, sitting down and stretching long legs out in front of him. 'Anything to do with what you and their lordships were talking about last night?'

'Yes, actually,' said Libby, her mouth full of salad sandwich. 'Constance Matthews.'

'What's she done now?' Harry poured coffee.

Libby told him.

When she'd finished, he shook his head at her. 'I don't believe it.'

'That's what Fran said.' Libby took another sandwich. 'And I'm not sure I do, either.'

'You realise we're actually all living in a Golden Age crime novel, don't you?' said Harry.

'And I'm *not* Miss Marple,' said Libby with a scowl.

Harry laughed. 'Nowhere near genteel enough, dearie.'

'Yes, all right, but I want to know what I should do now.' Libby raised her eyebrows at him. 'Should I call Lady Prudence?'

'And say what? That you know her corpse?'

35

'Well – yes.'

'And that will achieve what?'

'I don't know. But I could tell her who it is.'

'I expect our local fuzz will have done that. See if there's a – *connection*!' Harry waggled his eyebrows at her. 'Is Ian in charge?'

Detective Chief Inspector Ian Connell was a friend into whose investigations Libby – and Fran – had frequently stumbled.

'He's not actively involved in cases these days,' said Libby. 'Rachel seems to be in charge again.'

'The day Ian keeps out of a murder we'll have four blue moons in a row,' said Harry. 'And Rachel's only a sergeant, isn't she? She won't be the officer in charge.'

'She didn't say who's SIO, but she's doing all the work on the ground, by the sound of things.'

'Hmm.' Harry sipped thoughtfully at his coffee. 'So where exactly is this place where the dreaded Constance was found?'

'You remember Tyne Chapel?'

'Ah! The place with the nasty goings-on with the equally nasty nurse?'

'Nurse Redding, yes.' Libby shuddered. 'Actually, it was where we first met Ian. Well, the Tyne Estate adjoins the Howe Estate. I can't work out if the lake and the bridge are actually on one estate or the other. They merge into one another. Very pretty.'

'And Lady Howe is turning it all into affordable housing?'

'Rental properties, yes. I remember going past a few stone cottages on the way to Tyne Chapel all those years ago – I think those belong to Pru. And there's a lovely stream and a lake. I saw crested grebe.' Libby smiled, remembering.

'So perhaps Chronic Connie was intending to rent one of the cottages?' suggested Harry.

'Never. She wasn't a country type at all. I was surprised she lived as far out as Ashbury.'

'Ashbury is hardly far out. It's practically London.'

'Anyway, that wouldn't be why she was there.' Libby reflected.

'Actually, she was found in woods, so if it was the woods that came right up to the chapel walls, perhaps she was looking at the chapel.'

'Do the goings-on still go on?' asked Harry.

'No! Although we do still seem to have more than our fair share of that kind of thing round here, don't we? There's Grey Betty at Steeple Mount . . .'

'And that oak tree. What was it called?'

'The Willoughby Oak, where Cunning Mary was hanged.' Libby shook her head. 'All these so-called witches. But I don't think this has anything to do with all that.'

'Oh, I don't know,' said Harry. 'After all, it is almost Hallowe'en.'

'Anyway.' Libby leant back in the sofa and crossed her arms. 'What am I going to do?'

'Nothing, dear heart. As you said yourself, your august presence would probably make things worse. Go home and do some panto prep or something.' Harry patted her hand. 'Play to your strengths, poppet, play to your strengths. Oh – and I meant to tell you, I had a text from young Ricky this morning.'

Young Ricky and his dog, Barney, had met Harry during Libby and Fran's most recent adventure.

'Oh, lovely!' said Libby. 'What did he have to say? Is he enjoying uni?'

'He is. Although he misses Barney during the week when he's in halls, but he's coming here at the weekend and sleeping in our spare room, so you can see him. He says he's got some news from Mavis. Now!' Harry held up a warning finger. 'Don't go asking Mavis before you hear it from him. That would spoil his surprise.'

' OK, I won't. But what can it be?' Libby frowned. 'Is he going to move in with her? We said he'd like to, didn't we?'

Mavis owned the Blue Anchor café at the end of Harbour Street in Nethergate and had looked after Ricky and Barney for a while back in the spring.

'Too far from uni,' said Harry. 'Just contain your soul in patience, dear girl – difficult, in your case, I know.' He stood up. 'And now, get along with you. Time I went home to put my feet up.'

Libby wandered up the Manor drive thinking about Constance, Lady Howe and Ricky Short. Ricky's story had had a happy ending, unlike that of Constance, and as yet Lady Howe's was unknown. It was never a happy ending to have a dead body found in one's back garden. Libby pushed open the heavy oak door of the Manor.

'Hello!' she called. 'Anybody in?'

'Come in, gal.' Hetty's voice issued from her own private sitting room. 'If you want those lads, there's some of them in the big sitting room.'

'No, Hetty, I was going to talk to you, actually.' Libby put her head round Hetty's door.

Hetty cocked her head on one side and Jeff-dog, her black and white collie cross, jumped up to greet Libby, his second favourite person.

'Yes.' Libby perched on the edge of Hetty's small table. 'I wondered if you'd heard anything from Linda Davies – you know, young Ricky's grandma.'

Hetty smiled. 'Now, how d'yer know that?'

'I didn't!' Libby was surprised. 'So you have?'

'Surprised you haven't.' Hetty put her hands on the arms of her chair and heaved herself up. 'Bloody knees.'

'Why did you think I might have heard from her?' Libby followed Hetty and Jeff-dog into the huge kitchen. 'I wondered because Harry had a text from Ricky.'

'Ah. He'll tell you, then.' Hetty lifted the kettle. 'Cuppa?'

'I'm full of Harry's coffee, thanks.' Libby sat down at the table. 'Go on – what did she want?'

'Said she wanted to move here, remember? Bought Colin's flat, hasn't she?'

38

Chapter Six

Libby gaped.

'*She's* the one who bought Colin's penthouse?'

Hetty nodded, getting two mugs from the rack by the sink.

'Yes, I will have tea, after all,' said Libby, shaking her head. 'Why didn't she tell me? Tell us?'

'Reckons you weren't too keen on having her here.' Hetty gave Libby a knowing look. 'Weren't, were you?'

After Linda Davies had been introduced to Steeple Martin she'd said how much she would prefer to live in the village rather than her current sheltered accommodation. After getting to know Linda, Libby hadn't been so sure.

'She hasn't moved in yet, though, has she?' Libby fetched milk from Hetty's big fridge.

'End of the month – next week sometime.' Hetty poured water into her small brown teapot.

'Ricky's coming down to stay with Harry and Peter this week-end,' said Libby. 'He said he's got news about Mavis.' She thought for a moment. 'Oh, I do hope his nan being here won't stop him visiting. She'll expect him to stay with her, won't she?'

'Can say no, can't he?' Hetty sat down at the table. 'She just wants to make friends. Already taken her to Carpenter's Hall.'

Hetty's best friend Flo Carpenter lived in Maltby Close, in one of the retirement bungalows built by her late husband, and next to the converted barn, Carpenter's Hall, used by them all as a community space.

'What?' Libby gasped. 'To meet Flo and everybody? You didn't tell me!'

'She said not to.' Hetty laughed. 'Scared of you, I reckon!'

The kitchen door opened and Ben appeared. 'Who's scared?' he asked. 'Is there enough in the pot for me?'

Between them, Libby and Hetty told him about Ricky and Linda, and Libby went on to tell him about Constance and Lady Howe.

'I don't know,' he said, shaking his head. 'I turn my back for five minutes . . .'

'And the gal finds another body,' said Hetty, nodding.

Libby made a face.

'Well, I think it's rather nice that Ricky's nan thought we were all so nice she decided to move here,' said Ben, 'although how she'll feel when she finds out the other flats are being rented out to deserving families . . .'

'Why should that matter?' asked Libby sharply.

'All right, all right, we know you're on a crusade to help the homeless,' said Ben with a sigh. 'This Linda might feel differently, that's all I'm saying.'

'Yes, well . . .' Libby muttered.

'Can't take on all the problems in the world, gal,' said Hetty.

Into the silence that followed this remark came the shrill ringing of the telephone in the estate office. Ben stood up and left the kitchen, taking his tea with him.

'Don't mind him,' said Hetty. 'He was brought up here, wasn't he? Greg's son – landed gentry, like. Not like me and Flo, east Londoners born and bred, weren't we. Took me an age to fit in.'

'I know, Het.' Libby smiled at her almost-mother-in-law. 'And I'm a born and bred sarf Londoner. We both married out of our class, didn't we?'

Hetty snorted. 'You ain't married yet, gal!'

Libby laughed. 'You know what I mean.' She paused, suddenly serious. 'Do you mind that Ben and I aren't married, Hetty?'

'Course not.' Hetty winked. 'If we could've got away with it, Greg and I wouldn't have bothered.'

Libby choked on her tea.

Later on, Ben and Libby were eating their early dinner in front of the local television news when Libby's favourite news reporter appeared, telling the viewers that a body had been found in woodland on the Howe Estate.

'Let's just hope he doesn't get wind of you knowing the victim,' said Ben, 'or we'll be besieged by the media.'

'Not if he doesn't tell anyone else – and I'm hardly newsworthy, am I?' said Libby.

'Maybe not, but then the link to the Glover's Men will come out, and that *is* newsworthy,' Ben nodded wisely.

'Well, let's hope Pru won't let it out, either,' said Libby, 'although I don't hold out much hope of that.'

It was just as they were leaving to go to the theatre that Libby's phone began to ring in her basket.

'Libby, it's me!' gasped an obviously distressed Lady Howe. 'What's going on? The police said you know this body!'

Libby rolled her eyes at Ben.

'Yes, sorry, Pru. I—'

Prudence cut her off. 'But why didn't you *tell* me?' she almost shrieked.

Ben looked startled.

'Pru, calm down!' Libby tried to talk over the noise coming out of the phone. 'I didn't know either!'

'What do you mean, you didn't know?' Prudence barked.

'Until the police called me because my number was found in the victim's phone, I didn't know. How could I?'

'Oh.' Prudence subsided. 'Well, who was she? They wouldn't tell me. They said it was because her identity hadn't been confirmed.'

Libby frowned. 'That's odd. I would have thought they would have at least shown you a photo to see if you knew her.'

There was a short silence, then Prudence cleared her throat. 'Apparently the face was . . . er – well, it was, um . . .'

'Oh, no.' Libby stopped dead just as they were turning in to the high street.

'What?' said Prudence.

'Libby?' said Ben.

'I've got to go and identify the body.'

Half an hour later, Libby had been suitably restored by a large whisky in the theatre foyer bar and Prudence had been shocked enough to say sorry and goodbye. All appeared to be well with the Glover's Men and their highly anticipatory audience, who were excitedly milling around waiting to be let into the auditorium.

'I think we can leave them to it,' said Ben. 'I'll pop up later and check everything's locked up.'

'Are we going home, then?' asked Libby, waving across at Hereward as he entered the foyer down the spiral staircase from the lighting box.

'Of course not!' Ben put on a shocked face. 'It's Wednesday!'

It had become a tradition in Steeple Martin for Libby, Ben and their friends to meet in the Coach and Horses on Wednesdays. It had grown up after their friend Patti Pearson, the vicar of St Aldeberge, began coming over on her day off to see Anne Douglas, who lived in the village. They invariably had dinner at the Pink Geranium, where occasionally some of their friends joined them. However, tonight Ben and Libby went straight to the pub, where they were surprised to find not only Edward Hall, who lived not far from the village in one half of a beautifully converted small Georgian manor house, but his neighbour in the upstairs apartment, Detective Chief Inspector Ian Connell.

'We wondered if you'd be here,' said Edward, giving Libby a kiss on the cheek.

'What with all the theatrical shenanigans this week,' added Ian with a smile. 'Your usual, Libby?'

'She's already had a large whisky,' said Ben. 'Don't spoil her!'

'I beg your pardon?' Libby gave him a frosty look. 'I needed it!'

'Really, why?' Edward pulled out a chair for her at the large round table.

'She had a bit of a shock, poor old thing.' Ben grinned and he and Ian went off to the bar.

'Less of the old,' said Libby.

'I saw some of the fuss on Twitter,' said Edward.

'I know.' Libby sighed and sneaked a look at Ian. 'Nasty, wasn't it.'

'And I gather,' said Ian, returning to the table and placing a glass in front of her, 'we have you to thank for identifying her.'

'Eh?' said Edward. 'Identifying who?'

'The woman who stirred up the trouble on Twitter,' said Ian. 'And wouldn't you know it? She not only knew Libby, but she got herself murdered!'

'No!' Edward stared at Libby. 'I don't believe it!'

'Why does everybody keep saying that?' grumbled Libby. 'It isn't my fault.'

'You're like a magnet, Lib. You just attract the wrong people,' said Ben, patting her hand fondly.

'I take objection to that!' Edward gave Ben a friendly punch on the arm.

'Present company excepted,' said Ben. 'So, Ian. Libby said young Rachel was in charge of this murder, not you.'

'I didn't,' protested Libby. 'I said Rachel seemed to be the one on the ground, that's all.'

'And you're right.' Ian smiled at her. 'I'm supposed to be sitting in my office fastness supervising.'

'So you are involved in this, then?' asked Edward.

'Oh, yes.' Ian sighed heavily. 'As soon as the powers-that-be spot Libby's name anywhere near a case they hand it to me.' He raised an eyebrow at Libby. 'And I take it you're not exactly happy about identifying the body?'

'I didn't know until this evening that it was . . .' Libby looked round the table and bit her lip.

'Yes, I know.' Ian nodded. 'Believe me, if we could find someone else to do it, we would, but Rachel's had everyone and his dog ferreting around for someone else, but we can't find anyone.'

'I did a tour with her once,' said Libby reflectively, 'and she never once said she had friends or relatives anywhere. Most of us had people in at least one of the towns.'

'That's sad,' said Edward. 'Poor woman.'

'I suppose it was sad, but she didn't do herself any favours,' said Libby. 'She was quite a good director, although hardly inspired, but she seemed to go out of her way to alienate people.'

'Enough to drive them to murder?' asked Ian.

Libby shrugged. 'I wouldn't have thought so.' She shot a sly glance at Ian. 'So who found her? And did she have her cards and everything on her? She still had her phone, obviously.'

'You know I can't tell you,' said Ian, with a grin.

'I've just thought,' said Edward, flashing his bright white grin at Libby, 'if, as you've intimated, the poor woman is – er – somewhat disfigured, how will you recognise her?'

'Oh!' Libby turned quickly back to Ian. 'See? I won't be able to do it after all!'

Ian laughed. 'Don't worry, Libby. I'm sure Franklyn will find a way round it.'

Libby subsided and Ben changed the subject.

Patti and Anne arrived soon after that, Anne, as usual, whooping with laughter as her wheelchair got stuck in the doorway, followed, unusually, by Beth and John Cole. The conversation turned naturally to the production of *Much Ado*, and Ian adroitly kept it away from Constance's murder, in spite of a good deal of discussion about the Twitter debacle. It was some time later, when

Ben was preparing to go and check on the theatre, that both Libby's and Ian's phones began ringing.

Everyone stopped talking. Ben paused in the act of opening the door and Edward stopped halfway between the bar and the table with a loaded drinks tray. Libby and Ian exchanged wary glances.

'Right, thank you,' said Ian after a moment and switched off his phone.

'Pru!' Libby's voice was sharp. 'Thank you for telling me. I'll call you in the morning – I can't talk now.' And she, too, ended her call.

'What?' Anne was almost bouncing in her chair. 'What's happened?'

Ian frowned at his phone. 'That was DS Trent,' he said, and looked up at Libby. 'And your call was from Lady Howe telling you the same thing, I imagine.'

Libby nodded. 'I expect so. Constance was trying to buy all the Howe Estate properties to turn into holiday lets.'

Chapter Seven

'Oh, dear,' said Ben.

'Why is that important?' asked Anne.

Patti dug her friend in the ribs. 'Lady Howe is the leading light in our local homeless charity. You know that.'

'She's turning all her properties into low-rent housing,' said Edward. 'She's dead set against holiday lets, like Libby.'

'Oh.' Anne slid down in her chair and made a face.

'And apparently, Ms Matthews had already bought several other rental properties in the area,' said Ian. he turned to Libby. 'Did Lady Howe tell you that?'

Libby was looking anxiously at him. 'No.'

He gave her a crooked smile. 'It's all right, Lib. I won't arrest her on the strength of that.'

'It couldn't be that,' said Edward. 'No one would kill her for that.'

'Not unless she'd thrown them out of their home to turn it into a holiday let,' said Libby. 'We've seen some horrendous cases over the past few months.'

'Surely it's more likely to be a mugging?' suggested Ben.

'We don't know yet,' said Ian. 'And I'm not telling you anything else.'

'What about the actors?' asked Patti. 'They were upset, weren't they?'

'Because she spoiled the surprise? Or because she was horrible to them?' said Libby.

'It's still hardly enough for a motive for murder,' said Edward.

'That soprano must have been pissed off,' said Anne, with an apologetic look at her partner. 'I saw she was really nasty to him on Twitter.'

Libby sighed. 'You weren't supposed to see *anything* on Twitter.'

'I know,' said Anne. 'So the actors must have been really mad.'

'I think, for what it's worth,' said Ian, 'that this murder was committed in despair.'

Everyone went quiet and turned to look at him. 'Sorry,' he said.

He sat back in his chair and watched them throwing ideas back and forth, until the door burst open and Harry arrived, followed more slowly by Peter.

'OK, folks!' he said. 'What are we talking about tonight? The new murder?'

Peter rolled his eyes and went to the bar, where Ben joined him.

'I'm trying not to, Harry,' said Ian. 'But naturally, no one's taking any notice of me.'

'Oh, *I* will, petal!' Harry wiggled his hips suggestively and patted Ian's shoulder. 'Stop gossiping, you lot,' he said to the rest of the table, 'or I might have to patronise the alternative hostelry.'

Ben came back at that point, and grinned as he handed Harry his glass. 'I wouldn't mind,' he said. 'But Wednesdays wouldn't be the same.'

'We were just discussing motives for that woman's murder, Harry,' said Anne. 'You know about her, don't you?'

'Oh, yes, dear, I know about her,' said Harry, collapsing into a chair beside Libby. 'I had two sirs in the caff yesterday talking about her, didn't I, madam?'

'Sirs?' repeated Edward and Anne together. Libby explained.

'So what do you think, Harry?' Ian asked. 'Is it a dispossessed tenant or a defamed actor who did the deed?'

'Now, let me see.' Harry put a finger coyly to his chin. 'It could, of course, be a militant middle-aged lady who hates landlords?'

Libby looked indignant. Harry laughed.

'Actually, petal, young Ricky, via Mavis, might have some news for you on that front.' He raised his glass to her. 'But remember what I said – don't go quizzing Mavis before you've seen Ricky.'

'Oh, that's not fair,' said Libby. 'I shall be going down to Nethergate tomorrow.'

'After you've been in to meet Franklyn, of course,' interposed Ian.

'Who's Franklyn?' asked Peter, turning to join in the conversation.

'Franklyn Taylor–Blake,' said Libby. 'Forensic pathologist.'

'What a *lovely* name!' cooed Harry. 'I must meet him!'

Peter sighed and shook his head, while Ian and Libby laughed.

'Franklyn is almost aggressively heterosexual,' said Ian.

'Who is?' Anne squeaked. Ben and Edward looked round in surprise.

'Our pathologist.' Ian grinned. 'I don't know how you haven't come across him before.'

Patti chuckled. 'Want to meet him, Anne?'

Anne turned a delicate shade of pink.

'I'm not sure I do,' said Libby, 'not if it's over the top of a – a . . .'

'Body,' supplied Ben. 'No, but Ian says Franklyn will find a way round it. And, Libby,' he continued seriously, 'after getting involved in so many murders, it's your *duty*.'

Everyone round the table but Libby laughed.

Ben finally went off to make sure the theatre was locked up and Ian and Edward left for Grove House. Libby, Patti and Anne set off down the high street. Anne lived in New Barton Lane, just round the corner from Allhallow's Lane.

'Did that woman really upset everybody?' asked Anne. 'Was she really horrible?'

'Anne!' Patti reproved,

'I'm sorry, Patti, but Anne's right – she was really horrible.' Libby sighed. 'I should have realised when I picked her up. She'd taken it for granted that she was coming to stay with me for as long as she liked.'

'So why did she end up on the Howe Estate?' asked Patti.

'No idea.' Libby shrugged. 'She booked a taxi from the pub here to go to Nethergate on the Tuesday morning without saying a word to me. And when I called her to ask what was going on, she said she'd just decided to go and see it.' Libby frowned. 'Now, it seems she'd planned it all in advance.'

'Do you think that's why she wanted to see the play in the first place?' asked Patti.

'Maybe it was a combination of things,' said Anne. 'She'd heard about the Howe Estate and thought she could see the play at the same time.'

Now Patti was frowning. 'But how would she have heard about the Howe Estate? It's not as if Lady Howe has advertised it, and this Constance wasn't local, was she?'

'No.' Libby was looking puzzled. 'And if you were just going to visit Nethergate, you wouldn't hear about it. It's not as if there are local papers in all the shops anymore, so, you wouldn't catch sight of anything there.'

'You might find it online,' said Anne. 'You know – type Nethergate into the search engine and see what comes up.'

'That's true.' Libby nodded. 'It's still odd, though.'

'Even odder that she was murdered,' said Anne.

At the corner of Allhallow's Lane the friends parted, and Libby promised to keep Patti and Anne updated with whatever she found out.

'I did want to tell you about someone I met this week,' said Patti, stopping right in the middle of the road.

'Patti!' admonished Anne. 'We'll get run over!'

'I'll ring you tomorrow.' Patti gave a small wave and set off again.

★

Patti did ring in the morning. Unfortunately, it was just as Libby arrived at the mortuary in an unmarked police car, accompanied by DS Rachel Trent.

'I'll ring you later,' grunted Libby, struggling out of the car.

The mortuary looked like a modern office block. To Libby's surprise, it wasn't even attached to the hospital.

'There is one at the hospital,' Rachel told her as they passed through the automatic doors, 'but this is Franklyn's own domain. He does a lot of private work, you see.'

Libby made a vague sound of understanding, trying to calm her racing heartbeat. Rachel shot her a worried look.

'Are you all right?'

Libby nodded and tried a wobbly smile, 'No, not really.'

Rachel pressed the button to open the door of a sterile-looking lift. 'It'll be all right, honestly,' she said.

Libby nodded again and took a deep breath.

When they arrived at a frosted glass door bearing the legend *Professor F. Taylor-Blake* she almost turned tail and ran, but her pride kicked in and she allowed Rachel to usher her inside.

'Mrs Sarjeant!' The man behind the desk stood up, beaming. He wasn't very tall, about the same height as Ben, Libby thought, much younger than she had anticipated, and with a huge grin underneath a thatch of grey-striped dark hair. 'I've heard a lot about you.'

'Oh dear,' said Libby, taking his outstretched hand.

'Oh, all good, I assure you,' he said. 'Please, sit down.'

Libby and Rachel took the two seats in front of his desk, while he perched on the edge.

'Now, Mrs Sarjeant—' he began.

'Oh, call her Libby,' broke in Rachel. 'Everybody does.'

Franklyn raised an interrogative eyebrow at Libby, who nodded. 'Very well, then, Libby. I know you're here to tell us if the unfortunate woman we brought in from near Nethergate is someone you know called Constance Matthews.'

Libby nodded again.

'Under the circumstances,' Franklyn went on, with a quick look at Rachel, 'we decided to show you what she was wearing when we found her. Of course, the coroner might argue that we could have found the clothes anywhere – in a rubbish bin or a hotel room, for instance. But there is no way you could identify her face, so we decided – that's DS Trent, DCI Connell and me – that we would take the chance. Is that all right with you?'

Libby's breath came out in a whoosh. 'Oh, yes!' she croaked.

Rachel grinned at her. 'I told you it would be all right,' she said.

'Right,' said Franklyn, sliding off the desk. He went to the door, opened it and yelled: 'Roger!'

Returning to his perch, he said, 'You don't even have to move out of the office. We will get you to sign something, if you don't mind.'

Libby was so relieved she would have agreed to do anything.

'Mind you,' she said, and cleared her throat, 'she may have been wearing something different when she was found to what I saw her wearing on Monday.'

'Which is why we brought everything we found with her.'

The door opened and a giant with a wide grin entered, bearing in his arms a pile of transparent bags. Libby immediately recognised the dressing case that had accompanied Constance to Steeple Martin.

'That's Connie's,' she said, pointing.

Between them, Franklyn, Rachel and the giant, whom Libby assumed was Roger, laid the various items out on the desk.

Libby nodded. 'That's what Connie was wearing when I brought her down on Monday,' she said. 'And that's the dress she wore to the theatre on Monday night.'

'And we found a ticket in her handbag,' said Franklyn. 'I think that settles it, don't you?'

They made sure Libby checked over every item that had been found with Constance, then she signed a formal document and

51

sank back into her chair. Roger had disappeared and now returned with three mugs of tea.

'Rachel thought you'd prefer tea to coffee,' said Franklyn. 'Sugar?'

Libby shook her head, although she still secretly preferred sweet tea, and took a grateful sip.

'Well,' she said, 'thank you for making that so painless. I only hope you won't get into trouble with the coroner.'

'The coroner wouldn't dare,' said Rachel.

'Are you allowed to tell me anything about how she was found?' Libby sent Rachel a wary glance. 'DCI Connell wouldn't.'

'What I can tell you is that we don't think she was killed where she was found,' said Franklyn, sitting back in his own chair and putting his feet on his desk.

'And all of that stuff was with her?'

'Dumped nearby.'

'But no murder weapon?'

Franklyn sent Rachel an amused glance. 'I see what you mean,' he said.

'Can't tell you that,' said Rachel.

Libby sighed.

'But at least you've seen the mortuary,' offered Rachel, 'and met Franklyn. Ian said he'd make sure you did that, didn't he?'

'He didn't organise this, though,' said Libby. 'Not unless he organised Constance's murder.'

'Even he wouldn't go that far,' said Franklyn with a chuckle. 'Mind you, after all that business at the beginning of the year down at Heronsbourne . . .'

'He only stepped out of line to expose a bad apple,' said Rachel staunchly.

'I thought he often stepped out of line when Mrs Sarjeant and her friend were concerned.' Franklyn grinned at Libby. 'And your friend's psychic, isn't she? Definitely frowned upon by the hierarchy of the force.'

'But she's helped several times,' said Rachel. 'And we're not supposed to be a force, these days. We're a service.'

'Whatever.' Franklyn took his feet off his desk and stood up. 'And now, people, I'm afraid I must shoo you out. I have more bodies to cut up.'

'That reminded me,' said Libby, as she and Rachel returned to the car. 'Is that nice DS Stone still based down in Nethergate? I meant to ask if she was related to Sir Jasper, but I suppose "Stone" is quite a common name. Anyway, haven't seen her since what Franklyn called that business in Heronsbourne.'

'Claire? Yes, she's on this investigation with me.' Rachel drove carefully out of the mortuary car park. 'Actually, I didn't tell you.'

'Tell me what?' Libby looked sideways at Rachel. 'What's happened?'

'I'm – er. Well. I've been made Acting DI.'

'Rachel!' Libby was delighted. 'Congratulations! Ian told me back then you were on your way to becoming DI Trent. That's great. So you're Claire's boss?'

'Technically we're still the same rank,' said Rachel. 'And she's up for promotion soon, too. It's a question of openings. And,' she risked a quick look at Libby, 'there might be difficulties.'

'Difficulties?' Libby frowned.

'With Ian.'

Libby stared. 'She moved down from Dartford, you said,' she said slowly. 'And I wondered when we first met her. Was I right?'

Rachel kept her eyes on the road in front. 'Maybe. She and Ian – well, they'd started seeing one another.'

Chapter Eight

'Seeing one another?' repeated Libby. 'Not now?'

'No. You'd have known if they were, wouldn't you? You see Ian socially, and he's even moved near you.'

'I suppose we would,' agreed Libby. 'Golly! That's a bit of a shock! When did they split up?'

'They only got together just after all the Heronsbourne business,' said Rachel, 'but it wasn't going well, especially once Ian was back to full duties. And it all collapsed just about the time that woman asked him to look into the homeless person.'

'I suppose it would,' said Libby. 'That woman was an ex-girlfriend of Ian's – although when they'd been seeing one another I have no idea.'

'He always kept his private life to himself, didn't he?' mused Rachel with a little smile. 'I remember you didn't even know where he lived until he moved to Grove House.'

'Hmm.' Libby was frowning. 'Edward must have known. I wonder why he didn't say anything?'

'I don't suppose he thought it was any of his business,' said Rachel, in a faintly reproving tone.

'No.' Libby looked determinedly out of the side window. 'Of course not.'

'Anyway,' continued Rachel, 'I thought I ought to tell you, as you're bound to come across her during the investigation into Ms Matthews' death.'

'So I don't put my foot in it.' Libby nodded wisely. 'Very sensible.'

Rachel risked another look and giggled.

Rachel declined to come in for coffee when they arrived back at Allhallow's Lane, so Libby was free to call first Patti, whose phone went straight to voicemail, and then Fran.

'I said so, didn't I!' she finished triumphantly, after pouring out the whole story. 'I said she was a bit older than the average DS.'

'So you did,' said Fran, sounding amused. 'And now, please forget it. They both deserve their privacy.'

'But I want to know why he didn't tell us,' complained Libby.

'We didn't see that much of him between the end of the Heronsbourne case and the beginning of the last one, did we? We rarely do between cases – unless we're involved.'

'He and Edward come over on Wednesdays.'

'Not every week.' Fran sighed. 'Let it go, Lib. If Ian wants to he'll tell you. He probably didn't want you criticising.'

'I wouldn't criticise!' Libby was indignant.

'Yes, you would. Now, were you planning on coming down here this afternoon?'

'I don't know. Harry says I'm not allowed to talk to Mavis until I've spoken to Ricky, but I ought to go and see Pru, I suppose.'

'Well, let me know if you're coming. Now I've got to go and do something about our lunch,' said Fran, and was gone.

'Lunch,' muttered Libby, and went into the kitchen to look gloomily at the contents of the fridge.

She was just assembling the ingredients for an uninspiring sandwich when her phone trilled from the sitting room.

'You rang,' said Patti. 'Sorry, I was in the shop.'

St Aldeberge had a very successful community shop, run mainly by Patti's parishioners, in which Patti took the occasional shift.

'I was returning your call from earlier,' said Libby. 'I was on my way into the mortuary.'

'Oh, yes!' said Patti. 'How did it go?'

Libby told her. 'And now, what did you want to tell me?'

'It wasn't urgent.' Patti sounded as though she was settling down for a chat, so Libby abandoned her sandwich and sat down on the sofa. 'It was just about one of my parishioners. Well, not actually about—'

'Patti!' Libby laughed. 'Don't ramble! It isn't like you.'

'Right. This parishioner, old Miss Barton, she owns a house between here and Nethergate. Right on the cliff, before you get to the caravan park. Temptation House, it's called.'

'Good name. Victorian, is it?'

'How did you guess? Yes, it is – used to belong to her parents – huge place, it is. Anyway, it's much too big for her, so she lets most of it out and just lives on the ground floor herself. Well, recently, a lady called Karen has moved into the top floor, and she called me this morning.'

'What about?' prompted Libby when Patti seemed to have come to a stop.

'She said some woman had been trying to persuade Miss Barton to sell.'

Libby let out a breath. 'And you think . . .?'

'That it was your Ms Matthews, yes.' Patti sighed.

'When was this? Yesterday?'

'Oh, no.' Patti was definite. 'The last couple of weeks.'

'Couple of *weeks*?'

'Yes, turned up on the doorstep. And then she phoned. Actually complained that Miss Barton had no internet connection.'

'Blimey!' said Libby. 'How did Karen find out? Did Miss Barton tell her?'

'No, Nora did.'

'Nora? Who's Nora?'

Patti sighed. 'Sorry – I'm not being very clear, am I?'

'No,' said Libby.

'Nora lives in the house, too. She's got her own rooms, but acts

56

as a sort of companion to Miss Barton. She was worried about the letters and phone calls and told Karen. Karen asked Miss Barton, who pooh-poohed the whole idea. Apparently she won't leave Temptation House until she goes out in a box.'

'So why did Karen tell you?'

'Because Nora thought this person was threatening Miss Barton. And I *think*, although she didn't say, that Karen and Nora were threatened themselves.'

'Wow!' Libby sat back and stared at Sidney, who was glaring at her from the table

'Do you think you ought to tell Ian?' asked Patti hopefully.

'Well, no.' Libby grinned at Patti's gasp. 'Rachel's in charge – didn't we mention it last night?'

'Oh – er . . .'

'Well, actually, it's Acting Detective Inspector Rachel Trent.' Libby allowed herself a smug smile. 'Assisted by Detective Sergeant Claire Stone.'

'Who?'

Libby reminded Patti about Claire, but stopped short of explaining her relationship to Ian. She knew Patti would disapprove of gossip. 'Anyway, yes. I shall tell Rachel,' she said. 'If it was Connie, those tactics would certainly provide a motive for murder, wouldn't they?'

'It couldn't be Miss Barton, though,' said Patti. 'She's too old.'

'No, but maybe Connie has used the same approach to other people,' reasoned Libby. 'But how did she know about Miss Barton? Or Lady Pru?'

'Well, there was the estate agent.'

'The estate agent?'

'Yes – you know. Sells houses.'

Libby made an explosive sound.

'All right, all right. Guy must know about him. He'd been leafletting the area and approaching people with large houses – like Miss Barton. I bet he talked to Lady Pru, too.'

'So was he doing the same thing as Connie?'

'Trying to, I would have thought. Guy will know. Anyway, it's about time you got your investigating boots on, Lib!' Patti sounded more cheerful now.

'Ye-es,' said Libby slowly. 'I think so, too.'

Libby arranged to go straight to Howe House after eating her hastily assembled sandwich.

'I'm going now,' she told Fran as she climbed into the Silver Bullet, her rather inappropriately named little car. 'If I've got time I'll come to you afterwards. Unless you want to meet me there?'

'No, I'd better stay here. Guy's doing something about Christmas cards this afternoon, so I'm in charge of the shop. Give me a ring if you need to.'

Libby drove as fast as she dared along the Nethergate Road as far as the turning for the Tyne Chapel, where she turned off to the right. The road now became a lane that took her past the little stone bridge and the row of cottages to large, rusting iron gates, which stood wide open. She turned in and drew up outside the vast, towered Victorian pile that Lady Howe called home.

The front door stood ajar. Libby heaved it open and called, 'Pru! Where are you?'

A creak and hurried footsteps issued from the back of the huge hall behind the staircase.

'I'm here.' Lady Prudence, greying auburn hair escaping from its once-neat French plait, emerged in a flurry of woollen scarves.

'The door was open, Prudence!' remonstrated Libby. 'There's a murderer about, for goodness' sake!'

'But I knew you were coming, and I don't hear if people knock,' said Prudence. 'You can shut it now. Come into the kitchen.'

The kitchen was a vast affair, all pine shelves, Aga and a table even bigger than Hetty's at the Manor. Prudence insisted it was perfectly functional, and that it wasn't worth modernising it when the whole house was due to be remodelled. Libby supposed she could see the sense in that.

'So tell me about when Connie Matthews approached you,' she said, settling herself in the extremely tatty leather armchair next to the Aga.

Prudence switched on the electric kettle and looked around vaguely for mugs. 'A couple of weeks ago,' she said. 'Beginning of October.'

Same time as the approach to Miss Barton, thought Libby.

'Did she just turn up, or what?'

'Oh, no!' Prudence looked shocked. 'No, she wrote to me. All very proper.'

'And what exactly did she say?'

Prudence frowned. 'That she understood I had various properties that she would like to buy.'

'Did she say she wanted to turn them into holiday lets?'

'Oh, no.' Prudence gave Libby a knowing look. 'She'd hardly do that, would she? It might give me ideas!'

'Right.' Libby grinned. 'So what *did* she say?'

'That they obviously needed renovation, and she would be prepared to – er – take them off my hands.' Prudence smirked. 'As if!'

'Did you reply?'

'No.' Pru shrugged. 'I didn't see the point. But then she phoned.'

'And?' Libby watched as Prudence poured boiling water into the mugs.

'All sweetness and light at first. And I just kept refusing. And then she phoned again.'

'Did she threaten you?'

Pru looked surprised. 'Well – yes, actually. It was very vague. You know – "You're all alone out here, anything could happen" sort of threats. And then she turned up with this great big bruiser!'

'What – a heavy?' Libby sat up, wide-eyed. 'Did you tell the police?'

'Not then.' Prudence fished out teabags and waved a milk bottle at her guest.

'But you *did* tell them?'

'Yes – when they told me who the body was.' Prudence looked uncomfortable.

'When was the last time you saw her?'

'She only came the twice.' Prudence sat down at the table. 'As she was in the woods, I suppose she was coming again, just didn't quite make it.'

'Hmm.' Libby blew on her tea. 'It looks as though you weren't the only one she was going for, Pru. I heard of someone else today. At least, I think it was her.'

'Who? She said she already had property here.'

'She did?' Libby sat up straight. 'Where?'

'I don't know. Who have you heard about?'

'A woman called Barton,' said Libby. 'Has a house—'

'Oh – old Dorothy Barton.' Prudence nodded. 'She wouldn't have got much change out of her!'

'Oh, you know her?'

'Not really. She was a friend of Percy's mum. She must be about a hundred!'

'Yes, well – Connie got sent away with a flea in her ear apparently.' Libby put her mug down. 'But what I want to know is, how did she come to be here in Nethergate?'

'Because she's already got property here, like she said.' Prudence frowned.

'Yes, but how? Why?'

'I don't know!' Prudence shook her head. 'Perhaps this is her home town?'

'Never!' Libby looked appalled. 'I'd have heard. She couldn't have kept that quiet when I moved here.'

'Well, maybe she looked up where you lived and decided it looked a nice place?'

'Oh, no!' said Libby. 'That would make it all my fault.'

'Whatever the reason she came here, I wish she hadn't,' said Prudence grumpily. 'And I don't like being under suspicion.'

'You?' Libby was aghast. 'They don't suspect you!'

'It feels like it,' said Prudence. 'So you'd better get investigating, Libby.'

'You're the second person to say that today,' said Libby. 'But I don't know how.'

Prudence shot her a quizzical look. 'How do you usually do it?'

'Erm,' said Libby.

'You ask questions, don't you?'

'Yes, I suppose so.'

'Questions that the police don't ask?'

'Maybe.' Libby looked doubtfully at her friend. 'You sure you don't want to do it instead?'

'Oh, I wouldn't know where to start!' said Prudence. 'And I don't know as many people.'

'You know old Miss Barton.'

'I said, not really, and only because she was a friend of Percy's family. I don't come from round here, don't forget, and Percy and I lived mainly in London. I only came back here after he died to sell up.'

'Only you didn't,' said Libby, with a smile.

'No, well. And look how that's turned out,' said Prudence.

'What about the estate agent?' Libby asked, as Prudence saw her to the door. 'My friend Patti told me an estate agent had been pestering people with big houses. He spoke to Dorothy Barton, apparently.'

'Did he?' Prudence was vague.

'He didn't come here?'

Prudence shrugged. 'I don't think so. I'm not always here.'

'Right.' Libby waited, but nothing more was forthcoming.

'I'll be in touch, then,' she said, and Prudence closed the door.

Chapter Nine

Libby drove back to the main road and on into Nethergate. If Constance already had property here, there had been no need for her to ask Libby to fetch her on the basis that she knew nothing about the area. It also explained how she knew where Libby lived and her connection to the theatre and thus to the Glover's Men. And what, Libby asked herself, had all that been about? Had she really wanted to see *Much Ado*, or was it a pretext to poke around in Libby's local knowledge?

There were no parking spaces in Harbour Street, as usual, so Libby parked in the car park behind the Blue Anchor and the Sloop. Fran was waving to her from the doorway of the gallery, so she plodded down past Coastguard Cottage, taking note again of how many little key safes were on the doorframes of the pretty cottages.

'Checking all the holiday lets, were you?' asked Fran as she arrived.

'Yes.' Libby followed her friend into the warm shop, where she found half a dozen customers drinking coffee. She turned to Fran with raised eyebrows. Fran shrugged.

'Guy's idea. Coffee for customers.'

Guy shouted from the back of the shop, where he had a studio. Libby made her way through to him.

'It's the Keep Britain Warm initiative,' he said, grinning over his shoulder. 'I don't suppose any of them will buy anything.'

'That's very nice of you,' said Libby.

'Not just me,' said Guy. 'We all need to do our bit, don't we? So many people need help.'

Libby wandered back to Fran. 'I must tell you what Pru told me,' she said.

'Sit down, then,' said Fran, indicating a stook by the counter. 'Do you want coffee?'

'No, I've just had tea at Pru's. And guess what?'

Guy emerged to listen, wiping his hands on his rather scruffy smock.

'And that's why you were looking at the cottages along here,' said Fran. 'I wonder if she owned any of those?'

'I want to find out about this Miss Barton,' said Libby.

'I think I've heard about her,' said Guy. 'She lets out her house to what used to be called "indigent females". A good sort.'

'Barton,' muttered Fran thoughtfully. 'Don't we know a Barton?'

Libby frowned. 'Well, of course we do. Neil Barton, you can't have forgotten! He died.'

'Ye-es.' Fran was still looking thoughtful.

'You think he was a relation of this Miss Barton?'

'Hannah!' Fran looked up with a smile. 'Hannah Barton!'

'Yes?' said Guy and Libby together.

'Don't you remember, Lib? When we were looking into Jackie Stapleton's death? Her ex-boyfriend, Gary Turner's girlfriend!' Fran sat back, looking smug.

'Oh, yes! Lived in St Mary's!' Libby slapped the counter. 'I wonder if she was related to Neil? We never thought to ask, did we?'

'St Mary's?' asked Guy.

'Used to be a nunnery – or a monastery, or something,' said Libby. 'Turned into flats. Behind the Red Lion at Heronsbourne.'

'Ah.' Guy nodded. 'I think someone's had a go at turning some of those into holiday lets, too.'

'What we need to do,' said Libby, 'is find out what property Connie owned down here. How do we go about that?'

'We *need* to, do we?' Guy grinned.

'Yes.' Libby looked defiant. 'If she's trying to buy up rental property, she needs to be stopped.'

'I hate to mention it, Lib, but she *has* been stopped,' said Fran.

'Well, yes. What I meant to say was' – Libby took a deep breath – 'we need to find out so we can turn it back into proper rental homes.'

'And how are we to do that?' asked Fran.

'Find out who she's left it to, of course!' said Libby.

'And I doubt whoever that is would be inclined to change use just because we say so,' said Guy, reasonably.

'Haven't we found out any legal loopholes?' asked Libby. 'Your group has been working on it, haven't they, Guy?'

'Yes, we have, and we've got your pet solicitor working for us for nothing.' Guy beamed at her.

'Philip Jacobs?' Libby's eyes were wide. 'Really? I always knew he was a good egg.'

'I swear you get your entire vocabulary from P.G. Wodehouse!' said Fran, laughing.

Philip Jacobs was a resident of Steeple Martin, leading light of the local chess club, held in the upstairs room of the Coach and Horses every Sunday, and de facto leader of the Coach pub quiz team.

'There are several groups, nationally, as well as locally, trying to fight the no-fault eviction legislation,' said Guy, 'as you well know. It was first pledged by the government in 2019, and it's sent thousands into homelessness.'

'And it's still there,' said Libby, gloomily. 'I can't bear to think about it.'

'Well, if you want to find out who owns all these rental properties, I'll ask,' said Guy. 'We've been compiling a list. But most are companies; the few that are privately owned are usually someone's own holiday home, which is only let out when the owner isn't using it.'

'Which isn't so bad, is it?' said Fran. 'Our place was a holiday home once.'

Libby nodded, remembering. 'And old Jim Butler owned it, didn't he? Come to think of it, he had several properties in the town. I wonder if he still has?'

'No, he hasn't.' Guy shook his head. 'He sold them all – to private buyers, I might add. Lady Howe and I went up to see him a month or so ago. He said he wasn't happy about the town being gentrified. Went on a bit about posh coffee shops and sourdough bread.' Guy chuckled reminiscently. 'I have to say, I rather agreed with him.'

'So do I.' Libby slid off her stool. 'So we need to find out what places Connie owned and what she was trying to buy.'

'To see who had a motive for murder?' asked Fran.

'Well, yes. If she was trying to turn someone out of their home – or buy it in order to do that – it would be a bloody good motive, wouldn't it?' Libby sounded militant. A couple of the customers looked over at the sound of her voice.

'Better than the *Much Ado* actors taking umbrage at criticism,' agreed Guy.

'Who shall we talk to then?' Libby picked up her basket.

'We've still got Hannah Barton's number, haven't we?' said Fran.

'Good idea.' Libby pulled her collar up. 'I'll ring her when I get home.'

'I almost forgot,' she said, as she was going out of the door. 'Patti mentioned an estate agent who'd been approaching people with big houses. He spoke to Dorothy Barton, apparently, but Lady Pru didn't seem to know about him.'

'Oh, yes, we know about him. Trevor Taylor.' Guy scowled. 'Not the same thing as the holiday lets, though.'

'No?' Libby came back inside. 'What was his game, then?'

'Trying to get hold of large properties to turn into smaller units for sale.'

'So not actually that bad, really?'

'He was still trying to turn people out of their homes,' said Fran.

'Oh.' Libby looked round at the group of people currently enjoying Guy's hospitality. 'Pretty grim, then?'

But when Libby got home, she found Ben in the sitting room with Hereward Fisher and Oliver Marcus, all three looking decidedly glum.

'What's up?' Libby halted in the sitting room doorway. 'What's happened?'

'The police,' said Oliver.

'They've taken Freddie in for questioning,' said Hereward.

'*Wha-at?*'

'Quite.' Ben was looking angry. 'I can't imagine what Ian is thinking!'

'It isn't him,' said Libby. 'Rachel's in charge, I told you. She's Acting DI.' She collapsed on to a chair at the table. 'I don't believe this!'

'Can't you do anything, Libby?' Oliver stared at her with beseeching eyes.

Libby frowned at the cold woodburner. 'Why have they done it?' she asked.

'As far as we can tell, just because it was Freddie who that woman was particularly nasty about,' said Hereward.

'They haven't found any evidence?'

'I don't see how they could!' said Oliver. 'Freddie has been with us the whole time. And on stage for a lot of it.'

'I wish I knew when she was killed,' said Libby. She stood up again. 'I'll ring Ian. I expect I'll get my ear bitten off, but I can at least try, and then I'll try Rachel. Oh, and that nice Claire Stone – she's on the case, too. I'll go in the kitchen. Anyone want tea?'

Everyone refused and Libby retired to the kitchen with the landline and her mobile.

Ian's personal mobile went straight to voicemail, so she left a very brief message, then called Rachel.

'DS Trent,' came the crisp voice.

'Rachel – it's Libby.'

Rachel sighed. 'If this is about Freddie Cannon . . .'

'Yes, it is,' replied Libby, faintly surprised.

'He's been released for the time being.'

'But why was he arrested in the first place? He couldn't possibly have done it!' Libby's voice rose.

'How do you know that?' Rachel sounded tired. 'We have no idea when Ms Matthews was killed. Just because he was on stage every evening doesn't put him in the clear.'

'But how would he have known where she was? None of us did!'

'True, but he could have been in touch with her.'

'You had her phone. I bet there was no contact between them. And why on earth would they have been in touch?'

'Well, no . . .'

'And how would he have got to Nethergate, anyway? He came on the company bus.'

'He could have got a lift—'

'Oh, rubbish, Rachel!' Libby paused. 'This wasn't your idea, was it? You're protecting somebody. Please don't tell me it was Claire.'

'All right, all right.' Rachel let out another heavy sigh. 'You're right – someone jumped the gun. And no, it wasn't Claire. But he is still a person of interest.'

'Has he been sent back to us?'

'If you mean to Steeple Martin – yes. And now I must go. Don't go poking about too much.'

Libby heaved a sigh of relief and went back into the sitting room. 'It's OK,' she said, and watched three faces dissolve into smiles.

'But why the hell was he taken in in the first place?' asked Ben. 'He couldn't possibly have done it.'

'That's what I said. I gather someone jumped the gun – that's what Rachel said.' Libby shrugged off her cape. 'Would anyone like a medicinal Scotch? Wine?'

'I daren't,' said Oliver, 'although I'd love one. I'll buy you one later if you're coming up to the theatre.'

'Oh, we'll be there,' said Libby. 'I want to make sure Freddie isn't suffering from a sense of ill-usage – although he's every right to, under the circumstances!'

Oliver and Hereward departed, Hereward still looking a little white and shaken, and Ben poured Libby a healthy-sized pre-prandial whisky.

'Well done, darling,' he said, leaning down to kiss her cheek. 'Although I doubt Ian would have been so forthcoming.'

'No, but actually Rachel didn't tell me anything except that Freddie had been released, which Ian would probably have told me, too.'

'She didn't say who had jumped the gun?' Ben sat down beside her on the sofa. 'It can't have been anyone who knew about the theatre.'

'Because they wouldn't have taken in someone due to go on stage this evening?'

'Well, that, yes, but anyone who knew your connection to – oh, I don't know – murder investigations.'

Libby laughed. 'I would think if it was a DC who did know about us, they'd make a point of arresting any actor who came into sight.'

'Good job Rachel's in charge then!' Ben grinned.

'I wonder if any of Claire's former team are still around? They might have an axe to grind,' said Libby thoughtfully, remembering the recent police investigation that had nearly gone disastrously wrong.

'I doubt it,' said Ben. 'Now, hadn't we better be getting on? It'll soon be time to go.'

It didn't seem the right time to try to call Hannah Barton, now, so Libby decided to leave that until the following day. While she put together a hurried supper of stir-fried chicken and noodles, she told Ben of the day's conversations.

'It does all seem to hinge on the homelessness crisis, doesn't it?' he said, getting cutlery from a drawer. 'Not just this murder, but your last investigation.'

'I suppose so,' Libby agreed. 'Young Ricky and all the homeless of Nethergate ... Which reminds me, Ricky's coming to see Harry this weekend.'

'And he's got something to tell you about Mavis, Harry said, didn't he?' Ben gave her a dig in the ribs. 'I don't know how you've contained yourself!'

'I was very tempted to go and see Mavis this afternoon,' said Libby ruefully. 'Oh, and guess what Guy's doing?'

She told Ben about Guy's Keep Britain Warm initiative. 'Do you think Mavis is doing the same thing?'

'Maybe. Wait and see.' Ben took a plate from her and sat down. 'Eat up, or we'll be late.'

Chapter Ten

Tonight, the applause for 'Sigh No More' was even more rapturous than ever. In fact, the minute Freddie began to sing, he had to stop to allow for the cheers.

'The audiences don't realise that he's the one who sings,' Hereward whispered to Libby.

'Until he actually starts,' agreed Libby. 'He's doing awfully well, isn't he? I wondered if he might be very upset.'

Hereward laughed softly. 'Quite the reverse! He's revelling in the attention!'

At the end of the play, some of the cast came out into the auditorium to meet the audience. Freddie, inevitably, was surrounded.

'He'll get a terrible swelled head,' said Oliver, coming up to Libby at the bar.

'Not much chance of that while he's still a person of interest to the police,' replied Libby.

'Have you heard any more from them?' Oliver looked anxious. 'Jasper called earlier. Apparently, someone called him.'

'What – from the police?'

'No – the press.' Oliver shook his head. 'How *do* they get hold of these things?'

'But why Sir Jasper?' Libby was frowning. 'He's nothing to do with the Glover's Men.'

'No, but some bright spark had remembered the whole *Mrs Tanqueray* fiasco, and me, of course, and linked the whole thing together.' He shook his head. 'Hereward's told the press officer, and they'll try and put a lid on it.'

'Without much success, if I know the media,' said Libby gloomily.

'Look on the bright side,' said Oliver. 'The Twitter storm didn't do us any harm, after all – quite the reverse. Even if it did spoil the surprise. Hey – suppose Twitter had been around when *The Mousetrap* opened seventy years ago! They'd never have kept their secret then, would they?'

Oliver moved off to speak to a couple of audience members who obviously wanted him to sign their programmes, and Libby smiled. He was right, Constance Matthews' Twitter storm hadn't hurt the production; but – she sighed as she made her way to the front doors – murder was a different proposition altogether.

Hereward materialised at her side with a glass of red wine.

'Ben said this was what you'd like.' He dropped a kiss on her forehead. 'Thank you, Libby. You're a star.'

She smiled back, a trifle ruefully. 'I can't imagine you'll want to come back again, though. Two disasters out of three runs is a bit hard to take.'

'Oh! And there I was, thinking we might reprise the *Dream* next June!' he said with a grin.

'Really?' Libby beamed. 'It did go rather well this year, didn't it, despite the rush.'

The company had played *A Midsummer Night's Dream* at the Oast Theatre in June when another venue had let them down, and, as with *Much Ado*, they could have filled the theatre three times over.

'What I was thinking was,' Hereward went on as Oliver and Ben came to join them, while Libby began ushering the public out of the theatre, 'we could run it for a fortnight, and perhaps – I don't know what you think about this – have a sort of summer fair on your lovely green outside?'

Libby and Ben stared at him, open-mouthed.

'That's a bloody marvellous idea!' crowed Oliver. 'Libby, Ben – do say yes!'

Libby held the door open rather abstractedly for some departing audience members, nodded at them vaguely. 'What do you think, Ben?'

'I'm with Oliver!' said Ben, grinning broadly. 'As long as there's nothing in the book.'

'Looks like that's on, then,' said Libby, holding out her hand to Hereward, 'As long as there's nothing in the book, as Ben says, and as long as Peter agrees.'

'Of course he will!' said Oliver. 'We'll get on to the bosses tomorrow, won't we, Herry?'

'And Libby will solve the murder so there's no shadow over us!' said Hereward.

The lights were still on and customers still sat at the tables in the Pink Geranium when Ben and Libby went by twenty minutes later.

'After-show suppers,' said Peter, as he let them in. 'To what do we owe this visit?'

'Things to tell you,' said Libby. 'Would you like us to go out the back?'

'No, window seat,' said Peter. 'I'll come and join you. Nice drop of Merlot, Lib?'

Adam appeared in his long white Victorian apron and gave his mother a kiss. 'I won't ask,' he said. 'Bound to be this murder.'

'No, young man, it isn't!' said Ben. 'Makes a change, eh?'

Adam went off laughing, and Harry and Peter both appeared bearing glasses of red wine.

'Now,' said Peter, 'what's up?'

'Nothing's up,' said Ben. 'We've had a proposition.'

Between them, they told Peter and Harry about Hereward's suggestion.

'Brilliant idea,' said Harry. 'I can run a street food stall, like we did for the beer festival.'

'What about the bar, though?' asked Peter. 'Will Tim run it from his back door like before, or will you run a Hop Pocket bar?'

'That's a point,' said Ben thoughtfully.

'Never mind that,' said Libby. 'First of all, as Hereward said, we've got to solve this murder and clear Freddie's name.'

'Eh?' said Peter and Harry together.

'Oh – didn't anyone tell you?' asked Ben. 'Freddie was arrested.'

The explanation was interrupted frequently by Harry saying goodnight to his customers, but eventually he and Peter were up to date with the police investigation and Libby's own enquiries.

'So tomorrow I'm going to see if I can get hold of Hannah Barton, who we met over in Heronsbourne, and see if she's related to this Miss Barton who owns Temptation House,' Libby finished up, 'and see if I can track down any former tenants of Constance's who she might have annoyed.'

'From what I hear,' said Harry, 'any former tenant of the old bat's will be annoyed. Homicidal, probably, if she chucks them all out.'

'That's what I'm thinking,' said Libby. 'She can't have just bought up empty rental properties. Some of them must have had sitting tenants.'

'Which is why she'll have got them cheap,' said Peter.

'As I know,' said Ben. 'It's why the estate cut its losses and sold their farms to all our tenants.'

'Which was a very good thing to do,' said Libby. 'Now they've got security and you don't have to take final responsibility.'

'But he didn't make as much profit,' said Harry, rubbing his thumb and forefinger together with an evil grin.

'My cousin is trying hard to shed the mantle of the bloated plutocrat, I'll have you know,' said Peter.

'And become a simple brewer,' added Libby.

'You can mock,' said Ben. 'But it is actually embarrassing being a bloated plutocrat.'

'You're doing your best, cuz,' said Peter, patting him on the shoulder. 'You're employing people at the hop garden, brewery and the pub. And I bet you're not making a huge profit out of any of them, are you?'

'Not yet,' agreed Ben. 'But you never know. I might become a beer millionaire.'

'Anyway, back to Connie,' said Libby. 'I'm going to find out as much as I can about her empire. Neither Pru nor Freddie could possibly have anything to do with it – and if the police can't prove that, I shall.'

Peter grinned at his cousin and his partner. 'Here we go again!' he said.

Friday morning, Libby sat down at the kitchen table with her third cup of tea and found Hannah Barton's number in her phone. To her surprise, she was answered almost immediately, to the accompaniment of a high-pitched wailing.

'Hannah?' Libby asked hesitantly. 'Do you remember me? Libby Sarjeant.'

'Libby! Yes, of course. Just hang on a minute.'

There were shushing sounds, a hiccup or two, and then obvious slurping sounds.

'Sorry, Libby. Josh wanted a feed.' Hannah sounded tired. 'What can I do for you?'

'Well . . . I gather there's a junior Barton now?'

Hannah laughed. 'Oh, yes! You wouldn't know, would you? Josh was born two weeks ago.'

'Oh, goodness! Congratulations! I won't bother you, then – you must be up to your ears. And exhausted, of course.'

'No, no, it's lovely to have somebody else to talk to.' Hannah sighed. 'I *am* up to my ears, yes, in constant talk of babies and baby paraphernalia. It gets a bit wearing. And my brain's in danger of atrophy.'

'I can imagine,' said Libby. 'So you're on maternity leave, are you?'

'Sort of. I left my old job when Gary and I moved in together – oh, you won't have known that, either?'

'No, but it was obvious you'd got back together,' said Libby. 'Have you both moved out of St Mary's, then?'

'Oh, no! Gary's flat was bigger than mine, so I moved in there. We didn't even try and find anywhere else. We'd never have managed it.'

'Well, actually,' said Libby, 'that was partly why I wanted to talk to you.'

'Oh? Hang on – Josh wants to change sides.'

Libby imagined Hannah changing her baby from one breast to the other. Nice to know breastfeeding wasn't going out of fashion quite yet.

'There. So are you connected to our local action group? We saw that your friend Guy was, so we assumed you and Fran were, too.'

'Exactly,' said Libby, pleased that she didn't have to explain from the beginning. 'And I was wondering . . .' She paused, thinking how best to frame her question. 'Well – if you were any relation to—'

'Dorothy Barton,' interrupted Hannah. 'Yes, she's my great-aunt.'

'How . . .?'

'Did I know you were going to ask that?' Hannah laughed. 'Because a) she's a well-known character in the area, and b) Karen Butler told me that someone had been threatening her.'

'Oh.' Libby felt somewhat deflated. 'So you know all about it.'

'Not *all*, no. But I'm sure you're going to tell me.'

So Libby embarked on the tale of Constance Matthews. It took some time, but Hannah didn't seem to mind.

'And you wanted to know if this Matthews person was the one threatening Aunt Dorothy? And she's threatened Lady Howe, too?'

'Sort of,' said Libby. 'Lady Pru said it was more a reminder that she was all alone out there in a deserted woodland. Not, of course, that she is all alone. Not all of the time, anyway.'

'Yes, that was more or less what she said to Aunt Dorothy,' said Hannah. 'Nora and Karen were more worried than Aunt Dot, it has to be said – and I have to admit, I wondered what one old lady could do to another.'

'Yes, but Lady Pru said she came back with a heavy,' said Libby.

'A *heavy*? As in a gangland heavy?' Hannah sounded sceptical.

'Apparently.' Libby sighed. 'And when her body turned up in Pru's woods, she assumed – and so did the police – that she, Connie, was coming back again.'

'Yes, I see.' There was silence for a moment, while Hannah was obviously thinking this over. 'So what can I do to help?'

'For a start, I wanted to confirm that Connie was going round pestering people, and you've done that for me. And second, I wondered if you knew of anyone in the area who'd been thrown out of their home to make way for holiday lets?'

'Several.' Hannah's voice was harsh. 'As you obviously guessed, that was why Gary and I didn't even try to look for anywhere else. There isn't anywhere.'

'And do you know who gave the old tenants notice?'

'Some,' said Hannah. 'A couple of the original landlords jumping on the bandwagon. In several cases it was private landlords who could no longer afford to keep their rental properties. The buy-to-let boom is over, thanks to the rising bank rate – you know, mortgage costs and everything – so the small landlords were only too happy to sell. But we were all asked by the action group, your Lady Pru and Guy Wolfe, for any names we had. We didn't get any here, because St Mary's is owned and administered by a trust. When the convent sold it they tied everything up legally, so it can't be sold on.'

'So the action group will have all the names?'

'Of landlords and former tenants, yes,' said Hannah. 'And I'm sure the police will have gone through those. They'll be looking at former tenants particularly, won't they?'

'Yes.' Libby sighed. 'That was what I was thinking, but so far I haven't heard that they've done so. Neither Pru nor Guy have said anything.'

'I wonder why?' Hannah was obviously as puzzled as Libby was.

'Yesterday they were looking at the company who are playing at our theatre,' she said. 'Did you hear about that?'

'Yes,' said Hannah. 'Gary went to the pub the other evening and George was telling him all about it. You know George always likes to know what you're up to.'

'I know. Can't get away with anything,' said Libby.

'And it was this same woman?'

'It was. So the police decided it must be one of the actors.'

'The singer? The soprano?'

'Yes. They realised how daft that was and let him go again, but they're still being very suspicious.'

'Oh, how ridiculous!' Hannah hooted with laughter. 'I hope he's recovered? I just wish I could come and see it myself.'

'Yes, he's recovered – for the moment, at least. He's enjoying the attention. How he'll feel when the run's over and he goes back to normal, I don't know. Shame you can't come. No babysitters in the offing?'

'He's too young yet,' said Hannah fondly.

'Well,' said Libby, 'I'll be down nosing around Heronsbourne within the week, so I'll let you know when, and you can introduce me to Josh.'

'That'd be lovely,' said Hannah. 'And keep me in the loop. Actually, that will be easy, because after I left my old job I started working from home for a friend of yours who I met through the quiz.'

'Oh, yes? Who's that, then?'

'Philip Jacobs. And he's working for the action group.'

Chapter Eleven

'You're working for *Philip*? So why didn't you know all this already?'

'Because I've just had a baby, of course!' Hannah giggled. 'Philip is such an old-fashioned gentleman, he wouldn't dream of asking me to do anything while I'm – er – what's the term?'

'Lying-in, I think,' Libby told her. 'No, I can't imagine Philip wanting anything to do with all that messy baby business, can you? Well, fancy that! So you'll get to know all about everything anyway. When will you start working again?'

'Oh, fairly soon. My brain will go completely to mush if I don't start using it soon. So we'll keep each other up to date, shall we?'

'Oh, yes,' agreed Libby, 'but there was another thing, actually, Hannah. Not really to do with this case.'

Hannah sighed gustily. 'Barton is quite a common name, Libby.'

'How . . . ?'

'We were very surprised when you didn't ask back in May.' Hannah laughed. 'And yes, we are – were – related. Joan Barton, it was her single name, she never married, so "Mrs" was a – what do they call it?'

'Courtesy title?'

'That's it. Her father was my great-uncle, my grandad's brother, while Dorothy was their sister, so my great aunt.'

'So you were – what? Second cousins once removed, or something?'

'Something like that.' Hannah sighed. 'I'm just grateful they were victims rather than murderers.'

'One other thing before you go,' said Libby, 'what do you and Philip know about an estate agent called Trevor Taylor? Apparently he approached your aunt.'

Hannah sighed. 'Oh, him. He's a pain, but not really a problem. He's just been trying to rustle up business. He tried to get Aunt Dorothy to sell her house through him.'

'Guy and Fran said he seemed to want to turn big houses into smaller units.'

'Or knock them down and build new ones,' said Hannah. 'I don't think he got anywhere with anyone, though.'

After this cheering conversation Libby took herself upstairs for a shower, then, dressed in her favourite jeans, jumper and cape, set off for Nethergate.

However, she didn't get further than the high street, when Harry appeared on the pavement waving frantically.

'Want a passenger?' he called when she stopped.

'Who? You?'

'No.' Harry beckoned to someone inside the caff, and out rushed an excited liver and white springer spaniel cross, followed by a slightly less excited young man.

'Ricky!' Libby got out of the car and crossed the road. 'And Barney!' She bent down to make a fuss of the dog, who was wagging his tail furiously and trying to climb up her leg.

'Hello, Libby,' said Ricky, and suffered himself to be kissed.

'Ricky wants to go down to see Mavis, if you wouldn't mind giving him a lift?' said Harry. 'I assume that's where you're going?'

'To Nethergate, yes. Are you ready now, Ricky?'

'Yes, thank you, Libby.' Ricky turned to Harry. 'I'll see you later, shall I?'

'Well, yes, as you're staying here,' said Harry, giving him a friendly buffet on the shoulder. 'We're going to educate him, Lib.

Pete's got him a ticket for tonight with us. Your son and heir's taking on the management of the caff for the evening.'

'Blimey!' said Libby. 'What about the cooking?'

'Limited menu, pre-prepared. Donna's coming over, too.'

Donna was Harry's former right-hand woman, who now worked on his admin at home, having retired into motherhood.

'Come on, then, Ricky, let's go. All right if I leave you with Mavis while I go off and do some other stuff? I'll come and collect you later.'

'That's fine.' Ricky nodded.

'See you later, Hal,' said Libby, and led the way across the road.

Ricky in the passenger seat and Barney panting happily in the back, Libby set off once more for Nethergate.

'So what did you want to tell me about Mavis?' she asked, when they'd cleared the village. 'I've been dying to know.'

'Didn't Harry tell you?' Ricky seemed surprised.

'No, he refused. He's good at keeping secrets.'

'Well,' Ricky looked at her sideways, 'what she's doing is opening the Anchor as a warm space. For the homeless, but also for people who can't afford to heat their homes. And she's supplying tea and coffee and people just give her what they can afford – or nothing, if they can't.' Ricky beamed. 'Isn't that good?'

Libby's throat constricted and she had to blink away tears. 'That's wonderful!' she croaked eventually. 'Can she – I mean, she can't – well, can she?'

'Afford it?' suggested Ricky. 'I don't know. If people want hot food I think they have to pay, so ordinary customers can still go in, but how it works otherwise I don't know.'

'And we can't ask, really, can we?' said Libby, after clearing her throat. 'You remember Guy? Well, he's now giving customers coffee, even if they don't buy anything, and letting them stay as long as they want.'

'And Hal said there's a protest group about the holiday lets business,' said Ricky. 'You're involved in that, aren't you? And that woman who got murdered – she was a landlord?'

'How long have you been with Harry?' asked Libby with a laugh. 'You seem to have heard a lot!'

'I arrived this morning. Edward gave me a lift.'

'Oh, did he?' Libby was surprised, although she realised it was logical. Edward lectured at the Medway campus of Ricky's university, and had the use of a room there if he needed to stay.

'Yes – he offered when he heard I was coming down. He had something to do on campus last night.'

Libby wouldn't put it past Edward to have manufactured the circumstances for Ricky's benefit. The group of friends had rather adopted him and Barney after the events of the early summer.

'Well, she'll be pleased to see you,' she said aloud. 'And perhaps you can find out if any of the people there had anything to do with our murder victim. I haven't spoken to Mavis about it yet.'

'Yes, I will.' Ricky nodded. 'Will you talk to Mavis today?'

'Of course. And now,' said Libby, 'tell me about your nan. I hear she's moving into our village?'

'Yes.' Ricky shot her another quick look. 'Didn't tell you, though, did she?'

'No. Ben's mum says she's scared of me. I didn't think I was scary.'

Ricky laughed. 'Nan's used to getting her own way, and she doesn't think she'll be able to with you.'

'Oh.' Libby smiled . 'She could be right. But tell me – does she realise that the other flats – apartments – in the Garden will be rented out to families?'

'She didn't.' Ricky giggled. 'She does now.'

'Ah.' Libby tried to suppress a giggle herself, and couldn't. 'It's all part of our campaign to replace the long-term rentals that have been taken off the market. Did you hear about Lady Howe?'

'That's the lady who's letting her big house out?'

'Yes – and her cottages, and barns. That's where the murder victim was found.'

'Oh.' Ricky nodded wisely. 'So it could be a tenant who knocked her off? Hal said it might have been an actor?'

Libby explained, as well as she could without giving away Freddie's secret, assuming that Ricky wouldn't have seen the Twitter fuss. She was wrong.

'Oh, yes, I know about that. I'm really looking forward to seeing it tonight. I don't know much about Shakespeare, but Hal says it's brilliant.'

Libby had a feeling there would be rather a lot of "Hal says" larded through Ricky's conversation.

'And how's your mum?' Libby hadn't taken at all to Debbie Pointer, but thought she would probably have to be nice to her if Ricky and his grandmother were going to become fixtures in Steeple Martin.

'She's all right. Got over it all now.' Ricky turned to look out of the side window. Libby decided to leave well alone. Ricky's treatment at his stepfather's hands was not something to be remembered with any fondness.

They whiled away the rest of the journey with reports on Ricky's cultural studies and media with journalism university course and Libby's reports on life in Steeple Martin.

'So you'll be coming to spend a good deal of time in the village after Nan's moved in?' said Libby as they breasted the hill that led down into Nethergate.

'I expect so,' said Ricky. 'Although I'm hoping she won't mind if I stay with Hal and Peter. Their cottage has a garden for Barney, you see,' he added hastily.

'Of course,' said Libby, hiding a grin.

She parked in the car park behind the Blue Anchor and, before they'd even got the doors open, Barney was whining in recognition. Mavis, and Graham, manager at the Sloop, had been the ones to rescue Barney and keep him safe until Ricky came to find him.

After which, Ricky had worked for a time for Mavis in the café, so it was home from home for the dog.

'I wish I could leave him here while I'm at uni instead of Mum's,' Ricky said as they walked round the corner.

'But they couldn't look after him properly,' said Libby. 'And you go back home every weekend to see him while he's with your mum, don't you?'

Ricky nodded. 'Perhaps she could move to Steeple Martin, too,' he said suddenly, but then Barney let out a volley of barks and pulled the lead out of his master's hand in his eagerness to get at the short solid figure of Mavis, standing in the doorway of the café.

Libby stood and watched while the reunion took place, noticing how many people appeared from the Blue Anchor to greet boy and dog. When the effusion died down a bit, she walked over.

'Hello, Mavis,' she said. 'Nice to have him back?'

Mavis, a little red in cheek and bright of eye, nodded. 'I'd have him here all the time if I could,' she said softly, while Ricky took Barney to see Graham, who had emerged from the Sloop.

'At least he can come and visit now,' said Libby. 'And it looks as if you've got your hands full.' She nodded towards the crowded café. 'Ricky was telling me it's all about this warm space initiative.'

Mavis's expression turned militant. 'Couldn't stand by, could I?' She pulled herself up straight and turned to lead the way inside. 'You just look.'

And Libby did look. Every table was crowded with people, sometimes sharing chairs, sometimes standing. Some were obviously from the homeless community, others looked like Mavis's usual customers, although with a few more younger people than normal. She turned to Mavis.

'No one can afford heating?' she said quietly.

'Not just that.' Mavis went behind her counter and, without asking, began to pour Libby a large white mug of tea. 'See that table over there? That woman with the baby and the toddler?

83

Chucked out of their house, they was. We reckon by that woman what was killed.'

Libby looked, horrified. 'Where are they living?'

'B&B up King Edward Street. All of 'em, including dad. He's at work now, up at Darren's car repair shop. She – Kirsty – used to work, too, but they can't afford the childcare now, so she's had to stay home.'

'Oh, bloody hell,' muttered Libby.

'They ain't the only ones.' Mavis pushed the mug over to Libby. 'Your mate Guy's been trying to make people take notice, and you've been doing a bit, too, haven't you?'

'Yes, as much as we can,' said Libby. 'And Lady Pru—'

'Is a ruddy saint,' said Mavis. 'Kirsty and her kids will have somewhere to live soon as she gets all her places done up. And she's going to set up a crèche thing, as well.'

'Is she? She didn't tell me that!' Libby shook her head in wonderment. 'You're right – she *is* a saint. She didn't deserve to have that foul old woman killed on her land.'

'No – and this lot don't deserve the piggin' police treating 'em like suspects, either!' Mavis sniffed loudly.

'Oh, come on, now, Mavis – it isn't as bad as that!' said a new voice.

'Hello, Ian,' said Libby.

Chapter Twelve

'Yes, well . . .' muttered Mavis, going even redder and turning away to the coffee machine.

'Let's keep it low-key, Libby,' said Ian. 'I'm not here officially.'

'What are you here for, then?' asked Mavis. 'And how do you want your coffee?'

Ian eyed the machine. 'Plain black, please.'

'Go on, then,' prompted Libby. 'What *are* you here for?'

'I was going to talk to a couple of people.' Ian turned his back on the crowd, who by now were watching the group at the bar with considerable curiosity. 'Claire was a bit worried.'

'She was?' Libby's eyebrows shot up.

'I'll tell you later,' murmured Ian. 'Thanks, Mavis.'

He began to move towards Kirsty and her children, and halted Libby with a look as she made to follow him.

'Best leave him, gal,' said Mavis. 'He knows what he's doing.'

Luckily, at that moment Ricky and Barney reappeared. A sausage appeared magically beside Barney at the same time.

'Isn't it brilliant?' he said to Libby, and then, with a frown, 'What's Inspector Connell doing here?'

'Helping,' said Libby. 'He's not supposed to be here at all. He's a *chief* inspector, you see, so he's meant to stay in the office.'

Ricky spluttered into his Coke. 'Oh, yes! I remember.'

'Anyway,' Libby went on, 'yes, it is brilliant, but it's dreadful that it has to happen at all.'

'Well, you and the others will get everyone's homes back, won't you?' Ricky cocked an eyebrow at her.

'I don't know about that, but we're going to try and get people other homes, if we can.'

'What's going to happen to all the places she bought up now, d'you reckon?' asked Mavis.

'I thought of that,' said Libby. 'We've got a solicitor friend working on it, but we need to find Connie's will first – or the police do.'

'Connie – was that her name?' asked Mavis. 'Nice old-fashioned name. Doesn't suit her.'

Ricky and Libby grinned.

Ian was now sitting down at the table with Kirsty and two or three others. To Libby's surprise the toddler had climbed onto his lap, a circumstance that seemed to bother him not at all.

'What did you come down here for, anyway?' asked Mavis. 'Or was it just to see that Fran?'

'No.' Libby was still watching Ian. 'I came down to see if I could find anybody Connie had upset, but it looks as though Ian's doing that.'

'I could show you someone,' said Mavis thoughtfully. 'I reckon they'll be in in a bit.'

'They? Who?' Libby turned back to the counter.

'Old girl owns a house up there.' Mavis jerked her head backwards. 'Couple come in from there.'

'Do you mean Dorothy Barton at Temptation House?' asked Libby. 'How she does keep popping up!'

'That's her. Know her?' Mavis was surprised.

'No – but I've just discovered I know her great-niece.'

'That Hannah? Got involved with that golf course business, didn't she?'

Libby nodded. 'So you know about Connie approaching her?'

'Not just her. *She* give her what for.' Mavis gave a grim smile. 'No, she had a go at poor Nora. She'll be in with that Karen in a bit. Ask her yourself.'

Libby raised surprised eyebrows at Ricky. 'How about that, then?' she said.

Ricky shook his head. 'I don't really know much about it.'

Ian returned to the counter. 'Well, I can't see any of them banging Constance Matthews over the head,' he said, returning his mug to Mavis.

'Did you think they might?' asked Libby, while Mavis looked belligerent.

'The local sergeant was exploring the possibility,' said Ian diplomatically.

'And Claire told you?' Libby sent him a knowing look.

'I asked. She could hardly refuse to say anything to her commanding officer.' Ian gave what could only be described as a smirk.

'Well, here's someone else you can talk to,' said Mavis, nodding towards the door. 'Although I don't reckon Nora will want to say much.'

A thin, elderly lady was being ushered inside by a taller, middle-aged woman with untidy, fair hair.

'Karen, Nora,' said Mavis, as they approached the counter. 'Your usual? Dunno where you're going to sit – bit crowded today.'

Libby obligingly slid off her stool. 'Here,' she said. 'Have mine.'

'Thank you,' said Nora in a quavering voice. 'Most kind.'

'Thanks, Mavis.' Karen's voice was surprisingly soft. 'Hello.' She nodded at the other three. 'You're Ricky, aren't you? I remember you – and Barney.' She bent down to pat Barney, who had finished his sausage and was quietly dozing.

'This is Libby,' said Mavis, as Karen straightened up.

'Hello,' said Libby, holding out her hand. Karen shook it and looked quizzically at Ian.

'I'm Ian,' he said with a smile, and shook hands with both women.

Now what? wondered Libby, as silence fell.

'I was just talking to Kirsty over there,' Ian went on smoothly, 'and the other people at her table. About the rental properties.'

'Oh?' Karen frowned. 'Why?'

'He's a policeman!' cried Nora, in a muted shriek. 'I've seen him before!'

Mavis, Ricky and Libby all sighed wearily.

'Yes, I am.' Ian looked resigned. 'And there's nothing to worry about, I promise you.'

'That's what they all say,' said Karen. 'So why are you here? That Sergeant Powell already put the fear of God into Nora here, asking where she was when that dreadful woman was killed.'

Libby saw a look of annoyance flash over Ian's face.

'I'm sorry about that,' he said, smiling at Nora. 'He was only doing his job.'

'Yes, well . . .' Karen took a mug from Mavis, while Nora seemed to get smaller than ever on her stool.

Libby fixed her eyes on Ian and raised her eyebrows. He gave a slight shrug and an almost imperceptible nod.

'What we really wanted to know,' she said in a confidential tone, drawing closer, 'is what that woman told you. And did she threaten you? Or Miss Barton?'

'Yes!' said Nora and Karen together.

'All of you?' said Ian.

'Yes.' Karen pulled herself up straight, looking militant. 'She came to see Dorothy first – a business meeting, she said – and got turned away with a flea in her ear. Then—'

'When was that?' Ian interrupted.

'About a month ago,' said Karen, looking faintly surprised. 'Why?'

'Hannah said she'd been down here before,' said Libby.

'Did you think she hadn't?' asked Karen.

'She told me she hadn't. Said she knew nothing about the area.' Libby lips set in a firm line.

'Go on, Karen,' said Ian.

'Well, then she came back and tried again with Dorothy, but this time she told her she ought to be careful, a woman living alone

88

in an isolated house.' Karen shook her head. 'It was a threat. And when Dorothy laughed at her and said she wasn't living alone, that woman lurked outside until Nora and I came out. Then she tried to bribe us to leave. It was pitiful. As if we'd just get up and leave all for a paltry few thousand pounds—'

'And then,' broke in Nora, obviously taking courage from her friend, 'she said it might be as well if we went or we might get hurt.'

'Bloody— Good heavens!' Libby amended quickly.

'But she didn't follow it up?' said Ian.

'Not until Tuesday, when she came with some great lout,' said Karen.

'What?' said Ian.

'You too!' said Libby.

'I saw him,' said Mavis.

'I think I need more coffee,' said Ian with a sigh.

'Ricky,' said Mavis, casting a wary glance round the café, where several customers were beginning to take an interest in the group at the counter, 'take 'em up to the flat. Libby, you stay here and take the coffees up after.'

Ricky gently pulled Barney's lead, and ushered Nora, Karen and Ian to the door that led to Mavis's private quarters.

'Not good to have police questioning people in here,' Mavis muttered, lining up fresh mugs. 'You want tea?'

'Yes, please.' Libby leant in closer. 'Who's this Sergeant Powell they mentioned?'

'Don't you know him? Pain in the arse, if you ask me. That Sergeant Stone's much nicer – and that Rachel. She's an inspector now, isn't she?'

'Acting inspector,' said Libby. 'After that other one – er – retired.'

'Hmm.' Mavis loaded mugs on to a tray. 'That Powell was very thick with him. Still too much of that sort of thing in the police.'

'Yes.' Libby sighed. 'And when Ian tries to put it right, he's the one who gets into trouble.'

Mavis cocked her head on one side. 'Looks like he's trying to put things right now, though.'

'It does, doesn't it?' Libby gave her a wry smile. 'I'll take these up.'

Upstairs, Nora, seated in one of Mavis's armchairs, was in full flow.

'. . . and we told her, didn't we, dear? We aren't moving whatever happens.'

'Was that on Tuesday?' Ian asked, accepting a mug from Libby.

'Oh, no.' Karen shook her head. 'That lout was with her then, and she said they'd be back. We didn't get to say anything that time.'

'What did he look like, this lout?' asked Ian.

Karen and Nora looked at each other, frowning.

'Big,' said Nora.

'Broad. Not fat exactly, although he was going that way.' Karen thought for a moment. 'Bobble hat, so I don't know about hair. And he was tall – very tall.'

'Did he speak? Did he have an accent?' asked Libby.

'Not a word, dear,' said Nora.

'Would you both come in to the station and have a look at some photographs?' Ian looked from one to the other. 'He might be known to us.'

'Then again,' said Libby, 'if he's local, how would Connie have known him?'

'Well, we've learnt that she knew the area despite what she said to you,' said Ian.

'Yes, but to get to know local villains?' Libby shook her head. 'It seems so unlikely, somehow.'

'The woman was murdered, Lib,' said Ian. 'So not that unlikely.'

'We'll come in, won't we, Nora?' Karen looked quite pleased at the idea. 'I'll drive us in tomorrow, if that's all right?'

'That's fine,' said Ian. 'I'm sorry you'll have to come all the way into Canterbury.'

'Such a pity they closed the station here,' said Nora. 'So reassuring.'

'I know.' Ian smiled at her. 'I wish we could afford it.'

'The bobby on the beat,' Nora said wistfully.

Ricky shifted restlessly in his chair. 'Do you mind if I take Barney for a walk?' he asked.

'No, you go on,' said Ian.

'But be back here by four if you want a lift,' said Libby.

Ricky tipped an imaginary hat and he and Barney left.

'Such a nice boy,' said Nora fondly.

'He's at university now, isn't he?' said Karen.

'He is. And Barney lives with his mother during the week,' said Libby. 'Although I think that might change.'

'Oh?' Nora looked interested. 'Is he coming to live here?'

'No,' replied Libby, 'but Barney might go to Ricky's grandmother.'

'Yes, well that's good,' said Ian hastily, 'but could we get back to Ms Matthews?'

'We've told you everything we know!' said Karen, looking surprised.

'I just wondered if you'd heard anything from anyone else in the town.' Ian looked at Libby. 'What about your friend Lady Howe?'

'I was going to go and see her today,' said Libby. 'She mentioned a lout, too.'

'Maybe I'll come with you,' said Ian. 'If you don't mind.'

'No-oo.' Libby was wary. 'Don't frighten her, though.'

'Oh, he's not frightening, dear!' Nora smiled and patted Ian's arm. 'Not like that other one.'

Libby managed to subdue a giggle and Ian looked smug.

'Have either of you got a number I can contact you on if I need to?' asked Ian.

Nora looked disappointed. 'That isn't a verb, dear,' she said.

Ian looked puzzled.

'Contact, she means,' said Libby with a grin.

'Here,' said Karen, handing over a business card. 'My number and Temptation House are both there.'

Shortly after this, they left.

'My car?' suggested Ian. 'I wouldn't squash into yours.'

'All right,' agreed Libby, following him to the car park. 'What are you going to say to Pru?'

'Ask her about the lout, of course.' Ian, looking surprised, opened the passenger door and ushered Libby inside.

'What a gentleman,' she said. 'Nobody does that anymore, you know.'

'Yes they do,' said Ian firmly. '*I* do.'

He drove them up to the top of the Nethergate hill, then, to Libby's surprise, turned left into Canongate Drive, and right down to the end where Jim Butler lived, where he turned right into an almost concealed lane.

'I didn't know this was here!' said Libby. 'It must lead straight on to Pru's land.'

'It does. We're on it now. We think this is how Ms Matthews arrived on Tuesday.'

'It was Tuesday, then? Not Wednesday morning?'

'That was when she was found,' said Ian. 'Franklyn has now come up with a time of death.'

'Which is?'

'Between – approximately – eight p.m. and midnight.'

Chapter Thirteen

'So she was only here for one day?' said Libby. 'That means she knew where she was going in advance – *and* she must have already been in touch with her heavy. She had no time to cultivate a new one, did she?'

'No. I did take your point about him possibly not being local, though. We'll see what the ladies come up with tomorrow.'

He drew to a stop and pointed. They were now in fairly thick woodland and, over to the right, Libby saw the flicker of blue and white police tape.

'That's . . .' she began.

'Yes.' Ian started the car again. 'She must have known her way around here well.'

'Or the lout did.'

'But she'd been here before. She knew the layout of the Howe Estate.'

'Hmm.' Libby was quiet for a moment. 'How long has this lane been here? I've visited Jim Butler several times with Ben and never noticed it.'

'That's the old boy with the fat Labrador in the big bungalow?' Libby nodded.

'He's the one who opened it up. It was always there, but had got buried in vegetation. Your Lady Pru and he got together and agreed to open it. Not many people know about it, but she said she wanted people to be able to walk the land so she didn't want barriers. Mr Butler was quite happy – apparently he takes the dog for walks there.'

'Lady – that's the dog,' said Libby. 'I suppose it saves him having to take her all the way down to the beach. They're both getting on. Did you know he used to own Fran's cottage?'

'I think maybe I did.' Ian frowned. 'She seems to have been there for years.'

'She has been,' said Libby with a grin.

The lane came out at the edge of the woods, and soon Ian was parking in front of the main house, where builders were assembling scaffolding.

'She's certainly getting a move on, isn't she?' Libby was admiring. 'Perhaps some of those people you were talking to in the Anchor will soon have somewhere to live.' She turned to Ian. 'Did you speak to anyone Connie had actually thrown out? Or just people she'd threatened?'

'Everyone at that table – Kirsty, was it? – and the others had all been evicted. Not necessarily by Matthews.'

'Oh, bloody hell!' Libby was horrified all over again. 'Are they all in the B&B in King Edward Street?'

'No.' Ian's face darkened. 'A few of them are sleeping rough. Probably more than a few. Those were just the ones I spoke to.'

'And it isn't all to do with Connie?' asked Libby. 'Only a couple of people have mentioned an estate agent called Trevor Taylor.'

'It isn't all to do with Matthews,' said Ian, 'it's something that's been going on for some time. You know yourself how many holiday lets there are in the town. I haven't heard of this Taylor, though.'

'He doesn't work for Brooke's, does he?' Libby asked.

'Not as far as I know.'

'And speaking of Brooke's, what about the caravans?' Libby asked hopefully. 'They're still there, aren't they? They could be used as temporary accommodation.'

The caravans behind the Blue Anchor had been part of a case earlier in the year.

'Still part of the ongoing investigation,' said Ian, 'but I'll see what I can do.' He frowned. 'I don't know why Rachel hasn't suggested it.'

'Oh, don't be hard on her, Ian. She's finding her feet, isn't she?'

'I suppose so. But Sergeant Powell's been down here regularly ever since that last business. He should have done something.'

'So should Claire, then,' said Libby innocently.

'Hmm,' said Ian. 'So who else have you talked to?'

'Changing the subject?' Libby grinned at him. Ian's face darkened alarmingly. 'All right,' she said hastily, 'I'll tell you. Hannah Barton – remember her? From the Heronsbourne case? Her aunt's old Dorothy Barton, and it turns out she's working for Philip Jacobs – Hannah, that is, not Dorothy – and he in turn is working for the action group, with Guy and Lady Pru here. They've got all the gen on who owns what. I thought you'd know?'

Ian's face now wore an arrested expression. 'Who did they give it to?'

'I don't know. I assumed Rachel.' Libby frowned worriedly. 'Is it all going wrong again?'

Ian sighed and resumed walking towards the house. 'I hope not.' He shook his head.

'Claire's been reporting to you, hasn't she?' Libby quickened her pace to keep up. 'Is it that Sergeant Powell? Was he part of DI Winters' gang?'

'Not quite how I'd put it,' said Ian as they fetched up in front of the front door, which, once again, stood ajar. 'Not very security-conscious, is she?'

'Yes, I am!' Lady Howe emerged, hair even wilder than usual. 'I saw you coming, that's all.'

'Lady Howe, this is Chief Inspector Connell,' said Libby. 'He wanted to meet you.'

Lady Howe narrowed her eyes at Ian. 'Oh? Why?'

'I'm overseeing the case, your Ladyship,' he said, holding out a hand, 'and as Libby was coming to see you, I asked if she would introduce us.'

Prudence looked at Libby, then back at Ian. 'Do you want to ask me more questions? I've already talked to Inspector Trent and Sergeant Powell.'

Ian let his hand fall.

'Ian likes the personal touch,' said Libby hastily. 'Could you tell him what you told them, Pru?'

'I think I told them different things.' Prudence was frowning. She vainly tried to tuck a wayward strand of hair behind her ear. 'Inspector Trent came first – that was before she spoke to you, Libby. Then Sergeant Powell came afterwards.' She looked quickly at Ian, then away again. 'I'm afraid I didn't like him much.'

'Look, Pru – can we come in?' asked Libby. 'Then you can tell us what happened in comfort. We won't stay long, anyway – I've got to get back home.'

'Oh, very well.' Prudence held the door wide for them. 'Do you mind the kitchen? Nowhere else is very warm.'

'No. We were just at Mavis's Blue Anchor. She's got a lot of people in there who can't afford to heat their homes,' said Libby.

'And a lot who haven't *got* homes,' added Ian.

'Mostly because of that woman.' Prudence nodded briskly. 'Well, sit down, both of you. Tea?'

They both declined.

'Right.' Prudence perched on a stool, crossed her arms and thrust her hands up her sleeves. 'That woman called here first a couple of weeks ago – I told you, Libby – and started off fairly politely, but ended up telling me I should be careful out here on my own. And then she phoned me—'

'You didn't tell me that!' interrupted Libby.

'Didn't I? Well, she did, basically just to see if I'd changed my mind. And she said . . .' Lady Pru trailed off and stared at the floor.

'What did she say, Lady Howe?' Ian asked gently.

'She told me to look at all the homeless people in Nethergate who she could find homes for if only she had my property.' Prudence looked up. 'Complete manipulation, wasn't it?'

'I'm afraid so.' Ian looked grim. 'But she came again, didn't she?'

Prudence nodded. 'On the Tuesday. With this great lout. She was openly threatening that time.'

'What did he look like?' asked Libby.

Prudence's description was no more help than Nora and Karen's and, again, Ian asked if she would mind going in to the station to see if she could identify the man from the police force's gallery of criminals.

'Nora and Karen from Temptation House are going, too,' said Libby. 'Perhaps you could go together?'

'Have you got a number for them?' Prudence didn't look particularly thrilled at this suggestion.

Ian gave her Karen's number. 'Although I probably shouldn't,' he said. 'Data protection and all that.'

'What, even with phone numbers?' said Libby.

'Oh, yes.' Ian gave a tired sigh. 'So there's nothing else you can tell us, Lady Howe?'

'No.' Prudence shook her head. 'And at least the builders are here now, so I'm not on my own. And I didn't tell you, Libby – the cottages are almost ready. They didn't need that much work. I've already got some families lined up.' She beamed proudly.

'Kirsty and her children?' Libby nodded at Ian. 'And I hear you're going to set up a crèche?'

'That's right!' Prudence looked surprised. 'Do you know Kirsty?'

'We met just now at the Blue Anchor,' said Ian.

'Ah, she's a good soul, Mavis.' Their hostess slid off her stool. 'Now I must get back to my builders. You didn't want anything else, did you?'

Ian stood up. 'No, thank you, Lady Howe. You've been very helpful.'

'Have I?' Prudence looked surprised and faintly worried.

'Just one thing, Pru,' said Libby. Ian frowned at her. 'Who did you tell about Connie's visits?'

Prudence frowned. 'Um – well. Guy, of course.'

'Guy Wolfe?' It was Ian's turn to look surprised.

'I'm sure I told you about Guy being involved with the action group,' said Libby.

'Anyway, I told him,' Prudence went on, 'and the builders. She never came when they were here.' She looked puzzled. 'Actually, that was odd. How did she know? I mean, was that deliberate?'

Ian had his notebook out, now. 'Who are these builders?'

'Oh, they wouldn't have anything to do with her,' said Prudence. 'As I said, they were never here when she came.'

'That's just the problem,' said Ian, looking irritated.

'Who are they, Pru?' persisted Libby. 'Are they a local firm?'

'Of course!' Prudence was indignant. 'Brendan Birch – know him? He uses all local people, and takes on some school leavers, too.'

'I hope he has all the right cover.' Ian put his notebook away.

'I'm sure he's perfectly legal.' Prudence was now looking combative. Libby sighed.

'Come on, you two,' she said. 'This is not a battle. We're all on the same side here.'

Prudence avoided Libby's eyes, but Ian was still scowling.

'Come on, Ian.' Libby took his arm. 'I'll call you, Pru, OK?'

They made their way back to Ian's car.

'There was no need to be rude,' said Libby, as she climbed into the passenger seat.

'I wasn't rude.' Ian started the car.

'You were criticising her builder.'

'I was simply hoping all the right permissions and insurances were in place.' Ian swung back into the little lane. 'And,' he went on more mildly, 'I should have asked who else she'd told. Thank you for that.'

'Well, it seemed obvious to me. Especially now we know that Connie never appeared when Mr Birch and his minions were on the premises.'

'And how did she know that?' Ian nodded. 'I think we ought to look into Mr Birch.'

'Is that the royal "we", the police – or you and me?'

He sent her a sharp glance. 'The police, of course.'

'Surely somebody – Sergeant Powell, perhaps – will have done that?' Libby smirked out of the side window.

'I shall ask Acting Inspector Trent,' said Ian, as the car emerged beside Jim Butler's bungalow.

'Not DS Stone?'

Ian sighed gustily. 'All right, Libby, say what you've got to say and get it over with.'

'Me?' Libby turned a wide-eyed stare on her companion. 'What *do* you mean?'

'DS Stone and I went out a few times after the Heronsbourne Golf Club case.' Ian kept his eyes on the road. 'If you remember, I was on gardening leave for a few weeks.'

'And you're not seeing one another now?'

'No, Libby. It wasn't appropriate once we were both back on active duty, as it were.'

'How bloody daft,' said Libby.

Ian didn't reply.

Back at the Blue Anchor, they found Fran chatting to Ricky. Kirsty and her children had gone, as had Karen and Nora, but new people had taken their places.

'How was Pru?' asked Fran, after greeting Ian.

'She gave us some information,' said Ian with a warning glance at Libby, who bridled.

Fran laughed. 'He doesn't want it broadcast over the town,' she said. 'He knows you'll tell me.'

'Quite,' said Ian, with a sigh.

'Well, you might as well ask Mavis if she knows – you know.' Libby nodded significantly. 'Can't hurt.'

'Who?' asked Mavis and Fran together.

'Brendan Birch,' said Ian. 'A builder, apparently.'

'Brendan? Course.' Mavis folded her arms across her bosom and looked truculent again. 'What are you poking about him for?'

'No, no,' said Libby hastily. 'Just wondering if any of the people he employs ... er ...'

'Had anything to do with Connie's death?' suggested Fran helpfully.

Ian sighed. 'Not exactly.

'Good bloke, Brendan,' chimed in Ricky unexpectedly. 'He helped us when – when ... well, when we were turned out of the caravans.'

'He did? How?' asked Ian.

'Well, not exactly when we were turned out,' said Ricky. 'It was – um – sort of *before*.' He bent down to fondle Barney's ears. Barney looked surprised.

Libby narrowed her eyes at him. 'Got you in there, did he?'

Ricky blushed. 'I don't want to get him into trouble,' he said. 'But yes.'

Ian laughed. 'In that case, he's probably a *very* good bloke, Ricky,' he said.

Chapter Fourteen

Ian left soon after this, and Libby filled Fran, Mavis and Ricky in on Lady Howe's information.

'And it looks to me,' she concluded, 'as if someone in the local force is muddying the waters again. Ian's not been told about quite a lot, and inquiries haven't been made about some fairly obvious things.'

'Sergeant Powell,' said Mavis, glowering at the coffee machine.

'But he isn't in charge,' said Fran. 'It's Rachel Trent.'

'But she'll trust her sergeants,' said Libby. 'And that's Powell and Claire Stone.'

'Well, Claire Stone would tell Rachel if Powell is interfering, wouldn't she?' Fran raised an eyebrow. 'And surely, she'd suggest relevant lines of inquiry, even if Powell didn't.'

Libby frowned. 'I would have thought so. And I don't understand why Rachel hasn't thought of Pru's builders.'

"Ere! You leave Brendan out o' this!' Mavis barked.

'Not him, but one of his men,' said Libby. 'All we wanted to know was who knew about Connie threatening Prudence. Someone might have let that out.'

'All to the good, I'd've thought,' snapped Mavis.

'Yes, but it might have given someone the idea to look for her – Connie, I mean – on Pru's land and – well, and . . .'

'Bump her off,' submitted Ricky.

'Exactly,' said Libby.

'Someone like Nora, I s'pose?' suggested Mavis, her voice dripping with sarcasm. 'Or our Kirsty?'

Libby sighed.

'Come and have a word with Guy,' said Fran.

'I've got to be getting back,' said Libby gloomily.

'Just a quick word,' said Fran. 'Do you want to come, Ricky?'

'Guy won't want Barney in the shop,' said Ricky. 'Say hello for me, and I'll wait here for Libby.'

'He's very mature for his age, isn't he?' said Fran, as she and Libby walked down Harbour Street.

'Ricky? Yes. Must be all the trauma he's been through. That last episode on the beach earlier this year would have defeated anybody but he survived.' Libby shook her head. 'I don't know how he's coped.'

Fran opened the door of the Wolfe Gallery, and ushered Libby inside.

'Hello, Lib!' Guy came forward looking surprised. 'Didn't expect to see you today.'

'She's just come to tell you what she's been doing since Connie was murdered,' said Fran. 'I take it you don't want more tea or coffee, Lib?'

Libby shook her head and launched into a precis of her murder-related activities over the last couple of days.

'And I wondered if you'd got a list of affected tenants from Philip?' she concluded. 'We can't understand why the police haven't asked for one.'

Guy looked at her quizzically. 'Have you asked Ian?'

'Yes – he doesn't understand it, either.'

'Hmm.' Guy pulled thoughtfully at a loose thread in his disreputable smock. 'Well, it was offered.'

'*Offered*?' Libby squeaked. 'Who to? Please don't say Rachel!'

'No.' Guy looked up. 'Philip offered it to a Sergeant Powell.'

'What?' gasped Libby.

'You didn't tell me that!' said Fran.

'Didn't I? Sorry.' Guy patted his wife's arm.

'I'm sending Ian a text,' said Libby, scrabbling for her phone. 'He'll still be driving.'

'What about Rachel?' said Fran. 'She ought to know.'

'If I do that,' said Libby, laboriously typing her text, 'it's telling tales.'

'So it is if you tell Ian, surely?' Guy was looking worried.

'No, this is a conversation between friends — unofficial-like.' Libby pressed send. 'There.'

'I'd have a word with Philip if I were you,' said Fran.

'I shall, and Hannah.' Libby nodded. 'He needs to start sending her work, she's going stir crazy with that baby.'

'I bet she didn't say that,' said Fran with a grin. 'That's you twisting things to suit yourself.'

'Well, not quite,' conceded Libby, 'but nearly.' She sighed. 'I'd better collect Ricky and get off home. I'll let you know if anything else happens.'

The drive back to Steeple Martin was enlivened by Ricky's descriptions of all the people he'd talked to in the Blue Anchor and the Sloop, many of whom were worried about the increased cost of heating their homes this winter, and many of the rest either didn't have their own homes or were in fear of losing them.

'I'm lucky,' he said, turning to stroke Barney's nose, which had appeared between the front seats. 'I suppose I've got three homes, in a way. Uni digs — and that was dead lucky — Mum's house and Gran's place.'

'And no heating bills in any of them,' added Libby, with a grin. 'When you think of where you were only a few months ago.'

'I know.' Ricky sighed. 'I can't believe it.'

Libby drew up outside the Pink Geranium.

'Especially here!' Ricky turned to her with a huge grin. 'I'm so glad I met you all, Libby.'

'So am I!' said Libby, swallowing the lump in her throat that association with Ricky and Barney so frequently engendered.

Back at Number 17 Allhallow's Lane, Libby checked her phone, put the kettle on – she was ready for tea now – and even remembered to check the landline answerphone. To her surprise, the little red light was blinking.

'Hello, Libby! Reg Fisher here. Can you give me a ring back? It's about Samhain.'

Reg pronounced it correctly, as 'Sow-un'.

'Hallowe'en?' Libby said to Sidney. 'What does Reg—oh.'

Reg Fisher was the 'Squire' – leader – of Puckle Morris, from Pucklefield, a village a few miles from Steeple Martin. He had been helpful in the formation of the Steeple Martin Morris side earlier in the year. And Hallowe'en – or Samhain – was one of the traditional festivals at which Morris sides danced. Libby had forgotten all about it.

'Reg? Hello, nice to hear from you.' Libby sat down at her kitchen table with her tea. 'Are you dancing on the thirty-first?'

'Of course!' Reg laughed heartily. 'Wanted to know if your side was dancing or if you'd like to come over here and join us?'

'Not up to me, Reg. Have you called Ben? Or Duncan Cruikshank?'

'Tried 'em both, but can't get hold of 'em. Can you ask Ben to give me a ring?'

'Yes, of course,' said Libby. 'How are you? How's the Puckle Inn?'

'Excellent!' Libby held the phone away from her ear. Reg could be a little overwhelming. 'Charles Bertram's gone!'

'Gone? You mean he's sold up?' Libby was astonished, although not altogether surprised. Charles Bertram had been far too refined for a country pub in a working village.

'No – he's put in a manager and retired to Tunbridge Wells.' Another gale of laughter assailed Libby's ears. 'He wasn't best pleased about all the nasty goings-on round here.'

'I can imagine,' said Libby. 'So who's the manager? Good bloke?'

104

'Good *girl*, actually.' Reg lowered his voice. 'Right smasher she is, too. You want to come over here and meet her. Does good grub, too. Young Maria's right made up.'

Maria was the formerly downtrodden barmaid.

'Yes, I'd like that,' said Libby. 'We've got a lot on just now, but as soon as we can.'

'Yes, we heard about the murder. And that woman making people homeless. That's why you ought to come and talk to our Izzy.'

'Oh?'

'She got chucked out of her place, too.'

After speaking to Reg, Libby called Ben, whose mobile went straight to voicemail as the call from Reg had predicted. She called the estate office and was answered, in a rather fractious voice.

'What's the matter?'

'Bloody press!' Ben exploded. 'They've caught up with the whole story of Connie and Freddie and the murder and the fu— bloody phone hasn't stopped!'

Libby murmured sympathies until the explosion burnt itself out.

'Well,' she ventured into the eventual silence, 'a phone call you might have missed was from Reg Fisher.'

'Reg? Puckle Morris Reg? What did he want?'

Libby explained. 'So could you ring him, please? And could we go over there to meet the new landlady?'

'Why?' asked Ben suspiciously.

'Because I think she's got some information . . .'

'About the murder?' Ben sounded incredulous. 'Honestly, Lib, how do you do it?'

'I don't know – I don't do it on purpose. But can we?'

'Can't you go on your own? You haven't got time until next week, anyway.' Ben sighed. 'I suppose we ought to be doing something about Hallowe'en if the Morris side are to keep going. We haven't done much over the summer.'

'Will you dance here? Or over at Pucklefield?'

'Oh, here, I think. It's Monday week, isn't it, the thirty-first?'

'Yes,' said Libby. 'Plenty of time.'

Ben made a disbelieving sound.

'All right. I'll go over on Monday,' said Libby. 'I might get Fran to come with me. The Glover's Men will be gone by then, won't they?'

'Unless the police keep them here,' said Ben. 'All right, let me get on now. I'll see you later.'

The next phone call was from Liz Marcus, sounding rather overexcited about being away from the burdens of motherhood for a weekend.

'Can we meet up for a drink, Libby? Will you be here tonight? At the theatre, I mean.'

'I think I'm on house manager duty tonight, Liz, so I'll be a bit busy, but I'm sure there'll be time for a drink. You aren't watching tonight, are you?'

'No, tomorrow – and Olly says Sir Andrew's watching tomorrow, too.'

'Yes, he is. Shame you missed Sir Jasper.'

'I know, but Mum could only have Sebastian this weekend.' Liz paused. 'I do miss him, you know.'

'Of course you do,' said Libby. 'And you'll carry on missing him for the rest of your life. I still miss mine.'

'Really?' Liz sounded disbelieving. 'But one of yours is only round the corner from you, isn't he?'

'Yes, but the other two are in London, and I don't see them half enough.'

'Oh. Well, perhaps I won't let Sebastian leave home, in that case.'

Libby laughed. 'Good luck with that! Go on, get back to your husband. I'll see you tonight.'

Tea finished, Libby began to throw a quick Bolognese together before having a quick shower and changing into something more suitable for house manager than jeans and a rather out-of-shape sweater.

Ben arrived and reported that he and Reg Fisher had decided their respective Morris sides would dance together in Pucklefield on Sunday thirtieth, and in Steeple Martin on the thirty-first.

'And was Duncan Cruikshank OK with that?' asked Libby. 'And the rest of the side?'

'Yes, of course they were. Now, I'd better get changed – you don't mind clearing up, do you?' Ben gave her a winning smile and disappeared upstairs.

Liz was already in the foyer bar when Ben and Libby arrived, and started talking as soon as greetings had been exchanged.

'Go and sit down, Liz,' said Libby, laughing. 'I've got to see people in and check tickets. I'll speak to you after curtain up.'

Harry and Peter arrived with an excited Ricky, who had been persuaded to leave Barney with Hetty and Jeff-dog. 'So we'll have to rush off afterwards,' he said apologetically, 'Or I will, at least.'

Unfortunately the chat with Liz was doomed to failure; just before the auditorium doors were closed, Rachel Trent and a uniformed PC arrived, looking apologetic.

'You are NOT going to stop the performance!' Libby hissed, blocking their way immediately. The few last audience members turned to look at them, and Bob the butcher, tonight's bar manager, appeared swiftly at Libby's side.

'No, I know.' Rachel looked miserable. 'We just need to speak to Freddie Cannon and Noel Finch.'

'Well, you can't.' Libby's mouth set in a firm line. Her heart was beating like a sledgehammer and she felt slightly dizzy. 'Not until after the show.'

Rachel looked slightly surprised. 'They aren't on all the time, are they?'

Bob and Libby were aghast. 'You can't speak to them during the performance!' gasped Libby.

Rachel summoned up a stern expression. 'This is a murder inquiry,' she snapped.

'So you'll ruin the show for the audience and the company, will you?' Bob thrust a belligerent face into Rachel's. 'You don't know anything about theatre, do you?'

'Er . . .' said Rachel.

'You can't press pause, you know,' Bob went on. 'Once it's set in motion, the show goes on until the end.'

'What about the interval?' suggested the constable hesitantly.

'You must be joking!' Libby glared at Rachel. 'Why do you want to speak to them, anyway? You let Freddie go. And why Noel?'

'He drove Freddie Cannon into Nethergate on Tuesday.'

Chapter Fifteen

Libby was stunned into silence.

'You can speak to them after the show,' said Bob. 'They won't run away.'

'And you can go and guard the back door to make sure,' said Libby, finding her voice. 'In the cold.'

Rachel looked defeated. 'All right, all right. We'll wait.'

'Here?' Libby shook her head. 'A uniformed officer in the foyer all evening? I don't think so.'

'Isn't there somewhere at the back we could wait?' asked the constable reasonably.

'I'm afraid not,' said Libby more calmly, taking pity on him. 'It's a very small theatre. And I'm really sorry, but you would upset the whole cast, let alone Freddie and Noel, if you tried to speak to them before the end of the show.'

Rachel put a hand to her forehead. 'Oh, bugger,' she said.

Libby pulled forward one of the white wrought-iron chairs and gently pushed Rachel into it.

'Look, Rachel,' she said, and sat down herself. 'I know this is important, but you haven't actually come here to arrest Freddie, have you?'

Rachel looked up, her face woebegone. 'No.' She looked sideways at the constable. 'I think I've messed up.'

The constable looked embarrassed. Libby grinned at him.

'Don't worry, officer,' she said. 'We're old friends, Rachel and me. We'll sort this out. What's your name?'

'Constable Alleyn, ma'am,' he said, clearing his throat loudly.

'Oh, lovely! The name of my favourite fictional detective.' Libby beamed happily. Constable Alleyn looked confused. 'And what's your first name?'

Rachel sighed. 'It's all right, Mark. Sit down, we'll be here for a little while.'

Libby went to check on the auditorium doors, and came back to Rachel. 'Now, what's the problem?'

'We found out that your Freddie Cannon had been to Nethergate on Tuesday, driven by Noel Finch. Is he part of the cast here?'

Libby nodded. Noel, a slight, dark boy, was admirably suited to the part of Hero, which he played with an innocence quite foreign to his nature.

'Why did they go there on Tuesday? That was the day Constance Matthews put all that stuff on Twitter.' Rachel peered round the foyer. 'Could I possibly get a coffee?'

Libby waved at Bob, who had returned to the bar. 'Coffee?' she mouthed. He nodded and came over to take the order.

'How do you know they were there?' she asked, turning back to Rachel.

'Someone came forward.' Rachel wasn't looking at her.

'Who?' Libby looked from Constable Mark back to Rachel. 'Come on, Rachel. I'll only get it out of Ian later.'

'Oh, I don't suppose he knows.' Rachel sighed. 'This came from Sergeant Powell.'

'Ah.' Libby leant back in her chair. 'I take it he's been investigating on his own again?'

Rachel looked startled. 'What . . .?'

'What do I know? Well, I know he's been harassing people in Nethergate. Presumably one of those people saw Freddie and Noel. But how would they know . . .'

110

'One of those people turned out to be Freddie Cannon's grandmother.'

Libby sat staring at Rachel with her mouth open. Bob arrived with a tray and gave her a nudge.

'It gets worse,' said Constable Mark, seeing that his superior officer seemed to have lost her ability to speak. 'His grandmother happens to be losing her home.'

Bob put the tray down carefully. 'Shut yer mouth, Lib,' he muttered, and went back to the bar.

'This is a coincidence too far,' Libby said eventually. 'I don't like coincidences.'

'It's actually not as much of a coincidence as it seems,' said Mark. 'Apparently, it was one of the reasons Freddie Cannon was so keen to do this tour.'

'But how did Sergeant Powell find her?' asked Libby.

'He talked to people in the Blue Anchor,' said Rachel. 'You know the owner, don't you?'

'Yes, and I met some of the people Powell had terrorised only today. I hope it wasn't one of them.'

'Her name's Beryl Sampson – did you meet her?'

'No.' Libby was relieved. 'And she's lost her home?'

'She's going to,' said Rachel, taking a grateful sip of her coffee. 'She has a small flat in King Edward Street, apparently, and your Ms Matthews has bought the whole building to turn it into holiday lets.'

'It isn't Nightingale House, I suppose?' said Libby.

'No – I remember Nightingale House.' Rachel nodded. 'But they're all divided up one way or another. There's Nyebourne – that's a retirement home.'

'Yes, our friend Joe Wilson lives there,' said Libby.

'This one's Gleneagles, I think. Several of the other houses are already holiday lets.' Rachel drank more coffee.

'And Mrs Sampson goes to the Blue Anchor to save on her heating,' added Mark.

'I wonder why Mavis didn't mention her,' mused Libby. 'Surely she'd have known the grandson was in the play here.'

'I think Mrs Sampson keeps herself to herself,' said Mark.

'Hmm.' Libby scowled at her coffee cup. 'Why didn't that idiot boy tell anyone he'd been to Nethergate? Why didn't he tell you, when you were questioning him?'

Rachel and Mark exchanged glances.

'Oh, don't tell me. Sergeant Powell questioned him.' Libby made a face. 'Well, you did tell me somebody had messed up. I still wonder why Freddie didn't mention his grandma.'

'Because he thought it would make him look suspicious,' said Mark, who was relaxing considerably. 'Although the sergeant didn't know about Mrs Sampson at that point.'

'So now you do know and you think Freddie might have done it after all.' Libby sighed.

'We have to ask,' said Rachel tiredly.

'But what possessed you to come here tonight?'

'I didn't think. I knew the play was on and I just assumed . . .' Rachel shook her head.

'You're trying to mop up behind Powell,' said Libby shrewdly.

Rachel managed a small laugh. 'I won't be much of a DI if I can't control the sergeants, will I?'

Libby looked consideringly at Constable Mark. 'What do you think?'

He turned a delicate shade of pink. 'Not my place,' he croaked.

'Don't put him on the spot,' said Rachel, smiling across at him. 'He's in rather a – what d'you call it?'

'An equivocal position?' suggested Libby, grinning. 'This visit isn't by any chance unofficial, I suppose?'

'Not entirely,' said Rachel. 'Claire knows we were coming.'

'But Sergeant Powell doesn't. And Ian doesn't either.'

Mark looked quickly at Rachel.

'No,' she said. 'Will you tell him?'

'No.' Libby shook her head. 'Why doesn't Mark go home, you

stay here and talk to Freddie after the show. He'll be coming out to meet the public. Not ideal, for him or for you, but it would help.'

'We came in the same car – I couldn't get home,' said Rachel.

Mark reached over and patted her hand. Libby's eyebrows rose in surprise and realisation.

'Leave it to the morning,' he said. 'He'll be here then, won't he, Mrs Sarjeant?'

'Libby, please.' She smiled at him. 'Yes, he will. He won't run away, I can assure you of that. He's been loving all the attention.'

'I don't know what Gareth will say,' murmured Rachel.

'Gareth?'

'Powell,' said Mark. 'What he says doesn't matter, Rache. You got acting DI, not him.'

'Oh, and I bet he wasn't exactly pleased,' said Libby. 'But Mark's right, Rachel. It doesn't matter what he thinks. He reports to you, doesn't he? Or will he go over your head?'

'He might.' Rachel gave a half smile and sat up straighter. 'Oh, well, if we can come back in the morning . . . Shall we call at the Manor, then?'

'No, come and collect me and I can take you up there,' said Libby. She stood up. 'I'd better check on progress in there.' She looked at them both assessingly. 'Pity you couldn't have watched the show – or don't you like Shakespeare?'

'I love it,' said Mark, surprisingly. 'I did English at uni.'

Rachel grinned. 'Fast-track, Libby. I don't know much about it.'

'Are you both off duty tomorrow?'

'Barring accidents and more murders, yes,' said Rachel.

'Would you like to see it?'

'Yes!' Mark's face lit up.

'Right. You can have my seats tomorrow.' Libby grinned at them both. 'Now bugger off, both of you. I'll see you in the morning.'

'What was that all about?' Liz appeared at Libby's elbow, watching Rachel and Mark leaving and looking anxious.

'They just wanted to ask some questions and didn't realise they couldn't.' Although young Mark should have done, Libby thought, if he loves Shakespeare. Perhaps he didn't like to interfere – although once they'd got on to a more informal footing he had been keen enough to add his four-penn'orth.

'Do they still think Freddie could have killed that woman?' Liz lowered her voice.

'No, of course not.' Libby went to the auditorium doors and listened. 'We're all right for the time being. Now, are you ready for another drink?'

Libby said nothing to anybody about Rachel's visit until the cast started leaving the theatre to go back to the Manor. Then she stopped Hereward just as he was leaving, and told him.

'Oh, bloody hell,' he said. 'Why didn't he tell anybody?'

'That's what I said,' Libby agreed. 'Never mind, no harm done tonight, and I'll bring them up in the morning. I'd better get Olly to make sure those boys stay put, hadn't I?'

'They don't usually surface very early,' said Hereward. 'You know what it's like.'

Libby nodded 'Upside-down sleeping patterns. Comes with the territory. I'll just pop over now.' She told Bob to tell Ben where she was going and slipped out of the door.

The cast were all in Hetty's big sitting room enjoying a last night-cap. Libby managed to accost Oliver and Liz just as they were trying to slip away, and told them what she wanted.

'I'll try,' said Oliver doubtfully, 'but we don't always coincide with each other in the mornings. You know how it is.'

'I know,' said Libby, 'and I expect DI Trent will be here quite early, but just in case.'

She and Ben met up as he was locking the theatre doors. 'Trouble?' he asked over his shoulder.

'Not really.' Libby sighed. 'Come on – I want a drink.'

'Coach, Pocket or home?' asked Ben.

'The caff, if Harry's still open,' said Libby. Ben grinned.

The Pink Geranium had the closed sign on the door, but Harry, Peter and Ricky, still in their going-to-theatre clothes, Adam and a few diners could still be seen inside. Ben pushed open the door.

Harry turned, an arrested expression on his face, nodded towards the sofa in the window, gave Adam a look, and carried on saying goodbye to his customers. Peter came over to join them and Adam followed with a bottle of red wine and a handful of glasses.

'Don't let the boss see you carrying them like that,' said Peter. Adam pulled a face.

Harry closed and locked the door and came to join them.

'Something's happened,' he said. 'What is it?'

Libby launched into her story, with explanatory interjections from Ricky about the morning's visit to Nethergate, and including the phone call from Reg Fisher telling her about Izzy, the new landlady of the Puckle Inn.

'It looks to me,' said Harry, when she'd finished, 'as if this Powell is trying to make a name for himself. And prove all the decent coppers wrong.'

'It does, doesn't it,' said Libby. 'I think he must have been in DI Winter's camp during the Heronsbourne case.'

'Who is this woman?' asked Adam, who had perched on the arm of the sofa next to his mother. By the time he had received a multi-stranded explanation from five different people, he didn't look much the wiser.

'So what are you going to do next?' asked Harry. 'As if we didn't know.'

'Then why do you need to ask?' Libby took a sip of wine and gazed innocently at the ceiling.

'You don't know exactly where grandma lives,' said Ben.

'Rachel mentioned Gleneagles. I remember a Gleneagles in King Edward Street. Oh, and I think Rachel and that constable are an item!'

115

'Goodness me!' said Harry. 'How infra dig – an acting detective inspector and a lowly constable.'

'I think he's about her age,' said Libby. 'She said he's one of those fast-track people.'

'She's always seemed rather nice,' said Peter, 'not that I know her very well. Sad if she's got to deal with unpleasantness in the ranks on her first big case.'

Libby nodded. 'I felt sorry for her tonight. I've told her they can come and watch tomorrow. They can have the house seats.'

'Oh, that's all right, then,' said Harry. 'That'll make everything all right.'

'Don't be sarky,' said Libby. 'And anyway, did you all enjoy it tonight?'

It was almost midnight when Libby and Ben walked home arm in arm.

'Do you realise,' said Libby, 'none of you told me not to go and talk to Freddie's grandma?'

'Wouldn't have made any difference,' said Ben. 'And anyway, it's all part of the campaign, isn't it? And we're all for that. Even bloated plutocrat landlords like me.'

Libby smiled into the darkness.

Chapter Sixteen

Rachel and Mark had to wait for Libby to get dressed the following morning, and then spent the entire walk to the Manor apologising for being so early.

'I expected you to be early,' she said. 'It's my fault for offering to take you. Don't worry about it.'

Hetty met them in the hall looking surprised.

'Hello, gal – what you doing here?'

'Rachel here wants to speak to one of the cast,' explained Libby, indicating Rachel, who was doing her best to melt into the background.

Hetty cast her a fulminating look. 'Not that poor Freddie again?'

'Er – yes,' Rachel muttered.

Hetty sniffed. 'In the sittin' room,' she said. 'You can take this in with you.' She handed over the large coffee pot she was carrying.

'Thanks, Hetty.' Libby smiled at her and received another sniff in return.

Freddie Cannon was lounging in an armchair, one leg over the arm, his hair tousled and his eyes sleepy. He saw Rachel and sat up quickly.

'Now what?' he said.

His fellow cast members stopped what they were doing and turned to look. Including Noel Finch.

'Come to the office,' Libby murmured to Rachel. Out loud, she said, 'Just a quick word, Freddie,' and beamed at him. He stood up, glowering. Libby didn't blame him.

'And perhaps Mr Finch?' Mark whispered.

'Noel?' said Libby brightly. 'Could you come, too?'

The little party trooped out, leaving silence behind them. Libby hastily deposited the coffee pot on the sideboard and followed. She showed them into Ben's estate office and left them to it.

'Just pop into the kitchen and let Hetty know when you've finished,' she said as she left.

She walked down the Manor drive, feeling guilty. Freddie Cannon had no more to do with Constance Matthews' murder than she did. But then, she thought, cheering up, at least this chat with Rachel and Mark would clear things up and hopefully stop Sergeant Powell from hounding him.

Ben was just leaving for the Hop Pocket when she arrived back at Number 17.

'How did it go?' he asked, pulling on his ancient donkey jacket.

'Freddie didn't look pleased. I left them in your office – I don't think they'll pinch anything.' She gave him a kiss. 'Go on. Go and play landlords. I'm going to see Mrs Sampson.'

'When will you be back?'

'Not sure. We haven't got to do anything today, have we?'

Ben narrowed his eyes at her. 'What are you going to do?'

'I don't know yet.' Libby smiled sunnily. 'But I probably won't be home for lunch.'

After Ben had gone, Libby made herself a cup of tea and called Fran to tell her about Rachel's theatre visit and Reg Fisher's phone call.

'So I thought I'd pop down and try and see Freddie's grandma this morning, and then go on to Pucklefield at lunchtime to see the new landlady. I suppose you're busy?'

'Does that mean you don't want me with you?' Fran sounded amused.

'Of course not!' Libby spluttered. 'I just assumed, because it was Saturday . . .'

'Actually, it's not that busy at the moment, so I'm pretty sure Guy won't mind if I take today off. After all, it's almost protest group business, isn't it?'

'That's what Ben said. OK, shall I come to you first? I can leave the car there and we could walk to King Edward Street.'

'Fine,' said Fran. 'See you in – what? An hour?'

Just over an hour later Libby found a parking space on Harbour Street and stood for a moment gazing out at the sea, which this morning resembled rumpled grey satin.

Fran was waiting for her outside the door of Coastguard Cottage.

'Guy doesn't mind, then?' Libby grinned as they fell into step together.

'No, of course not. In fact this morning he's got a call scheduled with Philip Jacobs to talk about all things landlord and tenant. I've told him to ask Philip to give Hannah some work.'

'Oh, good. It's easier to keep in touch with her than Philip. He can be a bit intimidating in solicitor mode.'

Gleneagles, like many of its neighbours, had a doorway adorned by many bell pushes.

'At least it's the right house,' said Libby, peering at the handwritten label, which read 'Sampson'.

'No intercom,' commented Fran. 'That means the poor soul will have to come all the way down from her flat.'

A minute later, the door opened to reveal a small round woman with a brown, cheerful crab-apple face, wearing an obviously unaccustomed wary expression.

'Yes?' she said.

'Mrs Sampson?' asked Libby. 'I'm from the theatre.'

Mrs Sampson's face changed. 'Freddie's theatre?' she said. 'Are you Lizzie?'

'Libby, actually – yes, that's me.'

'Oh, how nice! I'm coming to see him tonight, you know.' Mrs Sampson stood back to allow them entry. 'Come in, won't you? What can I do for you?'

'We don't want to disturb you,' said Libby. 'This is Fran Wolfe, by the way.'

'Oh, you're from that nice shop in Harbour Street, aren't you?' Beryl Sampson held out her hand. 'Nice to meet you.'

'We actually wanted to know about this building being sold, Mrs Sampson,' said Fran, shaking her hand. 'I'm sorry if that seems impertinent . . .'

'No, not at all.' Mrs Sampson drew herself up to her full five feet. 'You're involved with that campaign, aren't you? Oh, do come in. I'm only on the first floor, not far to climb.'

Fran and Libby exchanged a grin as Beryl Sampson led the way to the stairs.

Once upstairs, in a neat, bright sitting room, they were offered tea or coffee, which they both declined.

'We just wanted to know if a woman called Constance Matthews had been in touch with you?' said Libby, once they were seated.

'No, but I know who she is.' Mrs Sampson frowned fiercely. 'She's the one who bought our lovely Gleneagles. And we've all had notice to quit.'

'Yes, we heard that from the police,' said Fran.

'Oh, the police are involved, are they? Perhaps it won't happen then?' Mrs Sampson's face brightened considerably.

'I don't know about that,' said Libby, 'but we're looking into it. Can you tell us when this happened?'

'About a month ago – maybe three weeks? No warning. We just got a letter from the agents telling us we had to quit. Gave us until Christmas. I ask you! Homeless at Christmas!' Mrs Sampson's voice trembled with emotion, and Libby felt something twist inside her. How bloody heartless Connie Matthews had been.

'Who are the agents, Beryl?' Fran asked gently.

'Oh, Brooke's, in the high street. Where that woman worked—oh!' Beryl Sampson's face broke into a grin. 'That's who you are, of course! You're the ones who—'

'Yes, that's us, Beryl,' broke in Libby hastily. 'You don't mind if we call you Beryl, do you?'

'Course not, dear. So you're looking into all this, are you? Freddie told me that woman had been murdered. You know they took him in for questioning? Cheek of it!'

'Yes, we know,' said Fran.

'She deserved it, if you ask me,' said Beryl. 'I know I shouldn't say that, but there's five of us in dear old Gleneagles that'll be homeless because of her, and none of us under seventy.'

'Really? How did you all happen to land up here?' asked Libby.

'Oh, it was such a lucky chance, really.' Beryl settled herself in her armchair, ready for a long chat. 'Jenny Peake – she's the other flat on this floor – well, she was a nurse down in Margate, and this lady patient found out she and her husband were going to lose their home. Oh, no dear,' Beryl noticed Libby's change of expression. 'This was years ago. Jenny's husband, Eddie, he worked for Sir Nigel Preece, you see.'

'Ah!' said Libby and Fran together. They'd had dealings with Sir Nigel before.

'Yes.' Beryl nodded wisely. 'And he was in a tied house. And Sir Nigel threw him out.'

'Well, he got his comeuppance,' said Libby.

'Yes.' Beryl put her head on one side. 'And that was you, too, wasn't it? It's all coming back to me, now.'

'Yes, well . . . So Jenny had this patient?' prompted Fran.

'And she told Jenny there was a flat going in her house.' Beryl smiled triumphantly. 'This house! This patient, you see, she lived at the top of this house, and she knew she wouldn't be able to manage the stairs, so she was going to move into Nyebourne. That's a retirement home just down the road.'

'Yes, we know Nyebourne,' said Libby. 'Our friend Joe lives there.'

'Not Joe Wilson?' Beryl looked delighted. 'Lovely man.'

'That's him,' said Libby. 'So this lady moved into Nyebourne. Then what happened?'

'Well.' Beryl leant forward confidentially. 'Jenny and Eddie moved in upstairs. But then next door – young chap, he was – he moved out. Got married, and they bought a house. So Jenny and Eddie decided to move in there – not so many stairs, you see – and they told old Mrs Bryant. So she got hold of her solicitors and made it so that only people over sixty-five could have the flats, and at a really reasonable rent. So as the flats became vacant, I moved in, and Eric on the top floor. And it was tied up tight, legally, so we both thought we were here for life.'

'What happened, then?' asked Fran, after leaving Beryl to ruminate on this for a minute or two.

'She died,' said Beryl flatly. 'And Brooke's had been handling it for her – well, she was nearly ninety by that time, and it was all a bit too much for her.'

'And whoever she left it to couldn't be bothered with it, I suppose?' said Libby.

'Well, I don't know, really.' Beryl was frowning again. 'There was something about probate, but what we gathered – the tenants, that is – was that this Miss Matthews just bowled in and said she'd buy it if they – Brooke's – could get rid of us.'

Fran and Libby exchanged another loaded look.

'It doesn't sound exactly legal to me,' said Fran. 'Have any of you asked a solicitor about it?'

'I think maybe Eric was going to.' Beryl looked hopeful. 'He said he knew all about this sort of thing. Something to do with his family, I think.'

'Have you informed the campaign group?' asked Libby, thinking that here was a case Philip Jacobs could get his teeth into.

'Do you think we should?' Beryl shrank a little into her chair.

'Of course,' said Fran robustly. 'I'll do it for you, if you like.'

'Would you?' Beryl sat up again. 'Oh, I can't tell you . . .'

'Can we give our solicitor your name?' asked Libby. 'And perhaps you'd better tell your fellow tenants what's going on. They won't mind, will they?'

'Oh, bless you, no! Especially Jenny and Eddie. They thought they were going to be evicted for the second time. Jenny kept saying she ought to have had some savings, but they never earned enough to save.'

'How are you getting to the theatre this evening?' Libby asked as they were leaving.

'Oh, I'll get the bus,' said Beryl, looking surprised.

'But what about getting back?' asked Fran. 'The last bus goes from Steeple Martin at around – what? Nine, Libby?'

Beryl's face fell. 'Oh . . .'

'Don't worry,' said Libby briskly. 'Leave it with me. You don't want to miss Freddie's performance, do you?'

Beryl brightened. 'Well, if you're sure, dear.'

As they reached the end of the road, Libby turned decisively in to Nyebourne. Fran raised her eyebrows. Libby grinned and, on entering the polished hall, rang the bell on the counter and asked for Mr Joseph Wilson.

Joe was surprised to see them to say the least, but unsurprised when he found out the reason for their visit.

'Yes, of course,' he said. 'Beryl Sampson. Nice woman. Keeps herself to herself – bit shy, I've always thought.'

'You do know her, then,' said Fran.

'Oh, yes. Comes on some of our outings now and then. So she can share my cab – and I'm not to allow her to pay. Is that right?'

'Yes, thank you, Joe.' Libby smiled at him. 'What a good job you were coming tonight!'

'And going home again!' said Joe, with a wink.

Chapter Seventeen

'What did he mean by that?' Fran asked Libby as they walked back to Harbour Street, after popping back to tell Beryl she had a lift to and from the theatre.

'He obviously isn't staying overnight at the Manor with Hetty,' replied Libby with a grin.

'What?' Fran looked shocked. 'They aren't . . .?'

'Don't know,' said Libby, 'but it wouldn't surprise any of us.'

'What are we doing now?' asked Fran after a moment.

'Pucklefield to see the new landlady, Izzy,' said Libby. 'You don't have to come if you'd rather not.'

'No, I want to. I've not been to Pucklefield, and I'd like to see it. I wish I'd met the old landlord, though.'

'You'd have scared him to death.' Libby laughed.

'Why? I'm not scary!' protested Fran.

'As far as I could see, Charles Bertram aspired to gentility. You're proper gentry and he would have been scared.'

'I'm not!' Fran was indignant. 'I'm proper working class, like you.'

Libby grinned. 'And people today would argue that neither of us are any more. We're both solidly middle class. Look at us both – dilettantes, the pair of us. Can you have female dilettantes?'

'I resent that!' Fran glared at her friend. 'We aren't dilettantes – we have a *professional* interest in the arts, for heaven's sake!'

'Hmm.' Libby sounded dissatisfied. 'But we're both amateurs, now.'

Fran stopped dead in the middle of Harbour Street. 'Is the Oast an amateur theatre?'

'Er . . .' said Libby.

'No, it isn't. It is run as a professional theatre, hosting professional productions and artists. And your own productions are pro–am, aren't they?' Fran stood, hands on hips, daring Libby to argue.

'Oh, OK, I give in.' Libby heaved a sigh and resumed her walk to the car. 'And see what I mean? You'd scare Charles Bertram to death.'

Fran, looking somewhat abashed, followed.

'Shall I follow you in my car?' she asked as Libby opened her door. 'Then you haven't got to bring me back here. And you must have a lot to do, with it being the last night . . .'

Libby laughed. 'Stop being humble! It doesn't suit you. And yes – that might be best.'

While Libby turned her car round, Fran fetched hers from its resident's parking bay in the car park behind the Blue Anchor. The route to Pucklefield took them past Steeple Martin, then turned right towards Itching, after which they turned left through apple orchards now denuded of their fruit. The country flattened out and, ahead, a church spire and a cluster of houses revealed themselves as Pucklefield.

Libby parked in the car park of the Puckle Inn.

'It's very pretty,' said Fran, getting out of her car.

'Rogation House is over that way,' said Libby, waving a hand. 'Never did get to see inside it.'

'Libby!' A voice boomed out from the doorway of the pub.

'Reg!' Libby found herself enveloped in a bear hug. 'This is Fran – you didn't meet her back in May, did you?'

'Not properly. Saw you though, when we all met in the Pocket.' Reg held out a hand. 'Reg Fisher. Pleased to meet you.'

He led them into the pub, which seemed a lot fuller than the first time Libby had visited.

'What can I get you?' he asked, shouldering his way to the counter.

'Tonic water, please,' said Libby, turning down her mouth. 'Driving.'

'Could I possibly have coffee?' asked Fran.

'Course you can. Maria! Coffee over here, love.' The large blonde woman who had spoken beamed up at them both. 'You must be Reg's friend Libby – and this is?'

Reg performed introductions.

'And this our Izzy – the Crown and Sceptre's loss is our gain!' He leant across the bar and gave her a smacking kiss.

Slightly bemused, Libby and Fran accepted drinks from a smiling Maria, who looked far happier and less harassed than when Libby had last seen her.

'They expected us?' whispered Fran, as Reg ushered them to a table in the window.

'I called Reg before we left Nethergate,' muttered Libby.

Izzy joined them at the table, having installed one of the regulars behind the bar to help Maria.

'Right,' she said. 'Reg tells me you're interested in that old bat Matthews.'

'Er . . . yes,' Libby agreed.

'I told you, didn't I, Libby. Izzy got turned out by her.' Reg nodded wisely.

'Out of a pub?' hazarded Fran.

'Crown and Sceptre up towards Canterbury.' Izzy shook her head. 'Isabel Maurice, licensed to sell wines and spirits, that was me.'

'Still is, Izz.' Reg patted her hand.

'But how?' Libby was puzzled. 'Didn't you own it? She couldn't have turned you out if it was owned by a brewery.'

'Brewery sold it, didn't they?' Izzy sighed. 'Wasn't making enough money. Well, no one was at the time, were they?'

'When was this?' asked Fran.

'July. I was dead lucky. A couple of the regulars from here used

126

to come in and they told old Bertram I was out of a job.' She shrugged. 'Simple as that.'

'Did Connie Matthews actually throw you out?' Libby was frowning.

'Came in one day, sweet as you like, and told me she was closing up at the end of the week and she'd be grateful if I was gone by then.' Izzy leant back in her chair. 'I'd been there nearly all my life, took over from my dad.'

'You weren't the tenant, then?' said Fran.

Izzy shook her head. 'Manager. Don't suppose she could have done it if I was the tenant.'

'The brewery would have offered it to you, if you had been,' said Libby.

'I fell on me feet,' said Izzy, hoisting a generous bosom up over her crossed arms. 'I landed here, and it's a great place. Bit out of the way, but still . . .'

Reg looked slightly nervous. 'We're really pleased to have you, Izz,' he said.

'I know, bless you.' Izzy smiled at him. 'They've been good to me, here,' she said to Libby and Fran, 'but I lost my home. And my kids don't see me like they used to. They both live in Canterbury, see, and they could pop in any old time. Have to make a special trip down here to see me.' She gazed out of the window. 'I hoped one of them might move out here, but they can't afford to.'

A depressed silence fell around the table.

'Back in July,' Fran said eventually. 'That's well before she seems to have started in Nethergate.'

Izzy looked surprised. 'Oh, no, dear! She was already in Nethergate. Keeping an eye on the area, she was – that's how she heard about the Crown and Sceptre.'

'Oh.' Libby and Fran looked at each other. 'Did she tell you that?' asked Libby.

'No, I've got a mate over there. Clive – tenant of the Sergeant at Arms – know it?'

'No,' said Libby.

'Yes!' said Fran. 'You remember, Libby – where we went to meet the Harriers that time.'

'Harriers?' Reg asked.

'A running club,' said Libby. 'Yes, I remember now. Real old-fashioned place, not touristy at all.'

'That's the one.' Izzy nodded. 'All his regulars are old Nethergate, and a lot of them in rented places. She was trying to get rid of them all. Managed it in some cases, too.'

'Yes, we know some of those she's managed to get rid of,' said Fran. 'We've actually got a campaign running to try and do something about it.'

'Really?' Izzy looked interested. 'Clive didn't tell me that. Could I join in?'

'We'll put you on the list,' said Fran with a smile. 'We've got a solicitor looking into everything for us at the moment, and trying to find out who inherits all her properties. We think a lot of it might be illegal.'

Izzy brightened, but then her face fell. 'Won't help me, though,' she said. 'Pub's sold. I couldn't go back.'

Nobody knew what to say to this, and another silence fell.

'So what's been happening down in Nethergate, then?' Izzy asked eventually. 'I don't know the details.'

Relieved, Libby and Fran fell to describing the Nethergate situation in relation to Constance Matthews, rent rises and homelessness, including what they knew about her murder.

'Oh, hang about!' Izzy turned to Reg. 'There was all that stuff on Twitter you showed me, wasn't there? About that play and that singer?'

'That's it!' Reg smiled happily. Crisis averted. 'It's Libby's theatre, see?'

Another ten minutes was passed describing the theatre and what went on there until, finally, Izzy stood up.

'I'd better get back to the bar,' she said. 'Glad to meet you.' She held out a hand in turn to Libby and Fran. 'And I hope you'll come again. Keep me in touch with what's happening with your campaign. I'd like to get me own back on the old bat – even if she is dead.'

Libby watched Izzy make her way back to the bar, speaking to customers as she went, then turned to Reg. 'She's popular, isn't she?'

Reg nodded. 'She was popular at the Crown, too. People knew her family. Caused a lot of bad feeling against the brewery.'

'I can imagine.' Libby sighed heavily.

'The trouble is,' said Fran, 'people of our parents' generation expected to stay in jobs for life, and often didn't have any savings.'

'And people didn't always expect to own their own homes, either,' added Libby. 'We both came from rented homes in London, didn't we?'

'I still rented when we first met,' said Fran. 'What I used to call my Betjeman flat.' She smiled reminiscently.

Reg was looking bemused. 'Never mind that now,' said Libby quickly. 'A lot of things have changed since then. Can I get you another drink, Reg?'

Reg declined politely and, after a few more minutes discussing the now established Hallowe'en celebrations, Reg having now made contact with Ben and Steeple Martin Morris, Libby and Fran took their leave.

'Was that helpful?' Fran asked, as they got back to their cars.

'In that we now know Connie was buying up Nethergate earlier than we thought.' Libby frowned. 'I wonder where she got the money? I mean – she can't have been getting rents at first, can she? So she must have had a hell of a lot of capital.'

'The police will be looking into her finances, won't they? They always do.'

'But will they tell us? And who will be doing that? They don't seem to have a very big team on the case.'

'Ask Ian,' said Fran, as she climbed into her little Smart car.

★

Libby drove slowly back to Steeple Martin thinking over what they had learnt since this morning. More and more it looked as though Constance had been empire-building, and more and more did Libby want to know who stood to inherit the empire. Whoever it was had to be a prime suspect. Then there were the displaced tenants, although none of them Libby had met so far seemed in the least bit likely to be a murderer. And of course, she realised, there were the existing landlords, whom Constance may well have been putting out of business. She sighed. How she wished she knew more about where and how the wicked witch had been killed.

Chapter Eighteen

It was mid-afternoon when she let herself in to Number 17 and tripped over Sidney. The red light was winking on the landline, and she fumbled in her basket to see if there was an unheeded message on her mobile. There was.

'It's Ian,' announced the mobile bluntly. 'Phone me back.'

Libby's heart sank, and she pressed the button on the landline.

'Libby, it's Andrew. I'm coming tonight, but I've got a bit of information, so I wondered if we could meet before the performance?'

Libby returned the call, but it went straight to voicemail.

'Never mind,' she said to Sidney. 'I'll see him tonight.'

She went into the kitchen to make a fortifying cup of tea before returning Ian's call.

'What have I done now?' she asked when he answered.

'I don't know! What *have* you done?' Ian sounded surprised.

'You sounded angry,' Libby explained. 'I assumed I'd put my foot in it somewhere.'

'No – I just wanted to tell you what happened when Rachel saw young Freddie and Noel this morning.'

'Oh.' Libby subsided on to a chair. 'Go on, then.'

'Very little actually. Noel confirmed that they had gone to see Freddie's grandmother in Nethergate and come straight back to Steeple Martin. Apparently grannie and one of her neighbours can confirm this – although we don't know if they stopped off on the way home, of course.'

'Even if they did, Connie wasn't killed until the evening, was she?'

'Pathologist's best guess, yes, but she was seen at around six thirty.'

'*What*? Then how the bloody hell did Freddie come under suspicion in the first place?'

Ian was laughing. 'Because we've only just found out about it.'

'Go on – where was she seen?'

'She had dinner in the Swan.'

Libby sat shaking her head at her tea.

'Say something, Libby. Even if it's only to swear at me again.'

Libby puffed out a breath. 'So obvious, when you think about it. She'd have had to eat somewhere.' She paused. 'And where was she staying? Do we know that yet?'

'She had a collection of key cards. Rachel's team are trying to find out which card belongs to which property. We assume she was going to stay in one of them.'

'That would make sense,' said Libby, wondering how much of the day's activities she should share.

'Thank you, ma'am.'

'I found something else out today, actually.' Libby waited for the reaction, which, when it came, was surprisingly mild.

'Go on – what?'

'Well, Fran and I went over to Pucklefield to see Reg.'

'Start again. Pucklefield. What did you want to go there for, and who's Reg?'

'Reg Fisher, of the Pucklefield Morris – remember?'

'I had very little to do with your Morris shenanigans, Libby. Why did you want to see him?'

'We're having a joint Hallowe'en celebration the week after next. Anyway,' Libby rushed on in case he asked for details, 'they've got a new landlady at the Puckle Inn. And she lost her job and her home at a pub near Canterbury when the brewery sold it.'

'Don't tell me – it was bought by Constance Matthews.' Ian let out a gusty breath.

'Yes. And get this – it was back in July, so she'd been at it for longer than we thought.'

'That's not quite true,' said Ian. 'We know now she'd taken over various properties almost from back in May.'

'Did she have a connection with Brooke's?' asked Libby with foreboding.

'How did you guess?' said Ian.

'Hmm.' Libby thought for a moment. 'You don't happen to remember who the letting agents were when we first found Fran's house, do you?'

'I wasn't really involved with the investigation early on, if *you* remember,' said Ian. 'We first met at—'

'Tyne Chapel,' Libby broke in. 'Don't remind me. While we were investigating Aunt Elephant.'

Ian chuckled. 'Actually, you know, you've calmed down quite a bit since then.'

'Have I?' Libby was surprised.

'Not quite so much "bull in a china shop".'

'You mean I don't rush in quite so quickly whether it's got anything to do with me or not,' said Libby.

'Something like that,' said Ian.

'Well, anyway,' Libby went on, 'what we were wondering was, where did Connie get so much money? And have you found out yet who were her heirs?'

'And, of course, why did she pick on Nethergate?"

'Yes! Why did she? It wasn't anything to do with me and the theatre, was it?'

'Why should it have been?' asked Ian reasonably. 'I doubt very much if she'd followed your life and times particularly, out of all her other theatrical acquaintances.'

'Oh, that reminds me! I had a message from Andrew this afternoon.'

'Andrew Wylie?'

'No – Sir Andrew.' Libby tutted. 'So annoying having two friends with the same name.'

'It must be!' Ian sounded amused. 'But all you have to say is *Sir* Andrew and all becomes clear. Anyway, what did he want?'

'He says he's got some information for me, but his phone went to voicemail when I tried to call him back, so he must already be on his way here.'

'Here? He's coming down?'

'Yes – to see *Much Ado*.'

'But I thought he saw it on Tuesday with Sir Jasper.'

'He did, but he was officially coming tonight. Oliver's doing his speech about the homeless charity and the proceeds of the performance are being donated.'

'Can I come?'

Libby laughed. 'I've already given the house seats to Rachel and Mark.'

'That'll be Acting DI Trent and PC Mark Alleyn, I take it?'

Libby cleared her throat. 'Er – yes. Shouldn't I have done?'

'It could be considered bribery,' said Ian solemnly.

'Oh,' said Libby in a small voice, and Ian laughed.

'On the other hand, it could be considered as helping the police with their inquiries. After all, it will show Rachel just how impossible it would have been for young Freddie to murder Constance, won't it?'

'Oh, yes.' Libby smiled in relief.

'So – can I come? I'd like to see what Sir Andrew has to say.'

'You might have to stand at the back,' said Libby doubtfully.

'That's all right,' said Ian. 'We're tough, us policemen.'

Sir Andrew telephoned just before Libby and Ben left for the theatre.

'I'm in the caff,' he said. 'Any chance you could join me?'

'Not tonight, Andrew – it's the charity performance and I've got bigwigs to greet.'

'Won't young Hereward do that?'

'Him and Oliver, yes, but I've got to be there, too, to usher them into their seats and all that stuff. But Ian's coming. He said he'd like a chat with you.'

'Oh, right,' said Sir Andrew slowly. 'Sort of off the record?'

'Oh, yes. He's coming as our guest – a friend, not a policeman.'

'Then I'll see you – and him – there.' Sir Andrew sounded slightly doubtful.

'Really annoying,' Libby said to Ben after she'd ended the call. 'Now I'll have to wait to find out what it is Andrew wanted to tell me.'

'You won't have to wait long,' Ben said. 'Unless Ian thinks you ought not to know, of course.' He shot her a wicked look.

'Stop it! He's actually being far more forthcoming these days.' Libby looked sideways at her best beloved. 'And do you know what he said this afternoon?'

'Surprise me.'

'He said I'd calmed down a lot since we were investigating Aunt Elephant.'

'I bet he didn't call her that!'

'No, but I always think of her as Aunt Elephant. She was always in the room, see?'

Fran's Aunt Eleanor had been one of the first victims they had investigated together.

Ben laughed. 'I suppose you have calmed down a bit.' He looked her up and down. 'Even your clothes have calmed down.'

'Have they?' Libby looked shocked. 'How?'

'Didn't someone once mention a carnival tent?' Ben couldn't suppress a chuckle at Libby's horrified expression. 'You were a lot more colourful in those days.'

'Was I?' Libby sounded wistful. 'Have I grown up, then?'

'Not completely,' said Ben, giving her a quick squeeze. 'I wouldn't allow it.'

★

Ian and Sir Andrew both arrived not long after the main doors had been opened to the public, and went into a huddle by the bar. The bigwigs arrived, with entourages, five minutes before the auditorium doors were opened. Libby was beginning to get stressed, especially when it transpired that said entourages expected to be seated in the auditorium. Explaining that this was not possible to both bigwigs and entourages took them right up to the time the audience were allowed in. Luckily, the bigwigs themselves quite understood, and seemed more than happy to leave their disgruntled retinues in the foyer.

'Honestly,' Libby muttered to Hereward, 'don't they know anything about theatre? Do they expect us to magic up seats just because they want them?'

Ian had been lucky enough to get a returned ticket, and was sitting two rows in front of Rachel and Mark, who had been slightly shocked to see him. Libby and Hereward had to stand. The audience gradually quietened after its first rapturous response to the booth stage, the lights went down and Oliver stepped out into a spotlight to begin his speech.

And once more, Leonardo and his daughter, Hero, and niece, Beatrice, were awaiting the return of Don Pedro, Claudio and Benedick from war. And once more, the audience rose to its collective feet as Balthasar began to sing. Libby was embarrassed to find that her eyes were stinging and there was an odd restriction in her throat. Hereward put a friendly arm round her shoulders.

Her plan to speak to Sir Andrew and Ian in the interval was doomed to failure as the bigwigs demanded attention, as did several other members of the audience. Rachel and Mark were over in a corner with Ian, while Sir Andrew was buttonholed by part of one of the bigwigs' entourages. Libby didn't even manage a quick glass of wine, let alone a comfortable chat.

And then it was over. The cast bowed, bowed again, reprised their curtain-call jig, bowed again and were finally allowed to leave the stage.

★

'Well, that went well!' said Hereward, retrieving a tray of filled champagne glasses from the bar after the departure of bigwigs, entourages and most of the audience. The cast had all come into the foyer in costume to receive congratulations, especially, of course, Freddie Cannon, who was positively bouncing with glee. It abated not a jot when he spotted Rachel and Mark, and he raised his glass and gave them an ironic bow. Libby grinned and went to join Sir Andrew and Ian.

'I suppose you want to know what Andrew wanted to tell me?' Ian said. 'And why haven't you got a drink?'

'On its way,' said Libby, waving a hand towards Ben, who was at the bar, 'and he wanted to tell me, not you.'

'I called you to ask if you thought I should tell Ian,' said Sir Andrew. 'So, as I've now told him, I'm sure he won't mind if I tell you.'

Libby raised an eyebrow at Ian, who gave her a wry smile.

'So, it was about Connie, was it?' she asked, accepting a glass of red wine from Ben.

Sir Andrew nodded and picked up his own drink. 'When I got back home the other day, the phone didn't stop ringing.' He made an apologetic face. 'I'm still happier with the old landline, I'm afraid. And my laptop computer – can't cope with looking things up on this thing.' He tapped his smartphone, which was sitting on the table.

'Me, too,' said Libby.

'And all the phone calls,' Sir Andrew continued, 'were about Constance's murder. And at least two of them had information. Not,' he said quickly, 'that they expected me to do anything about it, of course.' He stopped to sip his whisky.

'What were they about?' Libby asked, when Sir Andrew seemed to go into a brown study.

'Oh, they were both about the same thing. Connie had loaned money and foreclosed when the repayments didn't come quickly enough.'

'Surely that's illegal?' Libby looked at Ian.

'Somehow or other it was written into the contracts that she was allowed to do that,' he said. 'Andrew checked.'

'What was the money for?' Libby was puzzled. 'I'm not sure I understand.'

'There were two loans that I've heard about,' said Sir Andrew. 'One was for the Furnough School, and the other was for the Raincliffe Repertory.'

'Raincliffe Rep! I played there!' said Libby.

'Not any more you won't,' said Sir Andrew. 'Closed it down and sold it – the same with the Furnough School.'

'Wasn't that a bit like the Poor School?' Ben asked. 'Founded for people who couldn't afford drama school fees or get grants?'

Sir Andrew nodded. 'Polly Furnough founded it back in the early seventies. It always struggled for money, but managed to keep going. They applied to Connie thinking she'd make a donation, but she insisted it was a loan, and . . . well, that was that.'

'Iniquitous!' gasped Libby.

'When was this?' asked Ben.

'Both within the last year,' said Ian. 'I've already got someone on it.' He nodded towards Rachel and Mark, who were hovering on the outskirts of the little group. 'And Rachel's getting straight on to it in the morning.'

'Regretting your evening off now?' Libby asked them.

'No, it was wonderful,' said Rachel. 'Thank you, Libby.'

'It was,' agreed Mark. 'I'm almost wishing I'd . . .' He paused as he caught Ian's eye, and smiled. 'Well. You know.'

'We'd better get off, then,' said Rachel. 'I'll have to be up early. Thank you again, Libby. It was great.'

'And don't forget what we talked about, Mark,' Ian said. Mark blushed and they made their exit.

'What did you talk about?' asked Libby, diverted.

'Seconding him to the detective division. Just for now.' Ian turned back to Sir Andrew. 'Tell Libby what happened afterwards.'

'I only know what happened about the Furnough School.' Sir Andrew shook his head. 'Polly left it to Carl Robinson, and he ended up having to declare bankruptcy. He's been more-or-less sofa-surfing ever since.'

'He's homeless?' Libby's eyes were wide with disbelief.

'And we've come full circle,' said Ian.

Chapter Nineteen

'Should I know Carl Robinson?' asked Ben, as they walked home from the theatre.

'He was one of Polly Furnough's protégés – he went to the school and became quite a good jobbing actor. I'd heard that he became the senior tutor at the school, but I didn't realise Polly had left it to him. Bit of a poisoned chalice, that.' Libby shook her head.

'So she used the profits from selling the school and the Rep to fund her little empire,' Ben mused. 'Presumably it was just the buildings she sold – not the goodwill.'

'Yes, or they'd have kept going, wouldn't they? Raincliffe was a beautiful building just on the edge of Hampstead, and the school was in Hackney, before it became what it is now, so both prime locations.'

'I still can't get used to Hackney being posh,' said Ben, as they arrived at Number 17.

'Neither can I,' agreed Libby, avoiding Sidney's attempt to trip her up. 'Do you want a nightcap?'

Ben hung up his jacket. 'If you want one. And you want to talk.' He sighed dramatically.

'OK, we'll talk in the morning.' Libby grinned at him. 'Race you to bed.'

Sunday morning and get-out time for the Glover's Men. Libby and Ben arrived early at the theatre and found the huge lorry already there, waiting to be loaded with booth stage, props, costumes and other essential equipment, ready to be transported to the next tour venue. While Ben went into the theatre to help, Libby went on to the Manor to say goodbye to the cast. She found Liz sitting in the big sitting room on her own.

'Where are they all?' asked Libby.

'Packing,' said Liz with a sigh. 'Honestly – aren't actors disorganised?'

'Not sure how to answer that,' said Libby. 'We may not be working at the moment, but you and I are both actors.'

'All right, *male* actors, then,' amended Liz.

'Speaking of actors,' said Libby, 'do you know the Furnough School?'

'Oh, yes! Poor Carl! You know he's gone broke?' Liz looked sad.

'Yes. And what about Raincliffe Rep?'

'That's closed too, hasn't it? Oh!' Liz sat up and looked straight at Libby. 'You're not going to tell me this is something else to do with that woman?'

Wondering too late if she should have said anything, Libby nodded.

'Well, it wouldn't have been Carl.' Liz looked determined. 'And I'll tell them so. He's such a lovely bloke. He'd do anything for anybody – and does. And it was That Woman who got him closed down?' Now Liz looked positively incandescent. 'I'd bloody well have killed her myself!'

'Hey, hey!' Oliver appeared, carrying a suitcase and a sports bag. 'Don't say things like that around here, missus!'

'No – Olly! Have you heard?' Liz leapt up to face him.

'No, no,' said Libby hastily, 'he hasn't. Nobody has. I shouldn't have said anything.'

'No, you shouldn't!' Liz swung round angrily.

'Calm down, poppet.' Oliver put down his case and pushed Liz back onto her chair. 'Libby, you're going to have to tell me now.'

Libby sighed and complied. Various members of the company

141

drifted past on their way to the kitchen to say goodbye to Hetty, casting the three of them quizzical looks.

Oliver looked serious. 'A lot of people have been upset by the closure of the school,' he said, 'and the fact that Carl was forced out, but I didn't realise it was that bad. And really, you know, Libby, it shouldn't be kept quiet. Something needs to be done about it.'

'But what?' said Libby. 'The building's been sold. For all I know they could already have the builders in turning it into whatever—'

'No, they haven't.' Liz stated firmly. 'We don't live far from it, and it's just standing there, empty.'

'There is a board up outside,' said Oliver. 'I think it's going to be flats.'

'Why didn't Carl try and raise the money to pay off the loan?' cried Liz. 'Everyone would have helped.'

'He may well have done,' said Libby. 'Connie just wanted him out, so she foreclosed. Same with Raincliffe.'

'*What?*' Oliver was aghast. 'She did it to Raincliffe?'

'I'm afraid so.' Libby leant forward and kissed them both on the cheek. 'Go on, you've got to get off. I promise I'll keep you posted.'

Libby went in search of Hetty and found her surrounded by Glover's Men. She waited until they had all left to collect their belongings from the theatre, then sat down at the kitchen table.

'I've just made them all angry with Constance Matthews all over again,' she confided. 'And I need tea.'

Hetty moved the big kettle onto the Aga. 'Pokin' yer nose in again?' she said.

'Well, no, actually. Ian's been asking for our help again, but I may have spoken out of turn.' She thought for a moment. 'And yet, it may be all to the good.'

'What d'yer mean?' Hetty frowned at her.

'Yes, what do you mean?'

Libby jumped.

'Oh, Andrew! Where did you come from?'

142

Sir Andrew smiled, walked round the table to give Hetty a kiss and sat down opposite Libby. 'Ian drove me back to Edward's last night and back here again this morning.'

'Oh, Ian's here, is he?' Libby looked nervously over her shoulder.

'Briefly. He's on his way to Nethergate. He's going to meet that nice Rachel.'

'Yes, he would be.' Libby played idly with a stray fork. 'I do hope he isn't going to get into trouble again.'

'What do you mean — trouble?' asked Andrew.

'The powers-that-be in the police force don't like him interfering in investigations,' explained Libby.

Hetty made an incredulous noise.

'Interfering?' repeated Sir Andrew. 'He's the detective chief inspector — it's his case!'

'But Rachel is the acting detective inspector and she's the SIO. He's supposed to stay behind his desk and not get involved on the ground, so to speak.'

'Oh, how ridiculous,' huffed Sir Andrew. 'Sheer stupidity.'

'I agree, but unfortunately, he's done it a couple of times recently, and even had to take gardening leave for a month or two at one point. That was partly for bringing Fran and me into the investigation.' Libby made a face. 'And he's doing it again.'

'But you're involved,' said Sir Andrew, accepting a mug of tea from Hetty. 'You help!'

'But the force doesn't like that. It has protocols. Rules, regulations.'

'And it isn't always right!' Sir Andrew was becoming militant.

'No, but . . .' Libby shrugged.

'So tell me why you thought speaking out of turn might have been a good thing.' Andrew fixed her with a shrewd gaze.

'Because if Oliver and Liz tell the others, they might all get together and try and help Carl Robinson,' said Libby. 'Liz was saying why didn't he try to raise money before?'

'He did – that's why he had the loan,' said Sir Andrew.

'No – to pay it off,' said Libby. 'I explained about Connie fore-closing, but I think Liz was fired up enough to try and get something going to help.'

'Well,' said Sir Andrew thoughtfully, 'the Furnough doesn't have to be in *that* particular building, does it?'

There was a moment's charged silence. Hetty looked from one to the other, smiling faintly.

'Yes!!!' shouted Libby, waking up Jeff-dog, who had been snoozing peacefully under the table. 'So we find another building!'

'That was the idea,' said Sir Andrew. 'Although it wouldn't be in such a prestigious location.'

'When Polly opened it, it *wasn't* in a prestigious location!' said Libby. 'Hackney was still old East End then.' She stopped. 'Trouble is, everywhere's a good location in London these days. Even where I used to live the houses are going for millions. And where Fran used to live, too. So where could it be? It would have to be where industry people could get to it – you know, for showcases and so on.'

'Let's not get ahead of ourselves,' said Sir Andrew, laughing. 'Let me talk to a few people – young Oliver included—'

'And Liz,' broke in Libby.

'And Liz, and Sir Jasper, perhaps, and we'll try and come up with something. I agree. Poor Carl shouldn't have to suffer – and we need places like the Furnough.'

'And the Raincliffe?'

'One step at a time,' said Sir Andrew.

Due to the Manor having been overrun with guests, Hetty's traditional Sunday lunch had been cancelled this week, and Libby and Ben were going down to Nethergate to have lunch at the Sloop with Fran and Guy. On the way, the Glover's Men having been waved goodbye and the theatre locked up to await the cleaning company's arrival on Monday, Libby told Ben about her conversations that morning.

'I don't think you should have said anything.' Ben looked worried.

'No, I know, but as I said to Andrew, it may be all to the good.'

'Yes, and I'm sure he will do what he can to think of an alternative building for the school – but it isn't just a building, you know, Lib.'

'No, I know, there's all sorts of legislation to get through, but it might help.'

Ben sighed. 'I hope so. But from what I saw of Ian this morning, it didn't look good.'

'You saw Ian? He didn't come and see me!'

'It wasn't a social call. He dropped Andrew, had a word with Freddie, then he was off to see Rachel. He looked grim.'

'Oh, dear. Do you think something's happened overnight?'

'Well, he wanted to look into the whole business of the Raincliffe and the Furnough, didn't he? And he said he'd got someone on to it already, you told me. So yes, I would say something's happened overnight. Or at least, something's been discovered overnight.' Ben glanced sideways and gave a wry smile. 'Make of that what you will, Miss Marple.'

'Don't call me that,' growled Libby, and turned to look out of the window at the almost leafless hedgerows.

They called at Coastguard Cottage before going to the Sloop, and found Fran in an unaccustomed flap.

'It's Chrissie!' she said. 'Brucie baby's decided they are going away for a week and she wants to dump Cassandra on me!'

Chrissie was Fran's younger daughter, Bruce her husband and Cassandra, their arrogant and spoilt Siamese cat.

'Well, she can't!' said Libby indignantly. 'You've got a cat, too! What about Balzac?'

'That's what I told her! She then informed me that they were on the way over already!'

145

'Then you'll be out,' said Ben. 'She can't expect you to drop everything.'

'But she does,' said Guy, coming in from the kitchen. 'I've told my darling wife that we shall be out, and not to tell her where we are. Have you ever heard anything like it? Suppose we'd been – I don't know – abroad somewhere?'

'Let's just go to the Sloop and we can watch from the window,' said Libby.

'That's all very well, but I wouldn't put it past her to just dump the cat basket on the doorstep,' said Fran gloomily.

'Then you report her to the RSPCA,' said Ben. 'Come on. I can hear Graham's roast calling to me.'

Chapter Twenty

Fran was still uncertain, but they locked the door on Balzac and wandered over to the Sloop. Graham was waiting to seat them in their favourite window seat and ask about progress in the murder case. After bringing him up to date with a precis of events, they ordered and sat back to await their drinks. Fran suddenly shot up.

'Look! There they are!'

'Leave it!' said Guy, trying to coax her back into her seat, but Fran was adamant.

'I can't,' she said. 'She'll abandon the poor animal.'

In the end all four of them went out to confront Chrissie, who had, indeed, already placed the cat basket on the doorstep of Coast-guard Cottage.

'I said no, Chrissie,' said Fran, before her daughter could speak.

'But what will I do with her?' asked Chrissie, wide-eyed. 'I can't leave her in the house on her own.'

'No, you can't.' Libby elbowed Fran aside. 'You should have thought about that before you decided to go on holiday.'

Chrissie bristled. 'What's it got to do with you?' she snapped.

'The same as it has to do with all of us,' said Guy. 'The welfare of an animal.'

'Then why won't you take her?' said Chrissie triumphantly.

'Because if you leave her here,' said Ben, 'we will take her to the RSPCA for rehoming and report you at the same time.'

'You can't do that!' Chrissie shrieked. 'She's worth thousands!'

'Then you should think about her welfare,' said Libby. 'In fact, I think we should take her now to save her more trauma.'

Chrissie seemed to shrink. 'But what will I do?'

'What have you done before when you've gone away?' asked Ben.

'She goes to a cat hotel.' Chrissie's eyes were fixed on the now wailing cat basket.

'Why not this time?' asked Fran.

Silence.

'Come on, Chrissie,' said Guy. 'Why?'

'We can't afford it.' Chrissie cleared her throat at this shaming admission.

'But you can afford a holiday.' Libby was scathing.

'It's not exactly a holiday.' Chrissie finally looked up and fixed her eyes on her mother. 'We've got to move.'

The four friends looked at each other.

'This can't be resolved here and now,' said Guy, taking charge. 'Take your cat home, Chrissie. She can't come into our house – our own cat would definitely not approve. I suggest you then call your mother later this afternoon and explain.'

'I can't do that, Guy.' Fran turned anguished eyes on her husband. 'You three go and have your meal. Chrissie can come in with me and explain. I'll shut Balzac in the kitchen.'

Despite protests, Fran insisted, and the other three trailed back to the Sloop, where they found Graham waiting anxiously with a bottle of wine.

'Family problems,' said Guy, with an unconvincing laugh. 'She'll be along as soon as she can.'

And they settled down to wait.

In fact, Fran arrived sooner than expected, but looking more cheerful than she had earlier.

'Bruce has been made redundant,' she said, taking a healthy mouthful of wine, 'and they can't meet their mortgage repayments.'

'Golly!' said Libby. 'So definitely not a holiday.'

'No. They're going up to Lincolnshire.'

'Eh?'

'What?'

'Why?'

'Bruce has found a job up there . . .'

'Bloody lucky,' muttered Ben.

'And they're going up there to look at a house and schools and so on,' continued Fran.

'A house to rent?' asked Guy.

Fran nodded, taking a bite of her pâté.

'Couldn't get another mortgage if they've defaulted on this one,' said Libby.

'Actually, they haven't defaulted,' said Fran. 'They've been sensible and—'

'Jumped before they were pushed.' said Guy.

'Exactly,' said Fran.

'So what's happened about Cassandra?' asked Libby.

'She's going to the cattery.' A faint pink crept up Fran's neck.

'And you're paying for it,' said Guy, smiling.

'Why didn't she ask you in the first place?' asked Ben.

'Because she didn't want to admit it,' said Libby. 'Right, Fran?'

'Well, I haven't exactly been over the moon about her lifestyle choices in the past, have I?' said Fran with a cynical smile.

'Did she go away suitably cowed?' asked Guy.

'Not noticeably. There was a distinct air of it probably being all my fault in the first place,' said Fran, laughing.

'But,' said Libby, when they'd calmed down, 'it just shows you what a state the country's in, doesn't it? It isn't just the lower-paid who are suffering. Brucie baby was in a well-paid job. And now they're going to have to come down to the level of the ordinary people.'

'There were hints that if I was a decent mother I would stump up more funds to keep them in the style to which they are accustomed in Friar's Ashworth,' said Fran, who, in the past had made generous donations to all three of her children. 'I said if there was

149

a sudden emergency, she could come to me, but otherwise it was stand-on-your-own-feet time.'

'She could perhaps try and get a job?' suggested Libby.

'She could, but think how difficult it is to get a job – any job – at the moment.'

'Hospitality and care homes are crying out for people,' said Ben.

'But there's the childcare aspect,' said Fran. 'Like poor Kirsty we met the other day, Lib.'

They explained to Ben and Guy about Kirsty's situation.

'And I refuse to believe that all those people who gather in the Blue Anchor are just not bothering to find jobs,' said Libby.

'A lot of the time employers won't take people on if they haven't got a permanent address,' said Ben.

'Luckily, Bruce's new employers were only too glad to get him and are helping find the house,' said Fran, 'so they really are the lucky ones, except that they've got to move out of their comfortable life and surroundings. I don't suppose he'll be joining a new golf club quite yet.'

They managed to enjoy the Sloop's finest Sunday lunch despite the intrusion of, as Ben put it, the Interlude with Cat.

'It feels a bit self-indulgent though, doesn't it?' said Libby, as they lingered over their coffee. 'When so many people can't even afford basic food.'

Guy pulled a face. 'That thought isn't going to help with digestion.'

'Short of donating the cost to the crisis fund,' said Ben, 'what should we do?'

'Well, we could do that,' said Libby. 'Now that we've had a lovely lunch. Sort of extra payment.'

'We could go and donate to Mavis,' said Fran. 'To help pay for her heating and the food she's supplying.'

'I think my digestion might be eased,' Guy said. 'I'll go and pay Graham first.'

Ben stood up and Guy waved him down. 'My treat,' he said. 'That'll ease the digestion even more.'

'How do we do this?' asked Libby, as they approached the Blue Anchor. 'Shouldn't it be in cash? I never have cash these days.'

'We'll ask,' said Fran, and marched up to the door, past the few smokers huddled under Mavis's outdoor heater.

'Have to use the old machine,' Mavis said with a shrug, when they had explained what they wanted to do. 'All go into the same place, won't it?'

The crowd in the café was slightly different from that of the previous days, Libby noticed.

'Sunday,' said Mavis succinctly. 'Got the workers in. The others make way for 'em.'

'You know what you should have done with Chrissie,' Libby said to Fran as they left, 'brought her in here to see the people in real hardship.'

'It wouldn't have registered,' said Guy. 'I know my Chrissie.'

'He's right,' sighed Fran. 'Where did I go wrong with that girl?'

Ben and Libby drove home in time to have the traditional after-lunch drink with Peter and Harry.

'Really because he hasn't been able to indulge himself properly at lunchtime,' Libby told them, settling into her usual sagging arm-chair. Ben accepted a large whisky.

'And we all feel rather guilty about not being poor,' he added.

Peter sat down beside Harry – still in his chef's whites – on the sofa. Harry lifted his feet on to his husband's lap and lifted his glass.

'Cheers, dears,' he said. 'And let's be thankful that we aren't. After all, at least some of us were once.' He bent a minatory eye on Ben and Peter.

'It's a bit of a wake-up call when you realise people like Chrissie and Brucie baby can still become victims of – what? Society?' said Libby.

'Chrissie wasn't wealthy as a child,' said Peter. 'If I remember rightly, Fran was a struggling actor for a good few years. I never did know anything about her first husband.'

'Come to think of it, neither did I.' Libby frowned.

'Speaking of struggling,' Peter went on, 'do you remember Sadie O'Day?'

'Gosh – there's a name from the past!' said Libby. 'Of course I remember her. She's still working, isn't she?'

'Yes, and coming to Canterbury with a big band concert this week. I wondered if you fancied going.'

'Who's Sadie O'Day?' asked Ben.

'A singer,' said Libby. 'I knew her in the old days – she came from near us in London. Great voice – did all the old classics, you know, Ella, Billie Holiday. She did panto with me a couple of times before I retired.'

'Retired?' spluttered Harry. 'How old were you, exactly?'

'OK – left the business to have the kids,' corrected Libby. 'You know what I mean. Anyway – how did you hear about it, Pete? Her concert, I mean.'

'Social media, dear heart, what else? And actually, it was following one of those down-the-rabbit-hole trails. I was looking into the Raincliffe Rep. Andrew came in for lunch and told us all about it.'

'So where did the rabbit hole lead?' asked Ben.

'All the way back to' – Peter paused for effect – 'May!'

'May? Again?'

'There were a few one-nighters booked on the normal profit-sharing system and they were all cancelled. Sadie was one of them.'

Ben and Libby stared.

'Ha-ha! Surprise!' crowed Harry.

'This is a bit more than coincidence,' said Ben.

'Simply that your Ms Matthews had her fingers in many theatrical pies,' said Peter. 'Anyway, Sadie is now camping out with her friend, Cyd. I've told her we're coming—'

'But we haven't said we are!' said Libby.

152

'I've told her we're coming, and you'd like to speak to her,' Peter carried on, ignoring her.

'How, anyway? On social media again?' asked Ben.

'Oh do wake up, children!' said Harry. 'Of *course* soshul meeja. How else does one get in touch these days?'

'Sid,' mused Libby. 'Sid who?'

'Not Sid with an "S", Cyd with a "C",' said Peter.

'Oh! Like Charisse!'

'That's it. Only perhaps not as famous.'

'Oh – I know!' Libby remembered that she had met Cyd previously, some years before. 'Cyd Russell! She's a singer, too.'

'And was going to be doing the concert at the Raincliffe with Sadie. So both of them—'

'Would have an axe to grind,' put in Harry. 'She wasn't done in with an axe, was she?'

'I don't know,' said Libby. 'But I can't imagine Sadie or Cyd murdering someone. And anyway, if the theatre shut down, would they even know who was behind it?'

'Of course they would,' scoffed Harry. He leant back, looking at the ceiling. 'Sadie and Cyd – lovely double act, don't you think?'

Chapter Twenty-One

'Of course,' Libby said on the phone to Fran the following morning, 'she isn't really Sadie O'Day.'

'Oh?' Fran sounded distracted.

'No. She's plain old Judy Dale, actually. But she thought Sadie O'Day sounded better.'

'And now she's stuck with it,' said Fran.

'Something like that. Anyway, Pete's got us tickets for tomorrow, and I thought you might like to come?'

'Oh, I don't know,' sighed Fran. 'Not really my thing, big band stuff.'

'OK. Ben and I are going. We thought Hetty might like to go, seeing as a lot of the music will be her era, but you'll never guess!'

'She's already going? With Joe?'

'How did you know?' grumbled Libby.

'Joe – and Lenny, now – belong to a group of, er . . . mature people who go on outings. They call it the Old Codgers Club. Makes sense.'

'Yes, well . . . Anyway, the coach is picking them all up on the way to Canterbury.'

'All?'

'Flo and Lenny, too. Thank goodness Ricky's grandma hasn't moved in yet, or she'd have muscled in.'

Fran laughed. 'You really don't like her, do you? I thought she was quite pleasant.'

'Oh, she is. But a bit over-forceful.' Libby chuckled. 'I expect we'll clash.'

'I expect you will,' said Fran.

Libby was at the theatre with the team of cleaners who came to put everything to rights after, and between, productions when her basket began ringing. Retrieving her phone, she retired to the foyer to answer it.

'Is that Libby?' asked a female voice.

'Yes?' said Libby warily.

'It's Judy here – Judy Dale.'

'Judy! How lovely to hear from you! We're coming to see you tomorrow night – I gather you know my friend Peter Parker?'

Judy sighed with obvious relief. 'I thought you might not remember me,' she said. 'And yes – I came across Peter years back when he was with Reuters. I knew you'd moved after you split up with Derek – never liked that man – but I didn't realise you were Peter's neighbour.'

'Oh yes,' said Libby. 'In fact, he and his husband Harry found me my cottage. And my partner Ben is Pete's cousin.'

'Wow! What a lot I've got to catch up on.' Judy laughed. 'But actually, I wanted to talk to you, and I don't think there'll be much chance tomorrow.'

'Ri-ight,' said Libby. 'So what do you suggest? You're still living in London, or . . .' She suddenly remembered what Peter had said. 'You're – um – sharing a flat?'

'I'm kipping on Cyd's sofa.'

'Ah. Yes.'

'And that's what I wanted to talk to you about. So I wondered if I could come and see you?'

'Of course,' said Libby. 'When?'

'Well, I'm supposed to be coming down with the band tomorrow, but I could come down on my own and stay somewhere overnight. Have you got a pub in your village?'

155

'We've got two,' said Libby, 'but no need for that. We've got a spare room — why don't you come and stay with us? You won't be able to eat in the Pink Geranium because Harry closes on Mondays, but—'

'Hang on, Lib! You're going too fast! Pink Geranium?'

Libby explained about Harry and the caff. 'But we could have dinner at the Coach, and maybe Peter and Harry could join us.'

'Well, I . . .' Judy was hesitant.

'If it's private, you could come here first.'

'Are you sure you don't mind?'

'Of course I don't mind,' said Libby briskly, hoping that Ben wouldn't. 'I take it you'll be driving?'

'Oh, yes.' Judy sighed. 'In our business you have to be mobile, don't you?'

'Oh, yes,' said Libby, memories of wet and windy railway stations on dismal Sundays floating through her mind. Crewe, anyone? She gave directions, said goodbye to Judy and went to find Ben, who was overseeing some arcane process in the brewery.

'You don't mind, do you?' she asked, as he looked down at her from the top of a ladder resting up against one of the shiny mash tuns that contained the fermenting beer.

Ben sighed. 'I suppose not. I was looking forward to an evening with just us for a change.'

'Sorry.' Libby looked at her feet.

'Never mind.' Ben began to climb down the ladder. 'But could you please hurry up and solve this murder so we can get back to normal?'

Libby greeted his return to terra firma with a grin and a kiss. 'And panto,' she added.

'So I wonder what she wants.' Libby was back at Number 17, on the phone with Fran and foraging for lunch. The cleaners had promised to drop the keys in to Hetty when they had finished.

'Are you sure you don't want to check that we've done it properly?' the team leader had asked.

'Good lord, no! You've done it so often I'm sure it's all perfect,' Libby had assured her.

'Well,' said Fran meditatively now, 'as Peter already told you he'd more or less told her you wanted to speak to her . . .'

'She's obviously aware of our interest in the Matthews situation,' said Libby. 'Yes, I get that, but . . .'

'Look, you'll know later on today, won't you? Not long to wait, you impatient old biddy. Go and change the sheets on the spare bed.'

Libby ate her soup and went to do as she'd been told.

'Panto,' she muttered to herself as she came back downstairs. She really must concentrate on the panto. Auditions were coming up, although their resident performers were pre-cast, Tom as the Dame and Bob the butcher and his on-stage partner Baz the double act. However, this being *Cinderella*, another Dame was required to partner Tom as the Ugly Sister. Back in May Bob had suggested Ben, who, when informed of this, had reacted with horror.

It had become tradition with the Oast Theatre pantomime to have a mix of amateur and professional actors. They were lucky in that the trust that ran the theatre, under the guiding hands of Peter, Ben and Libby, was able to fund this slight departure from the norm. In fact, when Libby's friend Dame Amanda Knight had brought her production to the Oast last season, many of the amateur members had been paid as well, which had worried Libby slightly. She needn't have been concerned, as Bob had informed her.

'No getting out of it this year, young lady,' he'd said. 'We want to go back to normal and so do the audiences.'

Did that mean, Libby wondered, as she sat down on the sofa with a cup of tea and the updated script, an all-amateur cast? Or should she look into recruiting some professionals? She was still frowning over this conundrum when the doorbell rang.

Libby opened the door and beamed. 'Judy!'

Judy Dale, a tiny figure with a cloud of chestnut hair, beamed back. 'Libby!'

Ten minutes later she was seated in the armchair opposite Libby, who had made more tea in the brown teapot with proper loose-leaf tea.

'Now,' said Libby. 'Do we catch up with each other's lives, or do we get straight down to brass tacks? Which I assume has something to do with Constance Matthews.'

Judy nodded and gazed sadly at the empty grate. Libby immediately knelt down and began the business of lighting the woodburner. 'Comfort,' she said.

'Peter said you know about the Raincliffe being closed,' Judy began.

'Yes,' said Libby, 'taking your money with it.'

'Yes. It was a big thing for me.' Judy sighed. 'It was a concert built around me – "Sadie O'Day Sings", it was going to be called. Ray McCloud – know him? – brilliant pianist – well, he did it all. Arrangements, recruiting musos, everything. We both put money into it. I remortgaged . . .' Judy's voice trailed off.

'And it was pulled,' Libby said gently.

'The owners were really sorry.' Judy stared at the flames now licking round the kindling. 'They lost everything, too.'

'How did Connie Matthews come to buy it?'

'She bought up the loans – you can do that, apparently.'

Libby nodded. 'So they'd already borrowed?'

'Oh, yes. They were struggling to keep going. What with the pandemic and everything . . .'

'So what about the ticket money already received?' asked Libby.

'We managed to save that, or the solicitors did, so we could refund it. And left the Raincliffe without a . . .'

'Pot to piss in,' supplied Libby. 'Quite. And you couldn't meet your increased mortgage payments.'

'I had no idea it would happen so quickly,' said Judy, gazing into her mug.

158

They were quiet for a moment. Then Judy looked up. 'But what I wanted to talk to you about,' she said, 'was something else.'

'Not Connie Matthews?' Libby was surprised.

'Oh, yes – her.' Judy's face looked vicious. 'And Carl Robinson.'

'C-Carl?'

'You know Carl?'

'Oh, yes. And we heard about Connie buying the Furnough.'

'Oh, she didn't just *buy* it. She cheated him out of it.'

'How?' asked Libby, when she'd found her voice.

Judy heaved a sigh and put her mug down on the hearth. Sidney appeared and sniffed it. Judy smiled sadly at him and stroked his head.

'The Furnough was struggling financially, too. Well, it always has, really.'

'Because it was basically offering something for nothing,' said Libby. 'It relied on donations, didn't it?'

'And Arts Council grants, when it could get them.'

'So what did Connie do?'

'She went to Carl with an offer. If he raised a certain amount, she would double it.'

'And she didn't?'

'Not only that, but she bought the loan and foreclosed.'

'Bloody hell!' gasped Libby. 'That's got to be illegal!'

'You would have thought so, wouldn't you? But of course, you'd have to have written proof. A proper legal contract. And Carl, the idiot, had taken Matthews on trust. "She's part of the profession," he said. "She wouldn't cheat." Ha!'

'Bloody hell!' said Libby again. 'I don't believe that woman. Why was she doing this? She didn't need the money!'

'Power, I suppose.' Judy shrugged. 'She hadn't got it in the profession any more, so . . . Anyway, it turns out that Carl wasn't the only one she did that to.'

'Oh, no.' Libby closed her eyes and shook her head. 'So there are a lot more suspects.'

159

Judy nodded. 'I suppose there are, although I don't know anybody who slipped down to Steeple Martin to knock her off.'

'It wasn't Steeple Martin, actually,' said Libby. 'It was in some woods on the outskirts of Nethergate.'

Judy looked blank.

'It's a tiny little seaside town near here. My best friend Fran lives there.'

'What was she doing there?' asked Judy.

'Much the same as she was doing in London,' said Libby. 'Buying properties and throwing tenants out to turn them into holiday lets – that's always been a big business in Nethergate. Holiday lets, not throwing people out.' Libby stared into the fire. 'Now we're going to have to find out if she'd done any of this loan fixing in Nethergate, too.'

'Have the police got anyone in mind?' Judy lifted Sidney on to her lap. He purred loudly and sent Libby an evil look.

'They did have. I don't know if Peter told you, but we've just had the Glover's Men here for a week.'

'Hang on – aren't they the all-male Shakespeare troupe?'

'That's them. They're regulars here. Anyway, they had a male soprano, which was being kept as a surprise for audiences. Well,' Libby settled herself back into the corner of the sofa, 'Connie wouldn't believe he was a man. She wheedled me into picking her up from London and giving her a ticket, you see, saying she wanted to see Shakespeare as it was wrote. And then she put it all over social media, spoiling the surprise.' Libby grinned. 'And it backfired a bit, because there was so much interest we could have run it for another week. Anyway, she also accused the whole cast of being gay, in the most ghastly homophobic language. And she was particularly awful about young Freddie.'

'Freddie Cannon?' said Judy. 'Oh, I know him! He's lovely. We did a Prom together.'

'Well, the police thought he'd killed her for a bit.'

'No!'

'No, they gave up on that. It was fairly obvious he couldn't have done it.'

'So haven't they got anyone else?'

'They might have,' said Libby, 'but if so, they haven't told me.'

Judy frowned. 'Why would they? Tell you, I mean.'

'Ah,' said Libby. 'Pete didn't tell you everything about me, obviously.'

Chapter Twenty-Two

Libby was still explaining the Wolfe and Wilde adventure series to Judy when Ben arrived, just after five o'clock. After introductions had been made, Ben excused himself to have a shower.

'He's nice,' said Judy. 'You're lucky.'

'I know. I've never ceased to be grateful to Pete and Harry for bringing me here. I've got my lovely cottage, wonderful friends, my own theatre – almost – and Ben. Oh, and Sidney. What more could I want?'

Judy shook her head in wonder. 'I said you were lucky. I didn't realise *how* lucky.'

'I feel guilty sometimes,' confessed Libby. 'I expect that's why I've got involved in this protest group. Trying to help people who have been so unfairly treated. Not just by Connie, but the government, too.'

Judy nodded. 'But you're still involved in theatre, too, aren't you?' She nodded towards the pile of paper lying on top of the laptop by Libby's side. 'That's a script, isn't it?'

'Panto,' said Libby. 'One of mine. We've got auditions next week.'

'Amateur, is it?'

'No, pro–am usually. We've got our regulars who the audiences come to see, but we import people, too.' She looked up and realised the same thought had struck Judy that had occurred to her.

'I don't suppose—' said Judy.

'You wouldn't consider—' said Libby at the same time.

They both laughed.

'Do you do it these days?' asked Libby.

'Not really. The big ones always want names, don't they? I've done the odd run in the regionals – I did a *Mame* last year.' She pulled a face. '*Not* a success.'

'So . . .Godmother? Stepmother?' Libby put her head on one side. 'What d'you reckon?'

Judy's face broke into a huge smile. 'Do you mean it?'

'Of course. Do *you*?'

'Oh, yes! We've done it before, haven't we? You were the evil Queen and I was the goody-goody fairy.'

'Oh, *Snow White*, yes! At The Regent, wasn't it! And we did it the next year, too – *Sleeping Beauty*.' Libby smiled.

'I'd rather have go at the stepmother this time.' Judy sat forward, disturbing Sidney. 'If it's a decent part.'

'Oi! I wrote it!' said Libby. 'And yes. She's actually a witch. And not only does she have fights with the Fairy Godmother, she's under the whip hand of the Demon King. It's a great part,' said Libby, modestly and wistfully.

'Would you be Godmother?' asked Judy.

'No – I'm directing,' said Libby. 'Although I have done both in the past.'

They were still discussing *Cinderella* when Ben appeared and offered them both a drink. Judy excused herself to go and unpack her few belongings, and Libby told Ben what she had learned.

'Well, that adds a few suspects, doesn't it?' he said. 'Have you told Ian?'

'No – should I? Or Rachel? Or is it interfering?'

'They should have found out about it already,' said Ben. 'They'll have been looking into all her financial doings, won't they?'

'Yes.' Libby sipped her wine. 'And all the disaffected tenants and landlords, too.'

163

'And we haven't heard about other companies whose noses she might have put out of joint,' said Ben.

'Oh, no – so we haven't!' Libby sat up straight and dislodged Sidney, who had slunk on to her lap after being turfed off Judy's.

'I was thinking about it,' said Ben. 'The companies who run holiday lets in Nethergate. Has she snatched business from under those noses?'

Libby retrieved her computer from under the pile of script and typed in 'Holiday Lets Nethergate'.

'Here we are,' she said. 'Look! Quite a few of them.'

'Remember what Jim Butler said. It's turning into all coffee shops and sourdough bakeries.'

'Mmm. And look – Brooke's! There's a surprise.' Libby sat back. 'In fact, they were behind a distinctly dodgy deal with the house where Freddie's grandma lives.'

Ben frowned. 'We don't know anyone who works there now, do we?'

'No.' Libby finished her wine. 'In fact, we don't really know any suspects at all, do we? You can hardly count Lady Pru or Dorothy Barton – they weren't being affected, despite Connie's best efforts. And really, people like Freddie's grandma and Kirsty, the young mum I told you about, I can hardly see them bashing her over the head.'

'But somebody did,' said Ben. 'And I wonder if the police have been focusing on local suspects and ignoring the wider field?'

'They can hardly do that, surely?' said Libby. 'After all, Freddie isn't a local.'

'No, but he was here, in the locality. And his gran's a local. But it's easy enough to get down here from London, isn't it? Or from anywhere else, come to that.'

Judy reappeared and returned to the armchair. 'Are you discussing Constance Matthews?'

'Yes,' said Libby. 'And wondering about other suspects.'

'Me, for a start,' said Judy. 'And some of the other musicians who were doing the concert. Although they only lost the fee.' She picked up the glass Ben had left by her chair. 'Although there were a couple of others who I think had come up against her.'

'Oh?' said Ben and Libby together.

'I'm not sure of the details,' said Judy. 'Cyd might know – or Ray, of course.'

'Ray?' queried Ben. Libby explained.

'Would you mind, Judy,' he went on, 'if we told our policeman friend about this? I'm sure the police already know about Connie's financial dealings, but just in case.'

'No, I don't mind,' said Judy, looking resigned. 'It'll make me into an official suspect, but it might help. In fact, I did wonder why they hadn't got on to me already.'

'I'll call Rachel,' said Libby, standing up and depositing Sidney back on Judy's lap.

She took her phone into the kitchen and found Rachel's number.

'Libby.' Rachel sounded tired. 'What can I do for you?'

'Well,' said Libby, 'I just wanted to tell you a couple of things that I've learned today. About Constance Matthews. You probably know already, but just in case.'

'And you didn't tell DCI Connell first? Goodness.'

'But you're in charge, aren't you? You're SIO?'

Libby heard a heavy sigh. 'In theory.'

'Right, well, what I heard was this.'

And Libby went on to outline the facts she had learnt from Judy. Rachel didn't interrupt.

'So there you are. As I said, I'm sure you've got people on it already . . .' Libby trailed off. The silence was ominous. 'Say something, Rachel! Even if it's just "go away".'

'I've buggered this up, haven't I?' Rachel's voice was muffled. Libby had a horrible feeling she was trying not to cry.

'Of course not,' she said, wishing she'd brought her wine with her into the kitchen.

'I'm supposed to be in charge and I haven't even authorised a financials search.' Rachel sniffed. 'Oh, I expect the DCI has – he's in overall charge, after all – but if so, why didn't he tell me? And he keeps coming down and talking to people . . .'

'Rachel, stop it!' Libby was sharp. 'I'm sure you've been doing everything you should. That Sergeant Powell hasn't been helping, has he? He's alienating witnesses, as far as I can see. Why don't you start looking into what I've told you, and you might find it's already being done.'

'And then I really will look stupid, won't I?' Rachel sighed and sniffed again. 'I'm sorry, Libby. It isn't your fault. I can't see me getting my Inspector's badge at this rate, though.' She cleared her throat. 'Would this witness be willing to talk to me, do you think?'

'She's said she would. She's here overnight because she's performing in Canterbury tomorrow, but then she'll be going back to London.'

'What about tomorrow morning? I could come to you?'

'I'll just ask,' said Libby, and poked her head into the sitting room. 'She said yes, that's fine.'

'About ten, then?'

'That'll be great,' said Libby. 'I'll have the kettle on.'

She went back into the sitting room and retrieved her wine glass. 'Phew!' she said.

'I honestly don't understand it,' said Ben with a frown. 'Why haven't the financials been done already? And what about the will? The heirs?'

'I don't know.' Libby shook her head. 'And Rachel's always seemed so efficient in the past.'

Judy was staring at them wide-eyed.

'You really do know all about police investigations, don't you?'

Ben laughed. 'Unfortunately, yes. Hasn't Libby told you?'

'She told me about some of her – er – adventures. I didn't realise they were official.'

'They aren't,' said Libby. 'I'm sure any other police force would lock me up. And Fran.'

'No, they wouldn't,' said Ben, 'because Fran is actually *helpful*.'

Libby and Judy laughed. 'That's put me in my place,' said Libby.

'Come on,' said Ben, standing up. 'Let's go to the pub. We've got time to have a drink before dinner. Tim's not busy this evening, so he said it didn't matter what time we arrived. I think Peter and Harry are joining us.'

Much later, after an excellent dinner courtesy of the Coach and Horses' chef, Judy returned to the subject of the pantomime.

'I was thinking of auditioning,' she told Peter. 'I'd love to play the stepmother.'

'Oh, the Lady Aconite!' chortled Harry. 'I'd love to have a go at her myself.'

'Don't take any notice of him,' said Peter. 'And why not? Although I'm sure you wouldn't have to audition. Would she, Madam Director?'

'I don't think so,' replied Libby. 'I'd be delighted to have her.'

'I thought Libby should be the Fairy,' said Judy, not looking at Libby.

'Oh, *yes*!' cried Harry. 'Remember when the panto horse fell on the Fairy, and you did it before, Lib?'

'How can I forget?' muttered Libby.

'You directed that one,' said Peter. 'And I can always be your PA. Oh, go on, Lib.'

Ben was looking on, amused and taking no part in the conversation. Libby turned to him with a sweet smile. 'And as I recall, my darling, you were the King.'

'Oh, no!' Ben looked horrified. 'No way!'

167

'Oh, do you act, too?' Judy looked interested.

'Yes, he does,' said Libby. 'Don't worry, I'll work on him.'

'Right, now we've got that settled,' said Harry, 'what about this 'ere murder. You've usually got loads of suspects by now, petal, but apart from young Freddie, I haven't heard of any.'

'No, we were talking about that earlier,' said Libby. 'I'm sure the police have.'

'But they aren't telling you? How very unfair!'

'There'll be loads in London,' said Libby.

'And many down here,' said Ben. 'It's just that Acting Inspector Rachel isn't sharing.'

'Young Rachel? Why not?' Harry raised his eyebrows.

'I think she's being stymied by at least one of her team,' said Libby. 'I'm going to see if I can talk to Ian about it, but I don't want to drop her in it.'

'You can talk to her tomorrow,' said Ben. 'And now, let's think about where Judy's going to stay if she does panto with us.'

'That's a thought,' said Libby. 'It's a shorter run but a longer rehearsal period, Judy. We'll be rehearsing right through December and running all through January, so two whole months. How will that affect you? Have you got any gigs booked?'

'Yes, but mainly Saturdays,' said Judy. 'Anyway, where can I stay, if the situation's as bad down here as it is in London? I can't afford holiday rental prices.'

Peter, Harry and Libby all looked at Ben.

'Yes, all right, that's what I was going to suggest,' he said, turning to Judy. 'My mum has rooms at the Manor that visiting artistes use. That will work, won't it?'

Later they walked back to Allhallow's Lane, Judy and Libby on either side of Ben.

'I have the strangest feeling that my life has just changed completely,' said Judy. 'When I think how depressed I was when I arrived . . .'

'It's the Steeple Martin effect,' said Libby.

'Or possibly the Loonies effect,' said Ben, and then had to explain to Judy that Libby's Loonies was the name Harry had given to their group of friends who helped, hindered or criticised Libby's investigation efforts. It took some time.

Chapter Twenty-Three

Rachel, accompanied by Mark in plain clothes, arrived at two minutes past ten on Tuesday morning.

'Are you off duty?' asked Libby, surprised.

'No, I've been seconded,' said Mark, trying, and failing, to stop smiling.

'Oh, that's what Ian meant the other night when he told you not to forget what he'd said!' Libby patted his arm. 'Come and meet Judy.'

Introductions and tea supplied, Libby excused herself.

'No, please stay,' said Judy. 'You don't mind, do you, Inspector Trent?'

Rachel visibly sat up straighter on being addressed thus, and shook her head. 'No, Libby knows it all already,' she said, 'so, unless you've got things to do, Libby?'

'Oh, no,' said Libby. 'I'm fine.' She sat on a chair at the table, Rachel and Mark having appropriated the sofa.

Judy explained her own circumstances first, and then went on to relate what she knew of the other people and organisations that had fallen foul of Constance Matthews.

'What I can't understand,' said Rachel, when Judy came to a stop, 'is why this hasn't been picked up before. By the press, if no one else.'

'I thought that,' said Libby. 'Even if Connie wasn't named.'

'Have you spoken to Ian— DCI Connell about it?' Rachel asked.

'No,' said Libby, mentally crossing her fingers, knowing that she would at the earliest opportunity.

'Well, I don't mind telling you that we have a couple of people in our sights now.' Rachel looked and sounded far more confident than she had either yesterday, Saturday or Sunday.

'Really? Did you work overnight?'

Mark rolled his eyes.

'I take it that means yes?'

'I wanted to find out who had the opportunity.' Rachel looked down at her tablet and began scrolling. 'And it's rather difficult to find out who was in the woods last Tuesday evening, but we do have one witness.'

'Oh?' Libby and Judy both leant forward.

'I shouldn't really tell you,' said Rachel, with what could only be described as a smirk, 'but a resident of Canongate Drive did see a couple of people go into the woods from there at about six o'clock.'

'But the victim was seen about that time, wasn't she?' Libby frowned.

'Yes, but the people our witness saw didn't come back out again.'

'Your witness,' said Libby slowly. 'It wouldn't be Jim Butler, would it?'

Rachel looked slightly annoyed. 'Yes, it would.'

'And did he know the people he saw going into the woods?'

'You know I can't tell you that,' said Rachel.

'No, of course not,' said Libby. 'More tea?'

Both Mark and Rachel declined.

'Can you at least tell me,' asked Libby, 'if these people were together or separate?'

'No, I can't tell you that, either.' Rachel's lips snapped shut.

'Oh, well.' Libby sent Judy a wry smile. 'I expect you've been looking at all the holiday rental companies, haven't you? They won't have been pleased about Connie snatching all their business.'

Rachel gave in and laughed. 'It's no good, Libby, I can't tell you anything else – but yes, of course we have.'

'I thought so,' said Libby. 'I'd much rather it was one of them than one of the people she made homeless.'

'But now we'll be looking closely into the London end, thanks to what Miss Dale has told us.'

'Oh, Judy, please.' Judy smiled at Libby. 'And it looks like I'll be around here for a little while at least, so you can always get hold of me.'

'Oh?' Rachel raised questioning eyebrows.

'I'm – er . . .' Judy cleared her throat self-consciously, 'I'm going to be doing the Steeple Martin pantomime.'

'Oh!' Rachel looked surprised.

Mark grinned happily. 'Wish I could,' he said.

Rachel caught Libby's speculative look. 'Well, you can't,' she said, and stood up. 'Come on, we've got work to do.'

'Are you still based in Canterbury?' asked Libby. 'Such a shame the Nethergate station shut down.'

'I know.' Rachel shook her head. 'We've had to set up a small incident room down there, but there isn't the call for a permanent station these days.'

'Well, there has been in the last year or so,' said Libby. 'Where's the incident room?'

'Marine Parade – you know it?'

Libby nodded. 'Yes, it runs parallel with Harbour Street. Off the high street. I never seem to go up there these days. They used to have pretty gardens, didn't they?'

'Still have,' said Mark. 'The residents tend them now, as the council gave up on them.'

'*Are* there any residents?' aske Libby. 'Big houses along there – they'd be ripe for holiday lets.'

'Oh, there've always been holiday lets in Nethergate – there aren't many proper hotels.'

'Except the Swan,' agreed Libby. 'But there are B&Bs. I suppose she left those alone, didn't she?'

'Now, Libby!' Rachel smiled and stepped out into the grey autumn morning.

'She seemed quite nice,' said Judy, carrying mugs into the kitchen.

'She is,' said Libby. 'Just a bit overwhelmed, I think. And she's obviously looking into everything now, even if she wasn't before. I think all the London shenanigans surprised her a bit.'

'She must have known some of it already, surely?' Judy perched on the kitchen table and stroked Sidney, who had jumped up beside her.

'If she didn't, someone else will have done,' said Libby. 'So who do you think might have done it? From people you know, I mean.'

'I don't want to think of anyone I know being a murderer,' said Judy, shocked.

'No, it's not nice, is it.' Libby sighed and led the way back into the sitting room. 'That's the thing about murder. It's all very well in books or on TV, but in reality it's messy and terribly sad. There are always so many people who get badly hurt.'

'Is that why you do it, then? To help those people?'

Libby gave her a wry smile. 'I suppose so. I get very angry when people are taken advantage of. And, of course, I'm terribly nosy.'

Next on the agenda was a visit to Hetty at the Manor, to ask if Judy could take up residence there for the duration of the pantomime.

'Course, gal,' said Hetty, moving the big kettle on to the Aga hotplate. 'Mind, last time a friend of Libby's came down to stay for a bit, she ended up down 'ere for good.'

'Fran,' Libby said to Judy. 'She lived for a bit in the flat over the Pink Geranium. My son Adam lives there now.'

'I'd better be careful, then!' Judy laughed.

Libby took a mug of tea through to Ben, who once again was in the brewery.

'Jim Butler saw someone going into the woods last Tuesday,' she told him. 'Rachel wouldn't tell me who.'

'Just one person?' asked Ben.

'I don't know, she wouldn't be drawn, but she did say they'd been looking into holiday rental companies.'

'Like Brooke's?'

'She wouldn't say that either, but yes, I expect so.' Libby gazed up at the mash tuns. 'They'd be the obvious ones, wouldn't they?'

'You looked up some others, didn't you?' said Ben.

'Yes. There's Nethergate Holiday Homes, Harbour Holidays and a couple of others I can't remember, but they're all fairly small. They've probably already sold out,' she added gloomily.

'Shall I give Jim a ring and ask who he saw?'

'Would you?' Libby beamed at him.

'I'll do it now,' said Ben.

In the estate office Ben called Jim Butler while Libby went to see how Judy was faring with Hetty. They were at the kitchen table, deep in conversation, so she left them to it.

'Yes, Jim,' Ben was saying when she returned. 'She's been looking into it.' He winked at Libby. 'I'll ask her. No, I don't suppose they would, not if you know them. OK, yes, of course I will. And we'll come up and see you one day this week – Libby would love to see Lady again.'

'Well? What did he say??' Libby sat down in the chair opposite Ben.

'He saw several people,' Ben said. 'He didn't take much notice of most of them – people walk there all the time. That's why he and Lady Pru opened up the path.'

'But he did recognise someone?' Libby sat forward.

'Yes.' Ben looked at his notes. 'A couple. Er – Jenny and Eddie. Peace, I think he said.'

'Peake,' said Libby. 'Oh, no.'

'Do you know them?'

'Not exactly. They live in Gleneagles, the same place that Freddie's grandma Beryl lives.'

'And they're going to be made homeless by a combination of Connie Matthews and Brooke's?'

'That's right.' Libby closed her eyes and puffed out a deep breath. 'It can't be them.'

'Have you met them?'

'No, but all the residents are over sixty-five. The old landlady made that watertight.'

'Then they shouldn't have a problem,' said Ben.

'Not if the house is sold,' said Libby. 'But I did tell Beryl I thought it was illegal that they had been given notice to quit as the will hasn't been proved yet – Connie told Brooke's she'd buy it if they could get rid of the tenants. Fran was going to give their names to Philip.'

'Then let's ask Philip,' said Ben, picking up his mobile. 'I bet it is illegal. You can't buy a property – or anything else – if it's subject to an unproven will.'

'That's what I said.' Libby was triumphant. 'I'd better rescue Judy and Hetty. Back in a minute.'

By the time she returned with Judy in tow, Ben was writing furiously with his mobile on speakerphone.

'Yes, I've got all that, Philip, thanks,' he said. 'Let me know if you hear anything else.'

'I will. Bye, Ben,' said the phone.

'What did he say?' asked Libby.

'Well, he'd already written to Brooke's telling them that the eviction notice was illegal, which is the good news, but the bad news is that he also informed the police.' Ben looked up and pulled a face. 'The police in the shape of Sergeant Powell.'

'He's just not passing information on!' Libby gasped. 'What else does he know? We need to tell Ian about this.'

'Don't worry, Philip is going to tell him – and Rachel. The problem is that because Powell knows Mr and Mrs Peake's names, with Jim Butler's information as well they will definitely be pulled in.'

Judy was looking confused. Libby took pity on her.

'Sorry, Judy. This is all part of the murder investigation. The people we're talking about are pensioners living in a rented flat who were going to be evicted.'

'I gathered that,' said Judy. 'It strikes me that this murder was committed by someone in despair.'

'That's exactly what Ian said right at the beginning,' said Libby. 'Some of the people we've met have been truly in despair – truly desperate.'

'Or,' said Ben, 'it's someone trying to make it look like that.'

'Who?' asked Judy. 'A relative or something?'

'She hasn't got any,' said Libby. 'Ian told us, again at the beginning of the case, that Rachel and her team were pulling all the stops out ferreting in her background.' She stopped and looked at Ben. 'Didn't he? Do you remember? So why has nothing about all these financial problems emerged? Rachel was feeling upset because she thought she messed up by not looking into the financials, but it sounds as though it was being done after all.'

'I sense Sergeant Powell's fine hand in all this,' said Ben. 'Who else is in Rachel's team?'

'Well, I only know Mark – who was with her this morning and seems to be her partner in life as well – and Powell. There must be others.'

'In the CID office in Canterbury, I suspect,' said Ben. 'So it's Ian's job to assign her team, wouldn't you say?'

'Yes, but Rachel was also a bit huffy about him butting in,' said Libby. 'Oh, well. If Philip's going to tell him about the Peakes he might start butting in properly.'

'Let's hope so,' Ben said.

Libby stood up. 'Come on, Judy, we'll go home. You'll have to be sorting yourself out to get ready for tonight, won't you?'

Chapter Twenty-Four

After a lunch of soup and bread, Libby left Judy in the sitting room with Sidney and retired to the conservatory to gaze at her easel. This was a most peculiar case, she thought. First of all, there had been Connie's positively antediluvian attitude to the Glover's Men and Freddie Cannon in particular, then the revelation that she had turned into an evil landlord with countless numbers of the unfortunate dispossessed languishing in her wake. So, multiple suspects, all with good reason to hate her. And yet, there seemed to be no one actually in the vicinity of the murder site who could be linked. At least, apart from the Peakes. Libby scowled at the easel and picked up the paint-splattered notebook she kept on the table beside her.

Who else did she know about? Freddie's grandma Beryl and her fellow tenants, Jenny and Eddie Peake and – what was his name? – Eric, that's right. And there must be at least one other on the ground floor. Then there was Kirsty and her husband and the other members of the Blue Anchor warm space initiative, whom, she supposed, were all viable suspects, although she didn't know how many of them were actually victims of Connie's machinations. And Karen and Nora, who weren't threatened because old Miss Barton wouldn't sell to Connie – although that hadn't stopped her threatening them.

Lady Howe? No, she wasn't selling either, although Connie and her 'heavy' had been trying to persuade her. Other landlords? It seemed rather extreme – murder wasn't usually a recognised strategy in business. No – it looked far more like a spur-of-the-moment lashing out.

And then, sadly, there were Judy and her pianist Ray, the Raincliffe Rep and Carl Robinson and the Furnough School. And who knew how many more people and organisations Connie cheated with her policy of buying up loans?

She went back into the sitting room.

'Judy, I hate to ask this,' she said, 'but were any of the other musicians you know affected by Connie?'

Judy looked up, surprised. 'Well – I told you some of them were out of pocket because the concert was pulled, but I don't think—oh. Wait.' She frowned. 'Tara was. She told me last week at rehearsal.'

'Who's Tara?'

'Trumpet. Very good – comes out of the old brass band school. Her dad played. Anyway, she'd put money into the Raincliffe. I think she lost her home, too – couldn't afford to keep it on. Mind you, all she had to do was go back to live with mum and dad, except they're just outside Bradford.'

'So she has to travel a lot further for gigs?'

Judy shrugged. 'You know what it's like. We all have to travel. It's one of the reasons people give up. The general public only seem to think of pop bands travelling all over the place for gigs, but we have to do it, too. And we don't always have a band bus, either.'

'Was there one for today's gig?' asked Libby.

'Yes.' Judy looked down at Sidney.

'So you've had to spend on petrol to come down here?'

'It was my idea.' Judy looked up and smiled. 'And I'm glad I did. I'm going to do panto with you!'

Judy left a little later to drive to the venue in Canterbury to meet the rest of the band, and Libby fished something out of the freezer to feed herself and Ben.

178

'Philip called back,' Ben said when he arrived. 'He told Ian, and said he thought we might get a phone call.'

'Did he say if Ian knew all about everything?'

'He was non-committal,' said Ben. 'Hardly surprising.'

In fact Ian called the landline just before they were due to leave for the concert.

'I was going to leave a message,' he said. 'I thought you might have gone already.'

'No, we're leaving now,' said Ben.

'In that case I shan't hold you up. I'll call you in the morning.'

'Oh no!' wailed Libby, who'd been trying to listen in. 'I want to know now!'

Ian laughed. 'Too long to tell you now. If you could get a couple of addresses for me from your friend?'

'Did Rachel tell you she came this morning?' asked Ben.

'Yes. Now, go!' said Ian.

'But what addresses?' asked Libby, as Ben ushered her out to the car. 'Oh, how infuriating!'

'Anybody connected with what she told you about, I imagine,' said Ben. 'Although you would have thought that Rachel would have got that information this morning.'

'But they'll have the addresses of the Furnough and the Raincliffe by now,' said Libby, fastening her seat belt. 'And Carl Robinson. They've known since Andrew told us.'

'Then it'll be the members of the band Judy told you about,' said Ben.

'But no one's told the police about that yet,' said Libby. 'And it was only one.'

'Well, I don't know!' said Ben, exasperated. 'Now, can we please talk about something else? Like how much we're looking forward to the concert?'

The venue for the concert – not, this time, entitled 'Sadie O'Day Sings', but more prosaically 'Songs of the Swing Era' – was the purpose-built theatre of a school. Libby and Ben had been to events there before, and Libby was pleased to see that a bar had been set up in the foyer. Not something that was in evidence for school productions. Seated at a group of tables near the entrance were the members of Joe Wilson's Old Codgers Club, with the addition of the Steeple Martin contingent and Freddie Cannon's grandma Beryl Sampson.

'Did you enjoy the play last week, Beryl?' Libby asked her. 'I didn't get a chance to speak to you – I'm sorry.'

'Oh, I loved it, dear!' Beryl's face lit up. 'I've seen a couple of things Freddie's done in the past, but I've never been a great one for Shakespeare. Didn't understand it, I suppose, but I thought it was lovely. And I'm so looking forward to tonight's concert. You know Freddie did one of those Proms with this Sadie?'

'Yes, she told me,' said Libby. 'I wish I'd seen that.'

'Libby?' Joe called and gave her a slight nod. 'Got a minute?'

'Excuse me, Beryl,' said Libby, and went over to where Joe sat at the next table. 'What is it?'

'That Matthews woman,' muttered Joe. 'Found out yesterday she had tried to buy Nyebourne.'

'*What*?' Libby was stunned. 'She tried to buy a *retirement* home? She wasn't going to turn that into holiday lets, surely?'

'No – she wanted to – er – *tart it up* was how the owner put it. She – the owner – came round yesterday and asked us all if Matthews had approached us.'

'And had she?'

'No.' Joe shook his head. 'She wanted the whole package, far as I can see.'

A bell rang.

'That's us,' said Libby. 'I'll see you in the interval, Joe – if there is one.'

'If not, after,' said Joe. 'Got a couple of things to tell you.'

Much as she enjoyed the music, Libby was slightly frustrated that there wasn't, in fact, an interval. However, she was able to identify

180

Cyd Russell, the other female singer, with whom Judy had been staying, Tara, the trumpeter, a small, dark-haired woman who scowled a lot, and Ray McCloud, the pianist and band leader. The male singer was a well-known musical theatre performer who rather overacted his songs and, in Libby's opinion, deliberately tried to upstage and overshadow Judy. However, it was a joyous evening and much enjoyed by the audience, especially the more mature members, who comprised most of it.

Libby and Joe managed to catch up with one another before the private coach took him and his friends back home.

'Right, now,' he said, keeping his voice low. 'That woman – I don't know exactly what she was trying to do, but it was as though she was a bit – you know . . .' He pointed his finger at his head and gave it a twirl.

'Barmy?' suggested Libby.

'And the rest!' Joe made a face. 'It was like she was on some sort of a mission. Trying to grab everything she could lay her hands on. She told our owner she'd make Nyebourne into a "world-class" home, if you please! I take that as an insult! Nyebourne's already as good as it can possibly be. And then she wanted Gleneagles – Beryl's told you?'

Libby nodded.

'And – wait for it – she was trying to get Mavis out of the Anchor!'

'Bloody hell!' said Libby. Several heads turned in her direction. 'She didn't tell us that!'

'She wouldn't,' said Joe. 'This Matthews went to Mavis with an offer, which Mavis turned down, of course, then she started this – what do you call it? War of something?'

'Attrition?'

'That's it. She tried reporting Mavis to health and safety or whatever it is – you know, food standards or something. And said she hadn't got safety doors, or fire doors, and smoke alarms . . . Oh, she was going the whole hog!'

'But why?' Libby was aghast.

'Because Mavis wouldn't roll over for her, I reckon. And Mavis was helping the people the old cow had thrown out, wasn't she?' Joe looked round. 'I got to go. The bus is waiting. Give me a ring, Libby.'

And he was gone. Libby and Ben waved them all off and sat down to wait for Judy and the other musicians to appear in the foyer, which they did after a few moments, looking tired. Judy introduced them to Ray and Tara and Libby and Cyd exchanged hellos.

'Libby's looking into the murder of that woman Constance Matthews,' Judy explained. 'I said we'd all been affected.'

'Oh?' Tara glared at Libby. 'And what's it got to do with you?'

'I knew her,' said Libby, trying not to react aggressively. 'I actually drove her down to Kent last week.'

'Drove her to her death, did you?' Tara gave a mirthless laugh. 'Good for you.'

Ray looked at her with dislike. 'Unnecessary, Tara,' he said. 'We all suffered in one way or another, but no one wants to see anybody murdered.' He rubbed long slender fingers over his face. 'I'm shattered, kids. Shall we get on the bus?'

'You're coming back to stay with us tonight, aren't you?' Libby said to Judy. She – and Ben – looked surprised.

'Am I?' said Judy.

'Save you going back to London tonight,' said Libby, 'and the bed's still made up.'

'Oh, right.' Judy turned to Cyd. 'You don't mind, do you, Cyd?'

'No . . .' Cyd looked a trifle warily at Libby. 'I – er – I'll see you tomorrow, shall I?'

'What was up with Cyd?' asked Libby when the musicians had filed out.

'She wasn't very happy about me coming down to talk to you about the whole Constance Matthews thing.' Judy frowned. 'I don't know why.'

Libby exchanged glances with Ben. 'Never mind,' she said. 'You can tell her all about it when you go back tomorrow. And about the panto, too.'

'Yes.' Judy looked doubtful. 'I hope she won't mind. She's been saying how much she's enjoyed having me to stay.'

They all went out to their cars, and Ben and Libby waited while Judy loaded her dress bag and case into the boot of her decidedly old Seat Arosa, then drove out of the car park with her following.

'Well, we didn't get much out of that from the band, did we?' said Libby as they approached the roundabout that led them to the Steeple Martin road. 'Not even any addresses.'

'We were actually there to see the concert,' said Ben, 'not go detecting.'

'But then, I did get something from Joe.' Libby shot her beloved a triumphant look.

'Yes,' he sighed. 'So you'd better tell me what.'

So Libby told him what Joe had said.

'It does sound as though she was a bit . . .' Ben frowned out into the night. 'Unhinged.'

'It does, doesn't it? I mean, you'd have thought she'd have been satisfied with cheating people out of things in London, wouldn't you? Why did she pick on poor old Nethergate?'

'And was there anywhere else,' mused Ben. 'Was it simply an old-fashioned power complex?'

'I don't suppose they're called that now. It's probably some terribly scientific name for an illness,' said Libby.

'And what about Mavis?' said Ben. 'I'm sure she wouldn't have been guilty of any of the offences Connie accused her of.'

'Of course not,' said Libby. 'It was pure spite because Mavis wouldn't do what she wanted, as Joe said. And then she was helping the people Connie had made homeless. She wouldn't have liked that.'

'No,' agreed Ben. 'You know, I was thinking it would have been better if you hadn't brought her down to see *Much Ado* – but if you hadn't, none of this would have come to light.'

'But on the other hand,' said Libby, 'she wouldn't have been murdered.'

Chapter Twenty-Five

Judy didn't seem inclined for conversation when they reached All-hallow's Lane, so Libby said goodnight to their guest and poured herself and Ben a nightcap.

'I wonder if there's anything going on with Cyd?' she said, giving the logs in the woodburner a hopeful but unproductive poke.

'How do you mean?'

'Well, you know – she wasn't happy about Judy staying down here.'

'If you mean she wasn't happy because of something Connie had done . . .'

'No, nothing like that. I just wondered if she – um – fancied Judy?'

'Whatever gave you that idea?' Ben shook his head. 'Is Judy gay?'

'I don't know. I've never seen her with either a man or a woman.'

'Does it matter?'

'No, of course not. But if Connie had set out to ruin the Sadie O'Day concert . . .'

'But she didn't,' said Ben. 'It was the Raincliffe she ruined. The concert was a by-product.'

'I bet she enjoyed it, though,' said Libby. 'Ruining the concert.'

'Yes, I'm sure she did, but don't go looking for even more motives, Lib. The police have enough to contend with as it is.'

'And isn't that a bit suspicious?' asked Libby meditatively.

'How do you mean?'

'Well, all of a sudden all these dispossessed people coming out of the woodwork at once?'

'Look – we're only seeing it that way,' said Ben, with a forbearing sigh. 'It hasn't been all at once. She's been buying things up since at least May. Look at that landlady – what was her name?'

'Izzy at the Puckle Inn?'

'That's her. She got thrown out of her former pub – the Crown, was it?'

'Crown and Sceptre.'

'She got thrown out in May, didn't she say? So it's been going on since then.' Ben sat back in the armchair and gave an affirmative nod.

'Yes, but that's the whole point,' said Libby. 'It *was* sudden and sort of all at once.' She put her drink down and began to count on her fingers. 'The Raincliffe and the Furnough. It seems to be that's where it started, and she certainly cheated Carl Robinson out of the Furnough, and she probably did the same to the Raincliffe. At almost at the same time she bought the Crown and Sceptre. See? All at once. And then she started on Nethergate. None of those people were thrown out until then. At least, not by Connie. So what happened? What started it all off? And why Nethergate?'

Ben sat looking at her, his drink halfway to his lips. Eventually, he spoke.

'Bloody hell,' he said slowly. 'You're right.'

'See?' said Libby excitedly. 'It all looked haphazard – but it isn't. Something happened. Did she get a windfall that let her buy the Raincliffe, and then get a taste for power?'

'I would have thought it was more like someone cheating *her* out of something that set her off on a sort of revenge,' said Ben.

They looked at each other silently for a moment.

'I'll never get that over to Rachel,' said Libby at last. 'Nice though she is, she'd never listen.'

'Ian would,' said Ben, 'and tomorrow's Wednesday. Pub day.'

'He might not be able to come if he's tied up with the case.'

'He will,' said Ben. 'He's supposed to be in his office, isn't he? And it strikes me that he's trying to let Rachel plough her own furrow, so to speak, so he's just keeping a guiding hand on the tiller.'

'That was a fine collection of mixed metaphors,' said Libby with a grin. 'Shall I call him in the morning to warn him?'

'Send him a text. Then he needn't answer if he's busy.' Ben gave her an answering grin and finished his drink. 'And now, to bed, woman!'

Libby sent Ian a text before Ben left for the brewery, where he seemed to spend most of his time these days.

'We're getting orders from all over the place now,' he said. 'Every micropub in the area is ordering from us. And I've got to talk to the Morris guys, this morning – Duncan Cruikshank wants a rehearsal.'

'Not tonight,' warned Libby.

'As if I'd let anything interfere with the Wednesday Murder Club,' he said with a wink, and left the cottage.

Judy came downstairs with her case. 'I'll be off now,' she said. 'Now you are sure about the panto, aren't you?'

'Yes – I told you!' Libby gave her a pat on the shoulder. 'When do you want to come and move in to Hetty's?'

'When you tell me to,' said Judy. 'Do you want me to come to the audition? I feel I ought to.'

'Yes, please. I'll need you to read against the others, particularly the Demon King. It's Thursday week, and as long as I can cast it we'll start rehearsing the following week. Oh – and I'm going to put at least one song in for you. And I'll email you the script. Now, go on – shoo. Get back to Cyd and tell her all about it.'

Libby waited to see if anything further was forthcoming, but Judy merely smiled, gave her a kiss on the cheek and left.

Libby called Fran. 'I'm waiting to hear from Ian,' she said, 'but I'm hoping he'll come to the pub tonight. Ben's calling it the Wednesday Murder Club.'

Fran laughed. 'Well, we got there first, didn't we?' she said. 'Anyway, I think Guy and I ought to attend. Is there anything you need to tell me now?'

Libby recounted her conversations from the previous evening, including Joe's surprising revelation about Mavis.

'But why didn't she *tell* us?' said Fran. 'Guy would have taken that up immediately!'

'Joe said she wouldn't. I'm not sure why – perhaps in case the police suspected her?'

'But this was before Connie was murdered. And people were already talking about her – weren't they?'

'Yes, but perhaps not as much. Just talking about evil landlords in general, and not linking everything up. But I'm not sure why the owner of Nyebourne didn't report that to Guy and the protest group.'

'I suppose,' said Fran, 'they didn't feel the need to. After all, they weren't going to sell, the same as Lady Pru and Dorothy Barton.'

'That's true,' agreed Libby. 'But do you agree with me about something happening to trigger all this megalomania?'

'I can't see that it matters,' said Fran. 'She started buying up properties – that's surely all there is to it?'

'But *why*? There she was, a perfectly ordinary old lady—'

'Not quite,' put in Fran.

'All right, a perfectly ordinary, *unpleasant* old lady, sitting in her rather nice house on the outskirts of London, and she suddenly turns into a Rachman-look-alike.'

'A who?'

'Rachman – you know, that horrible landlord from the sixties.'

'Oh, yes. Wasn't he mixed up in the Profumo affair?'

'He was.' Libby had been looking it up. 'And the Krays. And he was only forty-three when he died, so he didn't have long to enjoy his ill-gotten gains.'

'Well, what's that got to do with Connie Matthews?'

'Nothing, except that she was doing the same sort of thing. Turning tenants out of their homes.'

188

'But he didn't do that, as far as I remember,' said Fran. 'He just overcharged and didn't maintain his properties.'

'That's an oversimplification,' said Libby. 'Anyway, something turned Connie into an evil landlord – and sent her down to our part of the world. I want to know what that was.'

'But it sounds as though her first sorties were in London. She cheated Carl out of the Furnough and the Raincliffe owners out of their theatre.' Fran was quiet for a moment. 'You're right. Something triggered that.'

'*I* think,' said Libby, 'that somehow she got wind of one of those being in trouble, offered to help them out and realised she could make money.'

'*Offered* to help them out? Never!'

'All right – saw how she could make money by buying up loans, or whatever she did, and realised she could do the same thing to other people. But then – how did she start the whole evil landlord thing?'

'And, as I said, does it matter?' Fran sighed.

'Yes. Because whoever got her interested could hold the clue to her murder!'

'Explain.'

'Well. She's sitting there retired and bored. She has no power over anyone any more. And someone shows her how she can get power. I don't suppose she thinks beyond the initial fact of being able to manipulate someone – or something – but then when she realises she finds – or looks for – other ways of being able to exercise power. And treads on someone's toes. Perhaps the very person who introduced her to the whole business.'

'Hmm,' said Fran. 'But I still don't see—'

'Oh, never mind!' said Libby, frustrated. 'I'll tell Ian tonight.' She put the phone down.

'And what do I do until then?' she asked Sidney, who took no notice.

There was the spare bed to strip, of course. That would take up

189

ten minutes or so. And the breakfast things to see to. And she could always do a supermarket run. She sighed and went upstairs.

When the house was more or less put to rights, she decided that a supermarket run was hardly necessary and a visit to the farm shop and the eight-till-late would suffice. And that would also mean that she would be near the Pink Geranium in time for a late-morning coffee, or possibly an early lunch.

In fact she was just about to cross the road from the farm shop on her way to the caff, when her mobile rang.

'Philip! Hello. What can I do for you?' Libby stopped on the kerb.

'I was just going to ask you if you had any more information for me about this whole Matthews business,' said Philip. 'I gather I muddied the waters a little the other day.'

'Muddied – oh! When you passed on info to Sergeant Powell.' Libby sighed. 'You weren't to know.'

'And I've told DCI Connell now, so I thought I ought to fill you in and see if there was anything else I ought to know.'

'I don't know, really. Are you around this evening? We'll be going for a drink at the Coach and I think Ian— DCI Connell will be there.'

'I can't tonight.' Philip sounded regretful. 'I don't suppose you're free now?'

'I was just going to Harry's for a coffee, actually,' said Libby. 'Are you at home? Why don't you join me?'

'Excellent idea! I'll see you in five minutes.'

Libby crossed the road and pushed open the door of the Pink Geranium. Harry looked up from behind the counter and raised his eyebrows.

'In need of succour and counsel, are we, ducks?'

Avoiding the curious eyes of a couple at the table in the right-hand window, Libby sidled onto the sofa in the left one.

'No – I'm meeting Philip for coffee,' she said.

'I'll tell Ben.' Harry leered at her. Libby made a face at him.

Philip appeared a minute later, every inch the country solicitor in his tweed jacket over a mustard-yellow waistcoat.

'Shall we have wine, Libby?' He consulted his watch. 'It is after midday, perfectly acceptable.'

'When did that ever make any difference to our Libby?' asked Harry, with a theatrical wink. Libby sighed.

'So tell me what you told Sergeant Powell,' said Libby, when Harry had provided wine, glasses and a bowl of crisps.

'Well, various things over the course of the last week,' said Philip, tweaking the crease in his trousers as he crossed his elegant legs. 'Until then, there was no real reason to pass on our information. Although,' he added thoughtfully, 'we had noticed Ms Matthews' name coming up quite frequently.'

'So you'd discovered she owned property here before she was murdered?'

'Of course.' Philip raised an eyebrow. 'I believe you know my new assistant?'

'Hannah? Yes, I do. I was surprised when she said she was working for you.'

Philip raised the other eyebrow. 'I don't know why. She's a qualified legal exec. Didn't you know?'

'No!' Libby gasped. 'Wow!'

'And, as great-niece of Miss Dorothy Barton, she knew all about Ms Matthews' approach regarding the possible sale of Temptation House.'

Libby grinned appreciatively at Philip's careful and correct phraseology. 'What?' he said.

'Nothing. So you knew about her approach to Miss Barton — and what about Lady Pru? You knew about that as well?'

'Yes, of course, but neither of those properties were for sale, so didn't fall under our remit.'

'No, of course not.' Libby took a sip of wine. 'So which ones did?'

'Mostly properties along Harbour Street, Victoria Place, Cliff

Terrace and Marine Parade. Nearly all of them were holiday properties already, mostly privately owned.' Philip paused to sip his own wine. 'But there were several that had been bought by Ms Matthews. Not directly, of course.'

'Don't tell me. Through Brooke's?'

Philip gave her a knowing look. 'Indeed.'

'And you told Sergeant Powell this?'

'Of course. Once there was an official police investigation in place.' He smiled. 'And I have now told DCI Connell.'

Chapter Twenty-Six

Libby gave a relieved sigh. 'You also told him about the illegal pro-spective purchase of Gleneagles in King Edward Street?' she said.

'I did. Unfortunately, he also now knows the names of Mr and Mrs Peake.'

'Who were seen going into Lady Pru's woods the day Connie – Ms Matthews – was murdered,' said Libby gloomily.

'I doubt very much that they were involved in her murder,' said Philip, 'and the sale of Gleneagles has been blocked now, anyway, and the original owner's wishes implemented.'

'I didn't know she had any,' Libby said, surprised.

'Oh, yes. The will was lodged with her solicitors, whom Brooke's had not informed of her death. Mrs Bryant wished the freehold of Gleneagles to pass jointly to those tenants in residence at the time of her death.' He shook his head. 'How they thought they would get away with selling it to Ms Matthews I have no idea.'

'So the tenants are safe!' Libby crowed delightedly.

'They are indeed.' Philip smiled at her. 'Drink up!'

'So can you tell me who *is* Brooke's?' asked Libby. 'Is there a Mr or Mrs Brooke? I really only know of it from that business with the caravan park earlier this year.'

'I can't tell you much, Libby.' Philip took a meditative handful of crisps. 'The company is now subject to a police investigation itself.'

'I suppose it would be.' Libby gazed into her glass. 'What about the properties they bought on behalf of Connie?'

'They remain within her estate,' said Philip, 'and, as yet, no will has been found. However, if there is one, a probate record will be lodged once it is proven. If there isn't, and no surviving eligible relatives are found, the estate becomes the property of the Crown, *bona vacantia*.'

'Bona what?'

'Legal term, don't worry about it. Anyway, the Treasury solicitor would decide what happens to the estate in that case. And it would take years.'

'Oh, dear. So we really need to find an heir?' Libby looked anxious.

'Except that you might find the new owner is just as – how shall I put it? – *unyielding* as Ms Matthews.'

'Supposing all the purchases were illegal?' suggested Libby.

'How would that be?' asked Philip. 'If money has been paid for a property it is hardly likely to be illegal.'

'But supposing the money was – I don't know – from ill-gotten gains?'

Philip laughed. 'Bank raids?'

'You know what I mean. Now listen. This is what we've found out over the last few days. I'd like your opinion.'

Over the next twenty minutes, while the level in the wine bottle grew lower, Libby told an attentive Philip about Constance Matthews' various activities, beginning with her acquisition of the Raincliffe Rep and the Furnough School. Unasked, Harry supplied bread and soup.

'Well,' said Philip, when the recital finally ended. He frowned at his soup plate and tapped an elegant finger against his chin. 'I think a proper search needs to be instigated into Ms Matthews' affairs. I'm surprised it hasn't been done already.'

'I think that's what Ian wants to do. Acting DI Trent has been rather – um – hindered, shall we say.'

'By Sergeant Powell?' Philip nodded. 'Yes, I gathered. Do you think Ian – DCI Connell – would let me look into matters?

Unfortunately, the purchase of loans is not illegal, but we may find some loopholes. I'm a barrister, not a solicitor, but I can wield a pretty big stick.'

Libby smiled at him. 'I'm sure he will.' She peered into her glass and sighed. 'I suppose I ought to go now.'

Philip drained the bottle into her glass. 'Before you do, tell me a bit about the Constance Matthews you used to know.'

Libby lifted her glass and frowned. 'I suppose I don't really know much. She was a reasonably well-regarded director – not with anything classy like the Globe, or National Shakespeare, but a fair few off-West End productions, a couple of tours, that sort of thing. She did seasons at some of the regionals. I never heard of her having any relatives, but she must at least have had parents, I suppose. Her house in Ashbury is quite big – and, as far as I know, that was where she lived when I knew her. I don't know whether she inherited it or bought it. It's a bit far out of London for her, I would have thought.'

'So she may have inherited it?' suggested Philip. 'Well, we can find out about that.'

'Do you think that's important?'

'It's one of her assets.' Philip shrugged. 'We'll see.'

'But what we really need to find out is who had the motive to kill her,' said Libby. 'Apart from all the dispossessed tenants.'

'Have you got any theories?' asked Philip.

'I wondered about landlords who'd had their properties snatched from under their noses,' said Libby. 'Are there any?'

'Only one that I can think of,' said Philip. 'Blue Sky Holidays. They owned a couple of buildings on Marine Parade. Ms Matthews bought them both, but it was hardly underhand. She made an offer and they accepted. She did the same with the rental properties she bought. The tenants had as much of a complaint against the original owners as against Matthews. There were a couple in Harbour Street and one or two in Victoria Place, and several flats in Marine Parade and King Edward Street, apart from Gleneagles – and Nyebourne, of course.'

'Yes.' Libby sighed. 'In fact, anyone could have done it.'

'I gather,' said Philip, after a moment, 'that Ms Matthews was accompanied by another person on occasion.'

'A heavy, yes. Ian asked Lady Pru and another couple of ladies to go and look at his rogues' gallery to see if they recognised anybody.' Libby shook her head. 'As I haven't heard anything, I gather they didn't.'

Philip nodded. 'And has Ian interviewed the estate agents? And the holiday companies?'

Libby frowned at him. 'You said she hadn't pinched any of their business.'

'I didn't exactly say that. I said her purchases were legitimate.'

'So, basically, it's only people who she got thrown out who have a motive?' Libby looked indignant. 'That's not fair!'

Philip laughed. 'I don't think murder is ever fair, Libby.'

Customers were beginning to come into the Pink Geranium for lunch, and Harry began making shooing gestures at Philip and Libby. 'Or eat!' he muttered, as he passed them.

'We'd better go,' said Libby. 'Half a bottle of wine at lunchtime's going to make me want to go to sleep!'

Philip stood up and took out his Gold Card, which Harry waved away.

'Pleased to help the forces of law and order,' he said. 'See you later, Lib.'

Libby and Philip parted on the pavement.

'I shall start looking into Ms Matthews' background,' said Philip. 'And see if I can find anyone else she's cheated.'

'It doesn't actually look as though she's cheated many people,' said Libby. 'Except the theatre and the school in London. The rest she's just deprived of their homes.'

'Unless she tried the same tactics on someone we haven't heard of,' said Philip. 'Maybe trying to buy a property like Gleneagles – that would have been illegal.'

'But that was more down to the estate agents than her,' said Libby. 'Are you sure you can't tell me who's behind Brooke's?'

'No, Libby, I can't. Your friend Ian would clap me in irons.'

'What about Trevor Taylor? Have you come across him in your inquiries?'

Philip paused as he began to turn away. 'You could always ask the property journalist at the *Nethergate Mercury*.'

'What? Would they know something?'

'They ran a piece on the elderly and home-blocking.' Philip grinned. 'You'll like that.'

Libby was left standing outside the Pink Geranium with her mouth open.

Ten minutes later, back at Number 17 Allhallow's Lane, she was ringing Jane Baker, the editor of the now online-only *Nethergate Mercury*.

'Listen,' she said, having got the pleasantries out of the way, 'you know about our protest group, don't you?'

'I could hardly fail to, Libby.' Jane sounded amused. 'Especially since this murder business. I assume the two things are tied up together?'

'Yes, sort of, but our solicitor—'

'You've got your own solicitor?'

'Of course,' said Libby proudly. 'Except he's actually a barrister. Anyway, he says you've recently run a piece on the elderly and home-blocking.'

'Yes, we have. In conjunction with *Kent and Coast News*.'

Kent and Coast was one of the regional television news programmes.

'And what exactly was it?'

'Oh, come on, Libby! You must know. There've been reports about it for years. This is just the latest flurry. Older people being accused of hanging on to their family homes instead of downsizing so that young families can buy them.'

'Oh, that.' Libby sighed. 'I thought that had all died down. It's reared its ugly head again, has it?'

'Yes.' Jane still sounded amused. 'Apparently, the latest argument is because old – sorry – elderly – people object to being ghetto-ised into sheltered housing complexes.'

'Hmm.' Libby nodded to herself. 'I've come across that myself, actually. Someone I know has just removed herself from one of those and bought a place in our village. For exactly that reason.'

'Really?' Now Jane sounded interested. 'Could our Damian talk to her, do you think?'

'I'll ask – but she isn't actually here yet. But our solicitor suggested I should talk to someone from your paper – can you still call it a paper when it isn't? – as they might have some information. Could I? Would that be your Damian?'

'Quid pro quo, Lib,' said Jane. 'You can talk to him as long as you introduce him to your friend.'

'OK.' Libby sighed. 'I'll ask her. I'm pretty sure she'd love to talk to him.'

'Right. I'll hand over his contact details when you hand over hers,' said Jane. 'Meanwhile, you can look up the issue online, can't you?'

Eschewing the lure of a cup of tea on top of a half a bottle of wine, Libby settled on the sofa with the laptop and began her search. It didn't take long.

The first thing she found, at the top of the written piece, was a link to an interview on Kent and Coast television, where a smart young man with 'Estate Agent' written all over him was explaining, very kindly, to viewers that the whole problem with the housing market was that the elderly refused to downsize and free up their homes for the deserving young. The subtext, as far as Libby could see, was that the elderly had no right to any more space than was needed to sleep, eat and bathe, and preferably in as few rooms as possible. Visions of estate agents' details of flats with one room for everything except bathing swam across Libby's

198

mind's eye and she gritted her teeth. She was unsurprised to find that the young estate agent's name was Trevor Taylor.

Now, why, she wondered, had Philip suggested she look into this? Connie was elderly herself, and wasn't evicting the elderly in favour of the young. She was just evicting everyone in favour of holidaymakers. In fact, it was more likely that Connie herself had been approached to sell Pendlebury Lodge to a young family. Libby sat up suddenly, dislodging Sidney, who had inserted a paw onto her lap. Was that it? Was that the event that had triggered the whole campaign? She rang Fran.

'Slow down!' Fran yelled. 'You aren't making any sense!'

Libby slowed down and tried to put her thoughts in order.

'So you think someone tried to persuade Connie to sell and it got her so angry she took it out on everyone else?' Fran said at the end of the still rather garbled explanation.

'Well, not exactly,' said Libby. 'But it might have alerted her to possibilities. See, there she is sitting at home with no one to boss around any more, and she sees her way to controlling people and making money into the bargain.'

'It's very far-fetched,' said Fran. 'And there's no way of finding out, is there?'

'Philip's going to look into whether she's got a will and the ownership of her house,' said Libby, 'although that should already have been done.'

'Except that Sergeant Powell managed to put the block on it.'

'We don't know that for sure,' said Libby. 'And I'm hoping Ian's managed to kick him off the inquiry by now.'

'He should have done,' said Fran. 'No doubt we'll find out tonight.'

'If he can get away,' said Libby. 'Meanwhile, I'll try and think of who else I can talk to and who might have a motive.'

Chapter Twenty-Seven

Libby and Ben arrived at the Coach and Horses just as a taxi deposited Edward and Ian outside.

'Grove House is beautiful,' said Edward, as he held open the door for the others to precede him, 'but it just isn't close enough to Steeple Martin.'

Grove House was the Georgian manor house divided into two apartments where Edward lived on the ground floor and Ian on the first.

'It's quite near enough for me,' said Ian, following them inside. 'What's everyone drinking?'

They had barely got settled at their usual table when Fran and Guy arrived.

'We've left the car at yours,' said Fran. 'I sort of assumed we'd be staying?'

'Good job I changed the spare bed, then,' said Libby with a grin.

'And I assumed,' said Ian, placing glasses in front of the two women, 'that I would be subjected to an inquisition. Especially as I had a long conversation with Philip Jacobs this afternoon.'

'Oh, good!' said Libby. 'And is he looking into Connie's financials?'

'As it happens, Libby, that is already being done. A little later than it should have been, but we've managed to get our act together, finally.'

'Have you sacked Sergeant Powell?' asked Libby eagerly.

'It's not as easy as that.' Ian sent her a minatory look. 'He's no longer on the case.'

'On gardening leave and being investigated!' translated Libby triumphantly.

'If you say so,' said Ian equably.

'So how far have you got with the case?' asked Guy. 'I'm just annoyed that none of us had noticed Matthews' name cropping up before she was murdered.'

'Philip said he did,' said Libby.

'Why should you, though?' asked Ben. 'It didn't mean anything to anyone until she turned up with us at the theatre.'

'And not even then,' said Ian. 'It was only when she turned up dead that it meant anything.'

'I was looking into something Philip mentioned this afternoon,' said Libby. 'Not quite the same thing, but I wondered if the protest group had come across it and whether Connie had been – well – involved.'

'What was that?' asked Edward.

'Elderly home-blocking,' said Libby, and looked round at the blank faces.

'I know about that,' said a voice from the door, and they all turned to see Patti manoeuvring Anne's wheelchair through the door.

Ben and Guy stood up to make room at the table while Edward went to buy drinks. Eventually everyone was established at the table, and Libby returned to the subject.

'So what do you know about home-blocking, Patti?'

'Oddly enough, I've heard about it several times over the years,' said Patti, 'but in particular, and recently, from Dorothy Barton.' She looked from Libby to Ian. 'That was Constance Matthews' first approach to her about Temptation House.'

'Oh!' said Libby. 'Hannah told me it was Trevor Taylor who approached her about that.'

'Karen didn't mention him,' said Patti, 'but she did say that

Constance Matthews wasn't the first person who had tried to get Dorothy to sell.'

'I think I need an explanation,' said Edward. 'Is home-blocking the same as bed-blocking?'

'Not dissimilar,' said Patti, and explained. 'So you see, it isn't as bad as evicting tenants to turn rentals into holiday lets, although, in the case of someone like Dorothy, once the house had been sold all the tenants would have been evicted, of course.'

'I wonder if Lady Howe was approached,' said Libby. 'She rather brushed it off when I asked her.'

'That would have been a real feather in an estate agent's cap,' said Guy. 'Selling Howe House and all the outbuildings as separate units.'

'But no one would have been evicted,' said Ian, 'and financially, it would have been a good deal for Lady Howe.'

'I wonder why she didn't go for it?' said Anne.

'Because she's too kind-hearted,' said Libby. 'Mavis calls her a saint.'

'It is an uncommonly benevolent thing to do,' said Ben. 'I don't know many property owners who would do it.'

'You haven't sold off the Manor,' said Guy.

'I'd hardly chuck my mother out, would I?' Ben laughed.

'And Colin's renting out his apartments in the Garden, not selling them,' said Fran.

'Except for the penthouse,' said Libby.

'He's sold that?' said Guy.

'Who to?' asked Edward. 'I didn't know that!'

'It's been kept a bit of a secret,' said Ben. 'He's sold it to young Ricky's grandma, Linda.'

'And Simon at the Pocket says he's met one of the renting families already,' said Libby.

Conversation turned naturally to the newcomers to Steeple Martin, and Ian persuaded Anne to move her wheelchair to allow him to slide in next to Libby.

'Tell me what you've been hearing about this Trevor Taylor,' he said quietly.

Libby repeated everything she'd learnt, including the clip from the television news.

'I can't honestly see that he comes into the case anywhere,' she concluded. 'It's all very up-front. He's just trying to make an honest buck, really, isn't he?'

'I suppose so, and there's been no effort at concealment,' agreed Ian.

'Whereas Connie kept under the radar, as far as I can see,' Fran butted in.

'And whereas evicting tenants wasn't actually illegal, the prospective purchase of Gleneagles was,' said Ian, 'and the rest of it was certainly immoral.'

'Who is he, though?' said Libby. 'I take it he isn't attached to Brooke's?'

'Don't fish, Libby.' Ian sent her a look over the rim of his glass. 'He appears to be an independent agent with an online presence only. We are looking into him.'

'Not Sergeant Powell, though.' Anne leant forward. 'Forgive me for saying so, Ian, but there do seem to have been various threads unpulled.'

'Nicely put,' said Ian, and sat back in his chair. The women waited for more, but he had obviously decided enough had been said.

'You know what,' said Libby, sighing, 'I have the feeling that Trevor Taylor will vanish like the autumn mist by tomorrow.'

'Because he'll get wind of all the interest,' said Patti, joining in. 'But why hasn't he already?'

'How do we know he hasn't?' said Fran. 'We – or the police – have only just picked up on his activities. The TV clip and the piece in the *Mercury* weren't recent, were they?'

'Yes, they were,' said Libby. 'Or – well, relatively, anyway. Couple of weeks ago?'

'Certainly not in the last week,' said Fran. 'We'd have noticed. Or someone would.'

'That's true. I expect he's gone to ground already.' Libby finished her drink. 'Anyone ready for another?'

More drinks were distributed just as Harry erupted through the door, ahead of Peter.

'OK, chaps,' he said, casting himself into a chair hastily vacated by Edward, 'tell me the latest.'

Peter rolled his eyes and went to the bar.

Libby and Fran gave a precis of what had been going on since the weekend.

'So much has happened,' said Libby. 'I can't believe it was only Sunday when you told us about Judy.'

'Who is now our Lady Aconite,' said Harry. 'I'm *sooo* jealous.'

'Tell me about the home-blocking,' said Peter. 'I'm sure I've come across it in the past.'

'If you look it up online it seems to have been a bone of contention for various governments over the years,' said Libby. 'And you said this Trevor Taylor had approached Miss Barton, Patti, didn't you? You didn't mention it before.'

'Well, he wasn't mentioned by name, there were no threats involved, and Karen only mentioned it in passing,' said Patti. 'Miss Barton said she was already providing homes, thank you very much, so there was no point in selling.'

'It's a bit of a coincidence, though, isn't it?' Peter steepled his fingers and frowned. 'Surely there's a connection?'

'Could he have told this Connie about possible pickings?' Anne was leaning forward eagerly. 'That would make sense, wouldn't it?'

'How would he have known her?' asked Fran.

'Don't worry,' said Ian, surprising them all by joining in. 'As I said, we're looking into Mr Taylor.'

'And that means stop speculating,' said Ben.

'I know what I want to ask,' said Harry, poking Edward in the ribs. 'Why haven't we seen young Alice recently?'

Immediately, the women round the table refocused their attention. Alice Gedding was a sheep farmer whose farm on the Heronsbourne Flats supplied Bob the butcher with premium saltmarsh lamb. Edward had met her during the same investigation that had introduced Libby and Fran to Hannah Barton.

Edward gave them his huge white grin. 'She's fine. She just doesn't get much time off.'

'So we lose him every weekend,' said Ian.

'And you brought Ricky down last weekend, didn't you?' said Libby. 'That was nice of you, Edward.'

'He's a nice boy,' said Edward. 'And from what he said, he'll be here more regularly, won't he?'

'Will he?' Patti looked surprised.

'His nan's moving to Colin's penthouse,' said Harry. 'The lovely Linda.' He cast his eyes up.

'And that's actually sort of connected to the home-blocking,' said Libby. 'Linda lives in a retirement complex and doesn't like it. When she came here back in spring, she decided she'd like to move here. Hetty's taken her under her wing.'

'Barney won't like being cooped up on the top floor,' said Guy.

'He'll stay with us when he visits,' said Harry firmly. 'Because of the garden.'

'But he did say perhaps his mum could move here, too,' said Libby. 'Then Barney could live here all the time.'

'How would you cope with Dear Debbie, petal?' Harry grinned at her.

'Nothing to do with me,' said Libby, with a shrug.

'We're keeping our eyes on the property market for her.' Peter made a face. 'Can't say I'm keen.'

'Oh, dear,' said Anne. 'Trouble in paradise.'

'Perhaps Trevor Taylor could find her something,' said Fran innocently.

'Oh, what a good idea!' said Libby.

Ian closed his eyes and shook his head.

Thursday morning after Fran and Guy had left, Libby decided she really ought to devote some time to organising herself ready for the upcoming pantomime audition. Audition pieces had been emailed to interested parties, something she was still getting used to; she still wanted to give out proper scripts, although she realised the advantages of the online system. A rehearsal schedule had been in place for some time, and that and a script she emailed to Judy; it made her consider the suggestion that she should perhaps think about giving herself Fairy Godmother. She rang Peter.

'I'm honoured, dear heart,' he said. 'It's usually my husband who's in receipt of your confidences.'

'Not when it's theatre,' said Libby. 'I want to know what you think – seriously.'

Peter gave it as his opinion that she would thoroughly enjoy herself, and, as the Godmother didn't appear in every scene, she would be perfectly able to direct as well, and he would be able to pick up the slack.

'And while you're there,' he said, 'I had a look online for Trevor Taylor.'

'Oh! I was going to do that,' said Libby.

'I've saved you the trouble. And I have various sources not open to you, don't forget.'

Although Peter no longer worked for Reuters, he was still a freelance journalist and indeed, had many sources of which Libby was jealous.

'So what did you find?'

'Very little. A very basic website, without even a contact form.'

'What does it say, then? Doesn't it have property details?'

'It doesn't. He puts himself across as a "property finder".' Peter sighed. 'I think Ian will have to get his IT gurus on to it.'

'How odd,' said Libby. 'There's definitely something fishy about him, isn't there?'

'Certainly is,' said Peter. 'So now we've got to look for Debbie's home somewhere else, haven't we?'

'Eh? Oh.' Libby pulled a face at Sidney, who was patting her arm with an insistent paw. 'Debbie. Yes.'

She ended the call and began to draft an email to *Cinderella* auditionees informing them of the parts no longer available. She felt guilty, but decided that if someone turned up who was a) desperate to play the Godmother and b) very good, she would stand aside. From time to time her mind returned to the puzzle of Trevor Taylor, but she firmly reminded herself that Ian and Rachel would be looking into that problem and it really wasn't her business.

Until Jane Baker rang her at lunchtime.

'What do you know about this?' said Jane. 'Is this my fault for putting you on to it?'

'Eh? What are you talking about?' Libby pushed the laptop away from her and stood up.

'Home-blocking. Trevor Taylor. You looked into it, didn't you?'

'Only a bit – why? What's happened?'

'Trevor Taylor. He's dead.'

Chapter Twenty-Eight

'*Dead*?'

Jane sighed. 'OK – you really didn't know.'

'Are you sure?' Libby was having difficulty absorbing this information.

'Of course I'm sure.'

'Where? How? How do you know?'

'You know perfectly well how we get our information,' said Jane, a little testily. 'As for how, I've no idea, but where – well, you'll like this, Libby – he was found on the steps of the Tyne Chapel.'

'What was he doing there?' Libby sat down heavily.

'How do I know? He could have been going to see Lady Howe, I suppose.'

'It's not really that close to Howe House,' said Libby. 'And why, anyway?'

'I don't *know*!' Jane heaved an impatient sigh. 'So it wasn't anything to do with you, then.'

'With me?' shrieked Libby.

'I meant – you weren't looking into it.'

'No. But the police were investigating him. His name kept cropping up.'

'Ah! So someone thought he had information and had to be silenced!'

'Maybe. When was this?'

'It came through about an hour ago,' said Jane. 'I don't know when he was found.'

'And I don't suppose anyone will tell me,' said Libby.

'I doubt it,' said Jane. 'But if you do find anything out, will you let me know? Oh, and did you get that person's details for me to give to Damian?'

'No, I didn't!' snapped Libby.

'All right, all right. I'll speak to you soon,' said Jane, and rang off quickly.

Libby sat for a long time staring at the cold woodburner. Sidney crawled stealthily on to her lap and began vibrating gently. Which was how Ben found them when he came in.

'Where were you? I thought you were coming up to the Manor for lunch with Hetty?'

Libby started and disturbed Sidney. 'Oh, golly! What time is it?'

'Half past one.'

'Why didn't you ring me?'

'I did – twice. You were on the mobile, so I didn't bother to ring the landline.' Ben sat down opposite her. 'What's happened? I can see something has.'

'Trevor Taylor. He's dead.'

'*What*?'

Libby nodded. 'That was my reaction.' She told him what Jane had told her. 'Pru's going to be devastated.'

'Why? She didn't know him.'

'The Tyne Chapel's virtually on her land. Why was he there?'

'Perhaps he wasn't,' said Ben. 'Perhaps he was killed somewhere else and moved there. Doesn't Ian think that's what happened to Connie?'

'Does he? I don't know.' Libby frowned. 'But all Connie's stuff was found with her, which was odd. You don't go paying calls with your case and all your clothes, do you?'

'No. And no one's told you if they found out where she was staying, have they?'

209

'No-o,' said Libby slowly. 'And actually, she wouldn't have stayed anywhere, would she? She only went to Nethergate on Tuesday morning, and she was killed Tuesday night, according to Franklyn.'

'So she might have had all her things with her!' said Ben.

'I wonder if they've checked all her properties in Nethergate?' said Libby. 'Nobody's said.'

'I'm sure they will have – unless Sergeant Powell's been interfering again.'

'No, he's gone, and they've been going through all the stuff he missed,' said Libby. 'At least, I think so. I wonder if Rachel would tell me?'

'Under the circumstances, I don't think so,' said Ben. 'Now, Hetty's got soup keeping warm, so forget about it for the time being and come and eat.'

Ben had driven down from the Manor, so he drove them back there, keeping up a gentle flow of conversation about the upcoming Hallowe'en celebrations and tonight's rehearsal for the Morris side.

'So it's drinks in the Pocket tonight, is it?' said Libby, as she climbed out of the car.

'Yes, we're rehearsing on the Bat and Trap pitch,' said Ben. 'We got Colin's permission.'

The Bat and Trap pitch was behind the Garden Hotel – or, as Libby must remember to call it, the Garden House – on land still owned by Colin and conveniently close to the Hop Pocket, which also hosted the occasional Bat and Trap matches, in which, not surprisingly, most of the Morris side also played.

'It'll make a nice change,' said Libby with a sigh. Ben smiled to himself.

It wasn't until Libby was walking home later in the afternoon that she received the call she had been expecting from Lady Howe.

'What am I going to *do*, Libby?' Prudence wailed. 'Why is this happening to me? I'm not throwing people out of their homes!'

Libby took a deep breath. 'I don't know, Pru, and I'm really sorry. What have the police told you?'

'*Nothing*! They just asked questions! It was that nice Sergeant Stone who came, not that horrible Powell.' Lady Pru huffed indignantly. 'But I don't see why they had to talk to me anyway.'

'Because Constance was found on your land, Pru, and the Tyne Chapel is too – well, almost.'

'And why? Someone's doing this on purpose.'

Libby paused to think about this.

'You could be right, Pru.' Libby turned the corner into the high street, and bumped straight into Flo Carpenter and her shopping trolley. 'Look, I've got to go now. I'll call you later.' She cut off the wail of distress and smiled at Flo. 'Sorry, Flo – wasn't looking.'

'Too busy thinkin' about murder, wasn't you?' Flo folded her arms and nodded wisely. 'You'll come a cropper one o' these days.'

'Yes, well, not today, eh?' Libby stepped round the trolley. 'See you Sunday if not before!'

Lady Howe could be right, she thought, as she hurried along the high street. She needed to discuss it with Fran, who presumably didn't know about the latest murder as she hadn't called.

'But then,' muttered Libby, as she turned into Allhallow's Lane, 'I haven't called her, either.'

'Hello, Libby!'

Libby looked up, startled, and came face to face with her next-door neighbour.

'Hello, Jinny!' Libby stopped and smiled. 'Haven't seen you for ages.'

'You've been busy with that theatre, haven't you, dear,' said Jinny Mardle. 'My Colin did ask me to go with them to see the play, but I don't go much on Shakespeare.' She hunched a thin shoulder.

Mrs Mardle had worked for Colin's parents at the Garden Hotel, and had almost brought him up while they were working the long hours demanded by the hospitality industry.

'No, it's not everyone's cup of tea, is it?' said Libby. 'Never mind – you'll come to the panto, won't you?'

'Oh, of course, dear! Are you going to be in it?'

'I think so.' Libby tried to look modest.

'Oh, good.' Mrs Mardle looked down at the floor. 'I was just going down to Flo Carpenter's for tea, actually, but I did want to have a word when you've got a moment.'

'I've just seen Flo,' said Libby. 'What did you want to see me about?'

'Oh, it's not urgent, dear, I'll see you later.' The old lady looked flustered, gave a quick smile and trotted off towards the high street.

'What was all that about?' Libby asked herself as she fished for her key.

But she forgot about Jinny Mardle as she laid a fire in the wood-burner and made herself a large mug of tea before calling Fran.

'Well, you took your time!' Fran sounded amused.

'What do you mean?'

'I heard about Trevor Taylor this morning, and I assume you did, too. I've been waiting for you to ring ever since.'

'Oh. Well, Ben carted me off to Hetty's for lunch and distracted me.'

'But now you want to think about it,' said Fran.

'I don't exactly *want* to,' said Libby. 'I would honestly rather forget about the whole thing.'

'Really? That isn't like you.'

'Yes it is. Over the last few years I've said time and time again I don't want to do this any more.' She sighed. 'My brain hurts.'

'OK,' said Fran. 'Why did you ring me, then?'

'To check whether you'd heard.'

'And see if I had any thoughts about it?'

'I suppose so.'

'And have you heard from Prudence?'

'Oh, yes.' Libby sighed again, gustily. 'Wailing at me.'

'Yes, she called us, too.'

'Was that how you heard? Jane called me. She'd heard on the wire, or whatever they call it these days, and thought it was because I'd been investigating. Cheek!'

Fran laughed. 'I can see her reasoning. If you – or I – started investigating something, that would suggest that there was something to find out. And that something might be dangerous to someone.'

'Yes, I know – but we didn't.'

'You brought it up, though, after Jane told you to look into the home-blocking thing.'

'Yes, but Ian obviously already knew about him – Taylor, I mean. I just don't see what it's got to do with Connie's death.'

'I wonder if the police have found any links between them?' Fran said thoughtfully. 'They might have done.'

'But they won't tell us,' said Libby. 'Ian only tells us stuff if we can help and his colleagues can't.'

'Or won't,' amended Fran.

'Like Powell and Winter,' agreed Libby. 'Bad, isn't it, that some of the police think they can use the law just how they like.'

'Or use it to cover up their own misdeeds.'

They fell silent.

'So what do we do?' asked Libby eventually. 'Abandon the whole thing? After all, Philip's managed to sort out the Gleneagles problem, and that was the only really illegal thing Connie was involved in.'

'Why don't we sit down and work it all out together? See if we can find any links. Even if they're completely speculative. You could come down here.'

'On paper,' said Libby. 'Yes, good idea. Tomorrow morning? You never know, something might have broken by then.'

'Not today?'

'We've got a Morris rehearsal this evening,' said Libby, 'and before you remind me that I don't dance, they want my support.'

'In the Pocket afterwards!' laughed Fran. 'OK, tomorrow morning. And if either of us can, we ought to find out anything extra that's relevant.'

Deciding that she wouldn't even try to find out anything else about either murder, at least for now, Libby poked up the logs, went and found something for dinner and settled down to read a book with Sidney on her lap.

'How very ordinary!' said Ben, when he arrived just before six. 'Have you given up detecting?'

'Just for now.' Libby grinned at him. 'I'll go and start the dinner.'

The discovery of Trevor Taylor's body was reported on the local news, but with no further details, other than an uncomfortable-looking Rachel Trent giving a statement and asking for any information from the public.

'It didn't say when he was found,' said Ben.

'No,' said Libby, getting up and going kitchenwards. 'Good job too. Fran and I will find out a bit more tomorrow.'

'What?' said Ben, but was interrupted by a tentative knocking on the door.

'Mrs Mardle!' he said in surprise. 'What can we do for you?'

'Oh, Jinny, please,' said Mrs Mardle. 'And I wonder – could I possibly speak to Libby?'

Libby came back out of the kitchen. 'Yes, Jinny, of course. Come in.'

Jinny Mardle stepped nervously over the threshold, and hesitated.

'I feel a bit of a silly, actually,' she began, hovering between the front door and the sitting room. 'Bothering you like this.'

'Come and sit down,' said Libby. 'Ben, could you pause the dinner for me?'

'Oh, dear! I've caught you right at the wrong time!' Mrs Mardle looked as if she was about to burst into tears.

'Don't worry!' said Libby, patting the armchair. 'Sit here.'

214

Mrs Mardle subsided into the cushions. 'I wouldn't have done, you see, dear, although I did want to talk to you, but then it was the news.'

'The news?'

'That man. The one I was going to talk to you about. Trevor Taylor. They said he was dead.'

Chapter Twenty-Nine

Libby tried to suppress her involuntary exclamation. This was just too much of a coincidence.

'So what were you going to tell me about, Jinny?' she said. 'And would you like a cup of tea? Something stronger?'

Mrs Mardle hesitated, and Ben appeared in the kitchen doorway with a bottle of wine. 'How about this, Jinny?' he said. 'Red or white?'

Mrs Mardle opted for the Sancerre, and Ben brought out two glasses.

'Now, go on, Jinny,' said Libby. 'Trevor Taylor.'

'Well, dear, I was going to tell you about him, because Flo Carpenter said you'd been looking into this murder in Nethergate.' She took a sip of wine and coughed. 'And that was all about people being forced out of their homes, wasn't it?'

'Yes – to turn them into holiday accommodation,' said Libby, nodding.

'And this Mr Taylor, he was trying to do the same.' Jinny Mardle looked suddenly militant. 'How he dared!'

'I thought he was simply trying to sell houses to young families?' said Libby.

'That's what he said. But he was trying to force us into these awful homes!'

'He was?' Libby was lost. 'How? What homes?'

Ben came to sit beside Libby. 'Tell us from the beginning, Jinny,' he said. 'When did you first meet him?'

'All right, dear.' Mrs Mardle smiled at him. 'Well, it was when I had the keys to Colin's flats.'

'Oh, yes! You were showing people round, weren't you?' said Libby.

'That's right, dear, because Colin couldn't always drop everything and rush over here, so sometimes I showed people the flats. Although there weren't many people.' She frowned. 'Too expensive, I think.'

'And then he decided to rent them.' Libby nodded.

'Yes. Well, that's a good idea, isn't it? And that Linda had already bought the top one. You know her, don't you? And she told us – you know our little group? We meet in Carpenter's Hall.'

'Yes, I know,' said Libby.

'Well, she said this man had gone to her flats, where she lives now, and asked to see her, as she would be giving hers up.'

'How did he know?' asked Libby

'This was Trevor Taylor?' said Ben.

'Yes, Mr Taylor. And she said he wanted to know if anyone was going to take her flat over.'

'How did he know about it?' repeated Libby.

'I've no idea. But the next thing we knew was there was a whole load of these little leaflet things at the hall, offering to buy our houses.' Jinny took another healthy swallow of wine. 'What do you think of that, then?'

'Why didn't Flo or Hetty tell us this?' Libby asked Ben.

'Oh, most people didn't take any notice,' said Mrs Mardle. 'Flo put them all in the bin. But then he turned up on my doorstep!'

'Goodness!' Libby's mouth dropped open. 'How did he find you?'

'I asked him that, dear. He wouldn't say, but when I talked to Flo about it today she reckoned he'd followed me. Probably followed several of us.'

'So what did you say? You didn't let him in, I hope?'

'Of course I didn't, dear! And luckily, that nice Beth was going into her gate and I could have called out to her, couldn't I?'

'Yes, of course. So what did he say?'

'He went on about the fact that my house needed a lot of work done, and I probably wouldn't want to be bothered with it – what a cheek, eh? And I would be much better off in – what do they call it? Protected something?'

'Sheltered accommodation,' supplied Ben.

'That's it. And he said he knew of a lovely place, and he would sell my house for me.'

'I thought he was only trying it on with big houses,' said Libby. 'To think he was right here, next door!'

'Flo said you'd know all about it,' said Mrs Mardle. 'And then he was on the news.' She shook her head. 'Do you think I should tell the police?'

'I'll tell them if you like, Jinny,' said Libby. 'I'm sure they'd like to know. They'll probably want to talk to you themselves, but I'll tell them first.'

'And is that what this woman was trying to do, too?'

'In a way,' said Ben, 'but she was actually throwing people out of their homes. At least this Taylor wasn't doing that.'

'Were they in it together?' Mrs Mardle said shrewdly. 'It sounds like it, dear, doesn't it?'

Ben and Libby looked at each other.

'You could be right,' said Libby slowly. 'I shall definitely tell the police.'

Jinny Mardle heaved a great sigh and put her empty glass down on the hearth. 'Oh, I do feel better now, dear,' she said. 'And now I must go and let you get on with your dinner.'

'Well!' said Libby, as Ben closed the door behind their guest. 'There's a turn-up. I wonder why she didn't tell Colin when Taylor got in touch?'

'She may have done. And after all, what could he have done? Taylor wasn't actually doing anything illegal, as we've said. And as a scam, it wasn't exactly effective, was it?'

'No.' Frowning, Libby made for the kitchen. 'In fact, he seems to have been remarkably *ineffective*.'

'Something to add to your investigations with Fran in the morning,' said Ben.

'And I think I'll send Rachel a text about it now,' said Libby. 'Just in case.'

Ben went off to his Morris rehearsal after dinner, and Libby sat watching an archaeology documentary without actually taking it in until she could legitimately take herself off to the Hop Pocket. It was just as she was deciding it was about time she left that her phone rang.

'Libby – what's all this about Trevor Taylor?' Rachel, as usual these days, sounded tired.

'Not me – it's my next-door neighbour,' said Libby. 'She told me, and I said I'd tell you. I don't know if it's any use.'

'Tell me, and I'll see.'

So Libby repeated Jinny Mardle's story.

'And he approached all the old dears?' Rachel sounded a lot more alert now.

'Don't you dare call them that!' said Libby. 'And no, he seems to have got wind of their little group through Linda – young Ricky's grandma, remember? And none of them took any notice. Flo Carpenter thinks he must have followed Mrs Mardle home.'

'Can I talk to them?'

'They won't know anything – only Linda and Mrs Mardle. But yes, you can talk to them, I should think.'

She gave Rachel Mrs Mardle's telephone number and promised she'd get hold of Linda's. This wasn't absolutely accurate, as she already had it, but she thought she ought to ask before passing it on. Then duty done, she made sure the woodburner was safe, flung her cape round her shoulders, picked up her purse and left for the Pocket.

As she turned in to Cuckoo Lane she could hear gales of ribald laughter, the rapping of stout sticks against each other and the wheezing note of a piano accordion. The Steeple Martin Morris were at full flood. She smiled and pushed open the door of the Hop Pocket. She was followed almost immediately by a breathless Beth Cole.

'I saw you go by, but I couldn't quite catch you up,' said the vicar, leaning against the bar counter. 'What will you have?'

Without being asked, Simon placed two half-pint glasses of lager in front of the women and waved away payment.

'Ben won't make any money that way,' said Beth, as they retired to a table under the window.

'I think he's more concerned with keeping the pub open,' said Libby, 'not profit. So many are closing these days, aren't they?'

'So Steeple Martin is going against the trend?' Beth raised her eyebrows. 'Opening a new one rather than closing one.'

'I suppose so,' said Libby. 'Listen, Beth. I want to run something past you.'

And Libby told Beth about Mrs Mardle's revelations, and how they related to the two murders in Nethergate.

'Yes,' said Beth pensively when she'd finished. 'I heard something about this. A couple of the Maltby Close residents were talking about it.'

'Really? Mrs Mardle thought no one had taken any notice of the leaflets. After all, they already live in what could be called sheltered accommodation, don't they?'

'Yes, that was the point.' Beth leant back in her chair and stretched her legs. 'They all thought he was a bit daft. That was how they put it.'

'Yes – he certainly didn't do his research, did he?'

'Except there are some of that group, like Hetty, who do live in large houses,' said Beth.

'I was just wondering,' said Libby, after a moment, 'if Connie wasn't pinching some of his business.'

'How do you make that out?' Beth frowned.

'Well, she was buying properties, sometimes big ones, and throwing people out, so he couldn't buy them, or sell them on, or whatever he was doing.'

'Perhaps she got the idea from him?' suggested Beth, sitting forward again and making the table rock. 'Perhaps he tried to buy her house? Was it a big one?'

'Oh, yes. A big, detached Victorian villa,' said Libby. 'But it was up near London, nowhere near here.'

'Well, maybe he didn't only operate near here,' said Beth. 'Estate agents have branches all over the shop, don't they?'

'Some do,' agreed Libby. 'But if that was the case, and Connie pinched his business, I could understand him bashing her on the head – but who killed him?'

'Oh, Lord, I don't know!' said Beth. 'Nothing humans do to each other should surprise me in my business, but I'm continually gobsmacked.'

They fell to discussing gentler village matters, including the newcomers who had come to live in the Garden House.

'Simon says one of the men comes in here sometimes,' she said.

'So I believe. Neither of the families are churchgoers, sadly. I don't know about the lady in the top flat.'

'Linda – no, I don't know either, although she seems keen to be part of the community, so maybe she will. And there's still one flat unlet. Maybe you'll get a brace of choir members out of that one.'

A burst of noise and a cold draught heralded the arrival of the Morris side, and within ten minutes Beth's husband, John, who had only recently been wielding a mean piano accordion, was installed at the old piano Beth had liberated from her church hall, a pint of Ben's best bitter wobbling dangerously on the top. Steeple Martin was its happy, rather noisy, self.

Chapter Thirty

On Friday morning, Libby deposited her laptop, phone, notebook and purse into her basket. collected her cape and keys, and told Sidney to be good. Ben had departed for the brewery looking very slightly the worse for wear, which made Libby glad that Steeple Martin Morris didn't rehearse more regularly.

'Although,' she told Fran, when she arrived at Coastguard Cottage half an hour later, 'if they did, I suppose it wouldn't always turn into a full-on party. And it would give him a hobby.'

Fran laughed. 'He hasn't got time for a hobby! He's got the hop gardens and the brewery, the holiday lets – sorry, dirty word – and the theatre. And you.'

'I don't take up his time!' protested Libby.

'No?' Fran cocked her head on one side. 'OK. Come on – let's sit in the kitchen. Do you want coffee?'

'Can I have tea, please?' Libby eyed Fran's smart coffee machine warily.

Fran, amused, switched on the kettle.

'Do you realise Harry's still got his old Cona coffeemaker?' Libby said, emptying her basket onto Fran's table. 'And it still makes perfectly good coffee.'

'And it's a design classic,' said Fran. 'I know. But he's also got a monster for people who ask for all the mad barista-style concoctions.'

'Which I shall never come to terms with,' said Libby.

'No, because you don't like coffee anyway,' said Fran. 'Come on, now. Let's get on with it.' She poured boiling water into a mug and pushed it and a milk bottle across the table.

'Right,' said Libby. 'I've got even more news for you.' She smiled smugly. 'Guess who came to see me last night?'

When Jinny Mardle's visit had been recounted, Fran sat back in her chair and pursed her lips. 'You're right,' she said. 'It is a bit too much of a coincidence.'

'The murders have got to be connected,' said Libby. 'Or at least, the victims have.'

'So let's go back to the beginning.' Fran drew her own notebook towards her. 'What was Connie's first foray into the property market?'

'Either the Raincliffe Rep or the Furnough School,' said Libby. 'She bought up Carl Robinson's debts and loaned him more capital.'

'Which proves he was a bit of an idiot.' Fran made a note. 'Someone told her how to do that, didn't they? She wouldn't have known how to do it otherwise.'

'Hmm.' Libby tapped her teeth with her pen. 'Was that Trevor Taylor?'

'If it was,' said Fran, 'how did they get in touch with each other in the first place?'

'Beth suggested he may have tried to buy her house, although I thought he only operated round here.'

'That's not a bad idea. He may have only come across our area when she did. Let's see – she bought the Crown and Sceptre back in May, didn't she? If she found that because of something he told her . . .'

'What, though?'

'How about that magazine that lists all that sort of stuff? Morning something?'

'Oh, yes! But she didn't go on to buy more pubs, did she?'

'No, but it introduced her to this area. The pub's near Canterbury, isn't it?' Fran drained her coffee cup.

'And then she would have had to find out about the whole holiday lettings business. Which I suppose Trevor Taylor could have told her about.' Libby stared at the blank page in her notebook. 'Perhaps he did try and get her to move out of Pendlebury Lodge and she got him talking about all the different wheezes for making money in the property market – including buying up loans. What's she done with those two places now, I wonder?'

'You told me Oliver said one of them was now flats – or was going to be,' said Fran.

'So it's still property!' Libby was getting excited. 'That's it! He was mentoring her in the whole property scam business.'

'Maybe,' said Fran, 'but there's no proof. And if that's what it was, the pupil certainly outstripped the master.'

'So we need to find proof,' said Libby. 'Do you think I could wangle my way into her house?'

'How, exactly?' Fran raised her eyebrows. 'The police will have searched it by now, despite whatever barriers Sergeant Powell put in the way.'

'Hmm.' Libby peered into her empty mug. 'Can I have another one?'

Fran got up. 'There needs to be a concrete link established between the two. And I refuse to believe there isn't one. As we've said, it's just too much of a coincidence otherwise.'

'Let's think about the properties Connie went for in Nethergate,' said Libby. 'There was old Miss Barton and Temptation House, Gleneagles and Nyebourne in King Edward Street, and – um – Blue Sky Holidays on Marine Parade. And Lady Pru's Howe Estate, and Mavis. Although what she would have done with the Blue Anchor, I don't know. The upstairs is too small to let to many people.'

'OK.' Fran placed Libby's refilled mug next to her and sat down. 'So who, individually, would be affected by those prospective purchases? And they were prospective, weren't they?'

'Except for Blue Sky – she bought them up. And then there were the individual flats in Marine Drive and King Edward Street and a couple along here. Although I think they were probably holiday homes already.' Libby sipped tea. 'I just hate to think of those poor dispossessed people like Kirsty being suspected of murder.'

'But think about it – certainly as far as Connie's concerned – a man and his family thrown out of their home . . . If he came across her on her own, at night, say, he may well be tempted to lash out.'

'But the same doesn't apply to Trevor Taylor,' said Libby. 'He wasn't, as I keep saying, chucking people out. Mostly, he was trying to persuade old people with big houses to move into small retirement flats so he could sell their properties at a huge profit.'

'Was he actually buying them?' asked Fran.

'I don't know. It would make sense if he was – which would explain why Connie kicked him into touch. If he was trying to buy them, he would be relying on the fact that the old people wouldn't know the current value of their properties and would let him have them for a knock-down price.'

'Or he'd sell their houses and tell the old folks they went for much less.' Fran nodded. 'It had to be something like that, or he wouldn't be bothering, would he? And it still gets us no nearer having evidence of him and Connie being in cahoots.'

'Except,' said Libby slowly, 'we do know he approached Miss Barton – at least, I think we do. That was prime property for him and for Connie. Which makes me wonder why he didn't approach Lady Pru.'

Fran sighed. 'We're no further, are we?'

'We could ask Philip or Hannah for the names of the sellers?' suggested Libby.

'What good would that do? The sellers weren't thrown out and presumably they made money.'

'Oh, yes.' Libby scowled at the table. 'Well, I don't know, then.'

'What was the name of the builder Lady Pru's using?' asked Fran suddenly.

'Lady Pru and Mavis both said he was honest and wouldn't have anything to do with Connie,' said Libby.

'Yes, but didn't you say she never went near the place when the builders were there?'

'Yes, but the builders wouldn't warn her off, would they?'

'No, but someone was doing the conversions, or updating the properties. It could have been the same builders. I thought they might talk.' Fran looked hopeful.

'No, honestly. Mavis particularly said Brendan Birch wouldn't have anything to do with it.'

'Brendan . . . Birch,' muttered Fran, writing it down.

'No!' protested Libby. 'I told you!'

'Yes, I know, but it's worth thinking about. Maybe Connie or Trevor Taylor approached him, even if he didn't do any work for them?'

'I suppose,' said Libby grudgingly. 'So where do we go from here?'

'We could ask Beryl Sampson at Gleneagles if she or her fellow tenants came across Taylor,' said Fran.

'I doubt it,' said Libby. 'As far as anyone knew, it was already divided into flats – Taylor couldn't have bought it.'

'Well, Connie couldn't either. Didn't stop her trying.'

'Yes, but that was different.' Libby shrugged. 'I suppose we could try.'

'After all,' said Fran, taking Libby's mug to the sink, 'it's the fellow tenants who were seen going onto Lady Pru's land, wasn't it?'

'True.' Libby put her unused laptop back in her basket. 'Tell you what – why don't we go up to see old Jim Butler? He's the one who identified them.'

'Could do,' said Fran, who was staring out of the window. 'But I keep thinking there's something we've missed. Or forgotten. Something someone's told us . . .'

'It'll come to you,' said Libby. 'Don't push it. Come on – let's go and see Jim. Then we can come back and have lunch with Mavis. We need to talk to her, anyway.'

'All right.' Fran sighed and went to collect her own bag and coat.

They went in Libby's car. They were halfway up the high street when Fran hit the dashboard.

'I've got it!' she exclaimed.

Libby trod on the brake. 'Got what?'

'The Sergeant at Arms! Remember? Izzy at the Puckle Inn told us!' Fran craned round over her shoulder. 'Look – turn down here. It's just on the right.'

Libby obediently made a sharp left-hand turn, to the loud annoyance of the driver behind, and pulled up on the right-hand side of the narrow street. The Sergeant at Arms listed slightly to the side, looking as if it belonged to a Nethergate from two hundred years ago.

'Right – what have I forgotten?' asked Libby.

'Izzy said Connie had her eye on the area and *that* was how she heard about the Crown and Sceptre! We got it the wrong way round.' Fran's eyes were alight.

'Oh . . . oh, yes!' Libby was enlightened. 'So she did! And she said the landlord here knew about it! What exactly did she say?'

'I can't remember exactly, but something about Connie trying to get rid of tenants. Let's go in and ask.'

There were only a few customers in the bar, which matched the exterior perfectly, being dark and slightly shabby.

'Hello!' said Fran brightly to the man behind the counter. 'Are you Clive?'

The man stood up straight, looking surprised. 'Yes – who wants to know?'

'Izzy over at the Puckle Inn said you were a friend of hers,' said Fran.

'And we wondered if you could answer a few questions about Constance Matthews,' added Libby.

Clive narrowed his eyes at her and rubbed his slightly bristly chin. 'You're not police.'

'No, but we've been trying to do something about all these

holiday let properties,' said Fran. 'And Izzy said some of your customers—'

'Oh!' Clive's expression changed. 'I know who you are now. And I saw you in here a few years ago.' He tapped his forehead with a finger. 'Good memory, see.'

'Yes – with the Harriers,' said Libby. 'You *have* got a good memory.'

'Yeah. You're the ones that solve the murders.' Clive nodded. 'Mavis was telling me.' His face darkened.

'So what can you tell us?' asked Libby. 'And could I have a tonic water, please?'

'And I'll have a white wine, please,' said Fran, grinning smugly at Libby. 'I'm not driving.'

'I don't reckon I can tell you anything you don't know.' Clive retrieved a bottle of wine from his cooler. 'You know all about the tenants she chucked out.'

'Yes, but Izzy told us she knew about Nethergate before she bought the Crown and Sceptre. We thought it was the other way round,' said Fran.

Clive looked surprised. 'Course she did. That cousin of hers lives here, doesn't he?'

Chapter Thirty-One

'*Cousin*?' echoed Fran and Libby together.

'Constance Matthews' *cousin*?' said Libby.

'Yes – didn't you know?' Clive looked surprised. 'He's one of my regulars. He was just as mad as everyone else. Thought it was all his fault.'

'Come to think of it, Fran, Beryl Sampson said Eric knew all about it – something to do with his family. Remember? I don't think she knew the ins and outs.'

'The police don't know,' said Fran. 'Can we tell them?'

'Oh, I don't know about that.' Clive shook his head. 'I don't want to get no one into trouble.'

'No, I understand that,' said Fran. 'But it was because of him she knew about the town?'

'Tried to buy his place, didn't she?' Clive scowled. 'Nearly managed it, too.'

'Nearly?' said Libby.

'I dunno. Some legal business – but he come in here a couple of days ago and bought drinks all round. Said it was all a mistake.'

Libby stared. 'Does he live in Gleneagles, by any chance?'

Clive's expression lightened. 'Yeah – that's it! You do know him.'

Libby turned to Fran. 'Beryl's fellow tenants.'

'The two who Jim Butler saw?' said Fran. 'The Peakes?'

'No,' said Clive, 'not Eddie Peake.'

229

'What was the other one's name?' Libby frowned and looked at Clive. 'You might as well tell us now.'

Clive sighed. 'Oh, all right. You'll find out anyway. And the police have talked to him already. Eric Bartlett.'

'Eric! That's the one.' Libby nodded. 'And the police have talked to him already?'

'Yeah, course. They talked to everybody.'

'Why didn't you want to tell us his name, then?' asked Fran.

'We-ell . . .' Clive looked uncomfortable. 'Not sure he told 'em he was that woman's cousin.'

'Ah.' Libby sipped her tonic water. 'So did he introduce her to any of his friends? His fellow drinkers?'

'No. She just asked around. Some other bloke came in here, though. He just asked a few questions – not that he got any answers.'

'Was his name Taylor?' asked Fran.

'No idea. Don't think he was anything to do with that woman, though.'

'Right,' said Libby. 'Thank you, Clive, you've been really helpful. Although I'm surprised we didn't know about this before.'

'Couple of the regulars told that group about it,' said Clive. 'You're part of that.'

'The protest group yes,' said Fran. 'I expect Philip got their names,' she said to Libby.

'Yes – he just didn't tell us.' Libby sighed. 'Oh, well, thank you again, Clive.'

'Hope you get whoever did it,' said Clive, coming to the door to see them off.

'I'm sure the police will,' said Fran. 'Thanks.'

'I suppose,' she said, as they got back into Libby's car, 'the police know all about this.'

'Hmm.' Libby fastened her seat belt. 'To be honest, I feel a bit of a fool now.'

'I know what you mean,' said Fran. 'Were we being used again, do you think?'

Libby drove down to the end of the narrow street where it turned into King Edward Street. 'You can see why that was Eric's local, can't you?' she said, as they drove past Gleneagles. 'And yes, I suppose we were being used, but for the best of reasons. I just feel an idiot for ferreting about trying to find things out when the police obviously knew all about it.'

'But they didn't at first,' said Fran. 'Because Powell was keeping a lid on it.' She frowned. 'I wonder why?'

'I don't know.' Libby hit the steering wheel. 'I can't see Connie paying him to do anything, can you? And what, exactly? Or Trevor Taylor.'

'Information,' said Fran. 'Perhaps Powell was telling Connie about rental properties. Or telling Taylor about big properties like Temptation House.'

'But why?' Libby came out at the top of the high street and turned left towards Canongate Drive.

'I don't know.' Fran sighed. 'It's all got a bit beyond me, now. Are we still going to see Jim Butler?'

'Might as well,' said Libby. 'Although what he'll be able to add, I've no idea. Seems a bit pointless I suppose.'

Libby parked outside Jim Butler's large bungalow and pointed out the new access point to the Howe Estate.

'And he and Lady Howe opened that up?' said Fran.

'Yes. And that's where he saw the Peakes going in.'

'Mmm.' Fran stared for a moment. 'Not exactly concealed, is it?'

'No.' Libby went up to the front door and rang the bell. Almost immediately, it swung open.

'Libby!' said Jim Butler, beaming.

'Jim!' said Libby. 'And Lady!' The elderly black Labrador waddled up, panting and wagging her tail.

'And this is Mrs Wolfe, isn't it?' Jim held out his hand. 'Good to meet you at last. Come in.'

Jim led them into the vast living room, with its wall of glass, at the back of the house.

'What can I get you?'

'Nothing for me, thanks,' said Libby. 'And we're sorry to drop in unannounced, but . . .'

'Oh, I knew you'd be round some time.' Jim sat down in a large, overstuffed armchair and waved a hand at the sofa. 'After your Ben called.'

'Yes.' Libby looked at Fran. 'We – er – we were wondering . . .'

'About Jenny and Eddie?' said Jim. 'Yes, well – I'm sorry I mentioned it now. The police have been asking questions.'

'Yes,' said Fran, 'but I can't believe they had anything to do with Ms Matthews' death, can you?'

'No.' Jim reached down and stroked Lady's head. 'Not sure how much you know?' He looked at Fran and then Libby.

'We know about some of the tenants she evicted,' said Libby, 'and that she was trying to buy Gleneagles.'

'Yes.' Jim nodded. 'And that lawyer you've got – he's been finding out all about that. So he'll have told you . . . ?'

'That it was illegal and the tenants have inherited it, yes,' said Fran.

'So you know about Jenny and Eddie.' Jim looked down again. 'And Beryl and Eric.'

'Beryl came to see the play at our theatre,' began Libby.

'Yes, I heard about that. And young Freddie.'

'And we've just found out about Eric,' said Fran gently.

'Ah.' Jim looked up and smiled. 'I wondered. Especially after I spoke to Ben the other day.' He sat back in his chair and Lady collapsed at his feet. 'See, he kept quiet about it, Eric did. Felt bloody guilty – pardon my French – because she came down here and started poking around.'

'Did she come down because of Eric?' asked Libby.

'Came down because she knew he lived in a big house. Course, he told her he only rented his flat and off she went. But he knew she was trying to buy some other places, like Dotty Barton's Temptation House.'

'Yes, we knew about that,' said Fran. 'So that's how she knew about Nethergate, then?'

'Guess so. But Eric said she didn't seem to know what she was doing at first. Course, he didn't know what she was doing afterwards, until people started talking about losing their homes.'

'No, we were wondering about that. How did she get the idea?' Libby was frowning.

'She had property up in London, didn't she?' Jim quirked an eyebrow.

'Ye-es, but not exactly the same,' said Libby. 'But we think the police know all about it now, although they didn't when she was first killed.'

Jim sat back, clasped his hands over his stomach and looked at the ceiling.

'Well, now,' he said. 'Let's see.' He paused for a long moment, then cleared his throat. 'Right. Now, first time she came to my attention was a few months ago. I pop in to the Sergeant now and then with Lady, and this particular day, Eric was in there – he usually is, of an evening – with Eddie Peake. Complaining about this relative of his, apparently.'

'Connie?' said Libby.

'No – not her.' Jim grinned wickedly. 'Ah! Got you there!'

Resisting the urge to say, 'Get on with it,' Libby smiled back.

'No it was his uncle, who was this Constance's dad. And he owned property up in London.'

'What!' gasped Libby.

'And Eric reckoned he should have got some of it, but instead his cousin got it all. Anyway, what had sparked him off was – this cousin had turned up in Nethergate. To see him, she said. And he reckoned she was going to buy property here – as if she hadn't got enough, he said. But she didn't seem to know what to buy. And then she tells him she's buying this pub.'

'The Crown and Sceptre,' said Fran. 'Did she say how she heard about it?'

'Don't think so,' said Jim. 'And then Eric hears she's buying up these flats. Including his own!'

'Didn't he try and talk to her?' asked Libby. 'What a rotten thing to do to your own cousin.'

'He left messages on her phone, he said, but she never came back to him. And then I heard she tried to buy Dotty Barton's house. Eric reckoned she started off trying to buy these big houses – like Gleneagles and Temptation House – and Nyebourne, o' course.'

'And then went on to smaller, privately rented properties when that didn't work?' said Fran.

'That's about the size of it,' said Jim.

'And the other man,' Libby said. 'Trevor Taylor. Have you heard about him?'

'He's the one trying to tell us all to get out of our houses so the youngsters can have 'em?' Jim threw back his head and laughed. 'What a prat. I suppose he must have managed that somewhere, but not here.'

'No, it is a bit of an idiotic idea, isn't it?' said Fran. 'Did he try that on with Miss Barton?'

'Dunno, come to think of it.' Jim sat up straight. 'Now – you sure you don't want a drink? Cup of tea?'

'Actually, I would now,' said Libby. 'Can I help?'

'No – you stay there. Won't be a mo.' Jim heaved himself up and went into the kitchen, a large room to the side of the sitting room.

'It doesn't sound as though Connie's business was quite as far-ranging as we thought,' said Libby, bending down to fondle Lady's ears.

234

'Nor Trevor Taylor's,' agreed Fran. 'I expect it all got blown up after Connie's murder.'

'Yes, but whatever it was like,' said Libby, 'it gave someone a reason to murder them.'

'You reckon it was all the holiday lets that did it?' Jim was leaning against the kitchen doorframe. 'See, I don't think there was that much bad feeling against that Matthews. People didn't know who it was. Not till after she was killed. *Then* people found out.'

'That's true.' Libby nodded. 'People didn't know who'd bought their homes and thrown them out. They probably just got a solicitor's letter, like the tenants at Gleneagles.'

'I reckon.' Jim went back to his kettle.

'So we've wasted all this time,' said Fran, 'trying to find out about rogue tenants and evil landlords, and they've got nothing to do with it.'

'Well,' said Libby, frowning, 'they must have *something* to do with it, or why were they both killed?'

Jim came back into the room carrying two mugs. 'I put milk in – is that all right? Do you want sugar?'

Both women declined, and Jim went to fetch his own mug and a biscuit for Lady.

'So Lady Howe didn't get bothered by the man – Trevor Taylor?' asked Fran.

'No, she just had the Matthews woman bothering her.' Jim shook his head. 'Couldn't understand that myself. Once Lady Howe had told the woman she was converting the whole estate, why did she bother coming back?'

'Did she talk about it much?' asked Libby.

'Nah. Doesn't talk a lot to me at all – keeps herself to herself, mostly. We talked about the right of way, o'course. She liked that idea. Said it wasn't fair to keep all the land to herself.'

'Yes, she's being remarkably generous, isn't she?' said Fran.

'Yes.' Jim frowned. 'Not like old Sir Percy.' He shrugged. 'Oh, he were all right, really, not that we saw much of him. Stayed in London most of the time. But tight! Wouldn't give you the drippings off his nose.'

'Perhaps that's why Pru feels she ought to spread it around a bit,' said Libby.

'Maybe. Old Lady Howe wouldn't have done.'

'Sir Percy's mother? Pru said she knew old Dorothy Barton.'

'Not Percy's mum – his first wife. Fenella.'

Chapter Thirty-Two

'Prudence is his second wife?' said Libby. 'I never knew that!'

'None of us did, either,' said Jim. 'Howes have been here for a couple of hundred years, but Percy went off to London. Didn't like the quiet life. His mum stayed here – she was the one who knew Dotty Barton – until she died. He came back for the funeral, with Fenella, then he buggered – sorry – off again and didn't come back until just before he died. And even then, he wanted to go back to London to die. So she hires private ambulances and what-have-you and off they go. No one invited to the funeral. We didn't even know he was gone till she tipped up back here. Didn't know Fenella had gone either, not until your Lady Pru come down with him.'

'Well!' said Fran. 'No wonder she wants to spread the wealth around – she feels guilty.'

'Because *he* didn't, you mean?' said Libby.

'Yes, exactly.' Fran finished her tea. 'You know, Lib, we ought to be going. I didn't think we were going to be out this long.'

'OK.' Libby put down her mug. 'Thank you Jim – it's been lovely seeing you and Lady, and you've given us a lot of information. Can we pass it on to the police?'

'Oh, I reckon they'll know it all already,' said Jim, levering himself to his feet, 'but help yourselves.'

He and Lady saw them to the door.

'Come by any time,' he said. 'And bring that Ben with you next time.'

'I will,' said Libby, and waved out of the window as she pulled away.

The women were silent as Libby drove them back down Canongate Drive and past Professor Andrew Wylie's penthouse flat.

'We haven't seen Andrew for a while,' said Libby. 'We ought to go and see how he's getting on.'

'Too confusing with two Andrews around at once,' said Fran. 'Wait until this case is over.'

Libby nodded. 'Edward sees him, though. And I believe he's taken Alice to tea there.'

'Wow!' said Fran. 'It's serious, then?'

'Looks like it.'

They fell silent again until Libby drew up in Harbour Street.

'What do we do now?' she said, before Fran could get out of the car.

'Tell either Rachel or Ian everything we've learnt today, even if they already knew it. And I still want to know why Sergeant Powell was keeping quiet.' Fran opened the car door. 'Are you coming in?'

'No, I'll go home.' Libby frowned out at the greying afternoon. 'I want to know about Sir Percy's Fenella, too.'

'Why?' Fran raised her eyebrows. 'She's dead.'

'I know, but I'm annoyed that we didn't know about her before.'

'Oh, Libby, for goodness' sake!' Fran got out of the car. 'Go home, light the fire and relax. This time next week panto will be starting – and no, I'm not going to audition. It's just too awkward going backwards and forwards every evening – especially if the weather gets worse.'

'Oh, OK.' Libby sighed. 'I'll ring you.'

By the time she had reached home, Libby had decided to ring Lady Pru and ask about Sir Percy and Fenella. Although she couldn't quite think of a reason why she needed the information – it was pure nosiness. And what she really needed to do was to pass on everything she and Fran had learnt today, as Fran said, either to Rachel or Ian.

Once inside, she went and collected some logs from the conservatory and lit the woodburner. And then called Ian's personal phone. To her surprise, he answered.

'I've just sat down,' he said. 'In my own sitting room. I am not in work mode.'

'Oh.' Libby was nonplussed.

Ian sighed. 'Go on, then. What do you want?'

'I just wanted to tell you something.'

'Something personal?'

'Er – not really.'

'Would you do better calling Rachel?'

'Um . . .'

There was a silence. Libby knew he was waiting for her to say something, but she had been completely wrong-footed.

'Oh, all right, you annoying woman,' he said eventually. 'Tell me.'

'OK.' Libby took a deep breath. 'Did you know that Eric Bartlett, one of the tenants who has inherited Gleneagles, is Constance Matthews' cousin?'

'Yes. Next?'

'Oh!' Libby was surprised. 'You knew!'

'Yes, of course we knew. Rachel and Claire questioned all the tenants. We've done a complete re-investigation over the last couple of days.'

'Oh. Well, you won't want to hear what we were thinking, then.'

'And what was it you were thinking?'

Libby settled back and began to recount today's events and conclusions.

'I suppose we were making bricks with straw,' she said, when she got to the end, 'but we were puzzled.'

'Not half as puzzled as we were, Libby,' said Ian. 'Rachel is feeling very guilty because she allowed Sergeant Powell to have his head, and is now frantically trying to make up for it.'

'Oh, poor Rachel,' Libby sympathised. 'Incidentally, Jim Butler was telling us about Lady Pru's background today. Did you know she was Sir Percy's second wife?'

'No!' At last, Ian sounded properly interested. 'But I suppose there was no reason for us to know it. She's not been around for long, has she?'

'No, only since Sir Percy died, really. Not that I knew him, either. Jim says he – Sir Percy – left home when he was young and didn't come back until just before he died.'

'And now Lady Howe's breaking up the estate,' said Ian. 'Very egalitarian of her.'

'You didn't take to her, did you?'

'I don't think I'd make a bosom friend of the lady, no.'

'Do you think Constance knew anything about the estate before she approached Pru? I was trying to see if there was any connection to Trevor Taylor as well, although Pru said he hadn't approached her, didn't she?'

'Did she? I can't say I can see any connection to nefarious goings-on there, anyway.'

'No,' agreed Libby. 'But Fran and I were wondering about Trevor Taylor. There doesn't seem to be any real motive for his murder, does there?'

Ian laughed. 'Don't worry, Libby, we're looking into it. Just because you can't see a motive doesn't mean there isn't one.'

'No, all right,' said Libby grumpily.

'There is something you could do for us, though.' Ian's tone changed.

'There is? What?' Libby sat up straighter.

'Have you any connections with those two places Matthews acquired in London?'

'The Raincliffe and the Furnough? Yes! Well,' Libby amended, 'certainly with the people who used to run them. I don't think I ever met Carl Robinson, but I know people who know him.'

'In that case, could you ask a few questions, for us? Strictly on the QT, of course. And don't say anything to anyone except me.'

'Of course! Is there anything particular you want to know?'

'I – we – are interested in how Matthews found out about the properties and how to get hold of them. It doesn't seem to have been her area of expertise until a few months ago.'

'Fran and I were wondering that, too,' said Libby. 'And incidentally, is that cousin of hers the heir? Will he inherit all her properties?'

'Still being looked into, Libby, I'm afraid, and not for public consumption,' said Ian, sounding amused. 'Don't push it!'

Libby called Fran.

'So who shall I call?' she said. 'Judy? She knew all about it, didn't she?'

'She talked to you, not me. But she certainly knew the Raincliffe people, because that was where her concert was going to be. So I'd try her. And perhaps Oliver? And even Sir Andrew – he was the one who first reported the London business.'

'OK, I'll give Judy a quick ring now, but I'd better not try calling anybody else after dinner, had I?'

'Better not, Lib.' Libby could hear that Fran was smiling. She chuckled in response.

'I know, overenthusiastic, that's me. I'll speak to you tomorrow. I wasn't supposed to be doing anything tomorrow, was I?'

'I don't know, Lib! When have you got your Hallowe'en celebrations?'

'Ours are on Monday, but we're going over to Pucklefield on Sunday. Are you coming up to watch?'

'Maybe. I expect Guy would like to. Anyway, call me tomorrow.'

Libby stared thoughtfully at the burning logs for a moment, then rang Judy's mobile.

'I'm in a rush, Lib – got a gig tonight.'

'OK – just wanted to know if you'd got any contacts for the Raincliffe as was, or for Carl Robinson? The police want me to have a chat,' said Libby, feeling important.

'Hold on.' Judy sounded frazzled, but came back in a moment. 'I'm sending you Carl's number and Tony Devonshire's. He was our contact at the Raincliffe. Lovely bloke. Now I must rush!'

Libby's phone pinged and there were the two numbers. She looked at the time. No, it was too late to call them now, it would have to be tomorrow. And she'd ask Ben exactly what she should say.

But she didn't get the chance.

'Is that Libby Sarjeant?' asked a pleasant male voice.

Libby gave her phone a surprised look and wiped her hands on a tea towel. Chicken and vegetables were part-chopped by the sink, and the wok sizzling gently with sesame oil.

'Yes,' she said, moving the wok to safety. 'Who's this?'

'My name's Tony Devonshire,' said the voice. 'Judy Dale gave you my number. She told me you were going to ring me and hoped I didn't mind.'

'Oh, goodness, I hope so, too,' said Libby.

'No, it's fine,' said Tony. 'I'm hoping I might find out a bit more about what exactly went on when the Raincliffe got closed down.'

'Don't you know?' Libby, surprised, sat down at the kitchen table.

'Well, yes. We'd got ourselves into a bit of financial trouble, then someone bought up our debts and closed us down. Sounds simple, doesn't it?'

'Er – yes.' Libby frowned down at the table.

'Put like that, it was, but we were given no chance to do anything else. Judy told you how we had to cancel her concert?'

'Yes, that was sad.'

'It was all sad. And we got the feeling that the person behind it was enjoying it.'

'How? I mean, how did you get that feeling? Did you meet the buyer?'

'No.' Tony heaved a frustrated sigh. 'I'm sorry, I'm not being very clear, am I? The thing is, we were left high and dry with everything in chaos. So was Carl – Judy says you know about him, too?'

'Yes, I do. Look,' Libby stood up. 'You've got me right in the middle of preparing dinner. Could we sit down and have a proper chat – perhaps a bit later this evening? Or tomorrow?'

'Oh, sorry.' Tony gave a sad little laugh. 'I was just so keen to . . . I'm sorry. Of course. Later this evening? What sort of time?'

They settled on eight o'clock, and Libby went back to her chicken and vegetables. When Ben came in, she told him what had happened and asked his advice.

'I'm not sure I understand any of this,' said Ben, pouring her a calming glass of wine. 'All these cousins, and first and second wives – it all sounds incredibly muddled. And frankly, I don't see the point of talking to these people from London either. Why does Ian want you to do that?'

'I think he wants to find out how she got involved in all these deals.' Libby perched on the table. 'So do we – Fran and me.'

'But what difference does it make? She's dead!'

'Yes, and somebody killed her. And that man Taylor. Why? There must be a link, and, if the police could find the link, they could probably find the murderer.'

'Put like that, yes, I suppose it does make a sort of sense. But what does Lady Howe have to do with any of it?'

'Oh, nothing! That was just a distraction that Jim told us about. Did you know Sir Percy had been married before?'

'No, of course not. I barely knew him – although Dad knew old Lady Howe, his mother.'

'Did Hetty know her?'

'No! Lady Howe would have looked down her nose at Mum. Now, come on, that dinner won't eat itself. And then you can sit down later and talk your head off to your theatrical type and leave me in possession of the TV, for once.'

Chapter Thirty-Three

Tony Devonshire rang back at exactly eight o'clock. Libby was sitting at the kitchen table with a cup of tea and her notebook.

'I suppose first of all,' she said, 'I'd better tell you why I wanted to talk to you.'

'Judy said something about the police?' Tony was hesitant.

'That's right.' She fell back on Fran's invariable explanation. 'My friend and I occasionally act as special advisors to our local force, and as this particular inquiry was to do with theatre, we were asked to help.'

'Oh – are you . . . ?'

'Both ex, although I help run a theatre,' explained Libby. 'Although much smaller than the Raincliffe.' She paused. 'The Raincliffe Old Time Music Halls would have been before your time, I suppose.'

'Oh, really? Did you do them?' Tony sounded delighted. 'That was my dad! Tommy Town – do you remember him?'

'Old Tommy? No! Of course I remember him!' Libby caught herself up. 'But I don't want to get sidetracked and waste your time.'

'Time's what I've got plenty of,' said Tony, 'but no, I see your point. So what exactly did you want to know?'

'How did Constance Matthews come to get involved with the Raincliffe? She was a theatre director, but I wouldn't have thought she had anything to do with you.'

'No.' Tony sighed. 'As you obviously know, we're a smallish hall, and we concentrated mainly on music hall, variety and small-scale musicals in the old days. I took over, with my brother, when Dad died, and we tried to make it pay. But we couldn't attract large-scale productions and the sort of thing that used to be our bread and butter had gone out of fashion. Even the music halls that did survive have gone now, more's the pity.'

They were both quiet for a minute.

'So, anyway, we staggered on,' said Tony, 'and began to build up a rep for medium-scale concerts.'

'Like Judy's,' said Libby.

'Exactly. But we weren't making a real profit, and we had to keep borrowing, although we were pretty sure we could get back on an even keel given half a chance. And then the Matthews woman arrived.'

'She came to see you? I'm surprised she knew about you. She was always rather snobbish about all things theatrical. Disapproved of the Hackney Empire, for instance.'

'Oh, yes, she knew about us. We had a mutual acquaintance, according to her. From what we could gather, it was an ex-performer – like yourself!' Tony allowed a chuckle to escape. 'It *wasn't* you, I suppose?'

'No, it certainly wasn't!' said Libby. 'She didn't give you any more clues?'

'She sort of hinted it was someone with a title – or someone who was part of a titled family, anyway. I don't know how true that was. Probably not at all. Anyway, there she was, saying she was thinking of hiring the theatre for a one-off production.' Tony made an explosive sound. 'All sweetness and light, she was. And when we said we couldn't afford the sort of lighting rig she was asking for, she said she'd bring it in. Got all our details, including our solicitor's name and address.'

'And that was just a ploy?'

'It was. Next thing, we get a letter via our solicitors, telling us she'd bought up our debts. I didn't know you were allowed to do that.'

'Neither did I until now. She did it to Carl, too, didn't she?'

'Yes, exactly the same – except she posed as Carl's guardian angel, helping him out of a hole.'

'Did someone introduce her to you?' asked Libby. 'What we can't understand is how she got into the business. She had no background in land deals or property, as far as we know.'

'But she knew theatre,' said Tony. 'And she's old school – knew us and the Furnough. We were part of the landscape, weren't we?'

'But how did she know about buying up debts, that sort of thing?'

'We-ell,' Tony said slowly, 'I don't know whether it's relevant, but Carl said he'd had a debt collector on his back before she arrived. And the debt collector was working for the company – loan sharks, I should say – who he'd borrowed from in the first place.'

'Ah!' Libby sat back in her chair. 'That's it, then. And she went to Carl before she came to you?'

'Yes, but how would she have known the debt collector?' Tony sounded puzzled.

'Yes, that's a point,' said Libby. 'I suppose I'd better ring Carl. Judy gave me his number.'

'Could you let me ask him?' said Tony. 'Poor sod's still sofa-surfing, and he's in a bit of a fragile state.'

'Yes, if you think that would be best. I don't want to intrude.' Libby paused. 'Like I did with you.'

Tony laughed. 'You didn't – I rang you. And I'm sorry if I was pushy. I'm still smarting, to be honest. Steve – that's my brother – and I were lucky to keep our homes after we lost the Raincliffe, and I'm still looking for answers. Well, excuses, really. I can't believe we were so idiotic.'

'But you don't expect people to be that – well – underhand, do you?' said Libby. 'And although we can't get the Raincliffe back, there are a lot of people hoping to get the Furnough up and running again, even if it isn't in the same building.'

'So I believe,' said Tony with a sigh. 'But without big names . . .'

'Well, we've got a couple of Sirs,' said Libby. 'Andrew McColl and Jasper Stone. And I'm pretty sure Max Tobin would get involved.'

'Really? Max Tobin? Of Tobin Dance? That's pretty high-flying.' There was a short silence. 'Well! You do know some important folk.'

'You know what it's like in the business. You get to know a lot of people. I'll let them all know I've talked to you.' Libby checked the time. 'Right – well, it's Friday night, and I've held you up for long enough. Will you ask Carl to ring me? Or ring me yourself when you've spoken to him?'

'Of course, and thank you so much, Libby.' Tony paused and cleared his throat. 'You've made me feel a lot better.'

'The trouble is,' said Ben when she'd repeated this conversation to him, 'you so-called "creatives" aren't necessarily good business brains. And so much is taken on trust, or done on a shoestring, that someone like Connie won't even register.'

'But there were always evil tour managers and people like that,' said Libby. 'Think how many times a company didn't get paid on tour, or at the end of a week.'

'Things are different now,' said Ben, 'with proper contracts and so on.'

'And the Musicians' Union for musos,' said Libby. 'Which makes me wonder why Judy and her crowd weren't protected when the concert got pulled.'

'Whatever the rights and wrongs, it looks as though you've got a lead on how Connie started getting interested in property,' said Ben, 'and what's the betting—'

'I know what you're going to say,' said Libby. 'What's the betting that Trevor Taylor was the debt collector?'

Saturday morning and Libby realised, regretfully, that a trip to the supermarket in Canterbury was required. Mostly, she was able to

248

rely on Ahmed and Ali's eight-till-late, Bob the butcher and Nella's farm shop, but now and then both she and Hetty needed a wider resource.

Before she left, she called Ian, but his private mobile went straight to voicemail. She left a brief message, gathered shopping bags, basket and cape and went out to the car. She was halfway to Canterbury when her phone rang.

'Ian,' she said.

'Where are you?'

'In the car on the way to Canterbury.'

'You're not driving, are you?'

Libby smiled. 'No, I've pulled in. I'm quite sensible, really.'

'Right.' Ian didn't sound convinced. 'Did you have something to tell me?'

Libby repeated the gist of her conversation with Tony Devonshire.

'Look, why don't you come in to the station when you get here? Are you in a rush?' Ian sounded positively friendly.

'OK. Before I go shopping, all right? Because of frozen food.'

'Fine. I'll see you in – what? Twenty minutes?'

Now why was this? Libby asked herself. The last time she had been to the police station to see Ian was with Ricky back in May, and before that she couldn't remember.

When she arrived, Ian himself came down to reception to meet her and take her back to his office.

'What's up?' she asked, as she settled into the chair opposite his desk.

'Nothing.' Ian steepled his fingers and put his head on one side. 'I just thought we should pool resources.'

'You – *what?*' Libby stared at him, open-mouthed.

Ian laughed. 'Is it that unusual?'

'Yes! And you got sent on gardening leave the last time you used Fran and me.'

'And now that I've managed to get rid of not only DI Winter but

Sergeant Powell as well, the powers-that-be are leaving me alone. Except that they would rather like me to go for promotion.'

'To superintendent? Haven't you refused that before?'

'I have. And it's becoming more difficult. But I do not want to be completely office-bound. At the moment I can still get out on the ground to a degree.' He pressed a buzzer on his desk and asked for coffee. 'And now, tell me again what this Tony Devonshire said.'

Libby obediently repeated the story, with slightly more detail.

'So your conclusion is that Trevor Taylor was the debt collector?' said Ian, when she'd finished.

'Well, Ben and I thought it was a – um – a workable hypothesis.'

Ian regarded her solemnly for a moment. 'And you'd be right.'

'Wha . . .?' Libby gaped. 'We were right?'

'We found where he was staying – in one of Matthews' holiday lets, incidentally – and there was enough there for us to confirm his identity. We already had it, as his murderer had conveniently left his phone in his pocket.'

'So were he and Connie in cahoots?'

'It looks like it. They each had the other's number in their phones – although there are no messages on either.'

'Canny,' said Libby.

'Indeed. But we still don't know exactly how they came to be in touch with one another. That was what I was hoping we might find out from your contacts.'

Libby frowned down at the desk. The door opened and a uniformed constable appeared with two paper cups of coffee.

'Sorry – the coffee machines and china cups of the detective novels don't seem to have made it to Canterbury.' Ian gave her a wry smile.

'What I want to know,' said Libby, ignoring the coffee, 'is how she knew about the Crown and Sceptre. We know now that her cousin Eric was her introduction – however unintended – to

Nethergate, and it looks to me as though *she* brought *Taylor* down, not the other way round, but how did she find out about the pub? Pubs weren't exactly her scene, so how could she have known?'

'Does it matter?' asked Ian. 'There was nothing underhand about the purchase; it was perfectly straightforward. In fact, all her purchases were. She simply used no-fault evictions to get rid of sitting tenants. And most of the properties she bought from private landlords – with one or two exceptions, because mortgage rates have doubled and the smaller landlords can't afford their buy-to-let properties any more.'

'Except for Gleneagles,' said Libby. 'She was pulling a fast one there.'

'She was,' agreed Ian, 'but she knew about that because her cousin lived there. And no, Lib, for some reason we still haven't found a will.'

'What about her solicitors?'

'The only ones we've found dealt only with her property deals. And searches of her house have revealed nothing.'

'Really? We wondered if Taylor had tried his tricks on her – you know, buying her house to sell on.'

'Not as far as we can see. And the house – what's it called?' He looked at his computer screen and tapped the mouse. 'Pendlebury Lodge. It was a family house. Her father inherited it, and several other properties in the area. Her solicitors had details of them all.'

'And no will.' Libby shook her head. 'That's weird.'

'It is.' Ian nodded. 'And how did she manage to find her accomplice?'

'Accomplice? Oh – you mean the heavy! Did none of the ladies recognise a face?'

'No. But Lady Howe's builder did.'

'Really?'

Ian grinned. 'Don't be so ghoulish! Yes, he did. Apparently he was a local bad boy – although not very bad. Got into all sorts of scrapes at school, got done for affray, small-time dealing, that sort of thing. But again – how did she find him?'

'She must have had a contact in the area,' said Libby. 'Are you sure it wasn't her cousin?'

'As far as we can see, Eric Bartlett has never put a foot wrong in his life.' Ian sipped his coffee and made a face. 'So we've come up against a brick wall.'

'Someone must have been pulling her strings,' said Libby.

'Or she was pulling someone else's,' said Ian.

Chapter Thirty-Four

'Pru, have you got a minute?'

Libby had put the shopping away, eaten a supermarket sandwich and lit the woodburner.

'Yes – what's up?' Prudence sounded tired.

'We've been trying to find out a bit more about why Constance Matthews came down to Nethergate.'

'Who's we?'

'The police and – well – Fran and me.'

'Does it matter?' asked Prudence.

'People keep saying that,' said Libby, 'but it does, because if we – or the police – know that, they might be able to find the murderer.'

'What about the other person they found? Taylor, was it?'

'Yes – same thing applies,' said Libby.

'I suppose so. Well, I don't know.'

'She gave you no idea how she'd come to hear about you?'

'Oh.' There was a pause. 'Actually, yes.' Another pause. 'She did say something. Now. What was it?'

Libby could hear movement. 'I'm just looking for that letter . . . wait a sec . . . Here?'

'You found it?'

'Yes! Here we are.' Libby heard rustling. 'Former husband . . . blah blah . . . Lady Howe . . .'

'Lady Howe? The previous Lady Howe?'

'One of them, yes.'

'I didn't know until the other day that you were the second Lady Howe.'

'In this generation, yes. Percy was married before.'

'Yes. So this letter mentions the first?'

'I assume so. It seems to say the Matthews woman knew her. Or possibly Percy's mother.'

'So she knew about the estate? And I suppose that was enough to get her interested in Nethergate as a whole.'

'I suppose so. Seems a bit tenuous to me though.'

'Did you not show this letter to the police?' asked Libby.

'No – should I have done? I didn't see the point. They knew she'd been to see me – that was why your inspector had me down as a suspect.'

'Yeah, I guess,' said Libby with a sigh. 'I wonder how she knew your predecessor – Fenella, was it?'

'Yes – the sainted Fenella.' Prudence laughed. 'Definitely Percy's mum's favourite. I was much too common!'

'Common? You?' Libby joined in the laughter. 'What happened to Fenella?'

'She died – ooh, years ago. Before Percy's mum. And I don't think she was as white as she was painted. She knew some very dodgy people.'

'Really? Including Connie Matthews?'

'Looks like it, doesn't it?' Prudence sounded slightly more lively now. 'Shall I see if I can find anything out?'

'Could you? How?'

'Everything's been moved down here from the London house, so I expect I could find some stuff. All Percy's stuff from his study is boxed up in the attic. I'll have a poke around—' Lady Pru stopped, suddenly. 'Hey – I bet I know!'

'What?'

'Fenella was a gambler! That bloke was a debt collector, wasn't he? I bet she had gambling debts! That's it! I bet you!' Prudence gave a crow of triumph.

'But I thought Sir Percy was wealthy? Or not short of a few bob, anyway,' said Libby.

'He was – but I know she didn't tell him about all her debts. He told me.'

'I wish I'd known all this before,' said Libby. 'I can tell the police, can't I?'

'As long as it isn't that Sergeant Powell! He's gone though, hasn't he?'

'I think so,' said Libby, not sure how much she was allowed to say.

'Do you know what's going to happen to all the flats that woman bought up?' Prudence now sounded as though she was settling in for a chat.

'No, not yet,' said Libby.

'She must have left a will? I know she was a lonely old . . . but she must have had family of some sort. Cousins, if she didn't have any immediate family?'

'I suppose she must have done,' said Libby, feeling a bit uncomfortable. 'Look, I'll let you know what the police say. I expect Ian – Detective Inspector Connell – will want to come and see you again.'

'Oh, OK – perhaps not this weekend, though. I'm supposed to be going up to town.'

'Monday?'

'Yes, that'll be fine. Will you come too?'

'If he lets me!' Libby laughed.

She ended the call, put the kettle on and called Ian.

'Stupid bloody women!' he complained. 'Why on earth didn't she tell us this in the beginning?'

'She said she didn't see the point. You knew Connie had been to see her, she just didn't see any reason to go into it any further.'

Ian sighed. 'I suppose we'd better go into this Fenella, now. And it's the bloody weekend.'

'So?'

'People stop working at weekends!' said Ian and ended the call.

'And thank you very much!' said Libby, and made her tea.

Fran was sympathetic.

'I'd say come down here for the evening, but I guess Ben might be rehearsing again?'

'No, I think he's got tonight off. We're off to Pucklefield tomorrow.'

'Well, let me know if you want to come down,' said Fran. 'Don't worry if you don't.'

But Ben wanted to stay in Steeple Martin.

'We've been gadding about a lot recently,' he said, 'and we've got two days of Morris performances coming up, so I'd really rather stay home, if you don't mind. We could pop out for a drink, if you like?'

'We've been doing a lot of that, recently, too,' said Libby with a smile. 'We could just stay in and watch telly.'

'If there's anything worth watching.' Ben sighed.

'We do have streaming services, you know,' said Libby. 'I'm sure we'll find something.'

They were halfway through an old episode of *Midsomer Murders* when Libby's phone rang.

'Is that Libby?' a hesitant female voice asked. 'I don't know if you remember me? Karen Butler?'

Karen Butler? Libby racked her brain – and remembered.

'Karen – yes, of course, Miss Barton's tenant. What can I do for you?'

'It's Miss Barton I'm ringing for, actually. She wondered if you could possibly come over and see her?'

'Really? At Temptation House? Did she say why?' Libby sent Ben a puzzled look. He paused the programme.

'I think it's about this Miss Matthews business. The police have been to see her, but she doesn't really like the police.' Karen laughed softly. 'I think she feels they should use the servants' entrance, if you know what I mean.'

'I see,' said Libby. 'When does she want to see me?'

'I don't suppose tomorrow would be convenient?'

'Tomorrow?'

Ben was frowning.

'I know it's Sunday, but . . .'

'I could come over in the morning,' said Libby, 'but I'm busy for the rest of the day, and on Monday.'

'Oh, dear,' said Karen. 'There's church on Sunday morning . . .'

'She attends St Aldeberge, doesn't she? The Reverend Pearson's a friend of mine.'

'Yes. Well, she's usually home by eleven thirty . . .'

'I'll be there at eleven thirty, then,' said Libby, 'but I won't be able to stay longer than about three-quarters of an hour.'

'Oh, dear,' said Karen.

'It's that or nothing.' Libby was beginning to feel irritated.

'All right, thank you. Do you know where we are?'

'Yes,' said Libby, who actually didn't. 'I'll see you then.'

'What was all that about?' asked Ben, standing up to refill their glasses. Libby explained.

'You could have just said no.'

'But she might have something important to tell us.'

'Then she should have told the police,' said Ben.

Sunday morning dawned grey and blustery.

'Take my car,' said Ben, surveying the weather. 'Or would you like me to come with you?'

'No, you've got a busy couple of days, I'll be fine. And I'll be back by one for lunch.' Libby gave him a kiss and ran across the road to the big four-by-four. Ben was right, in windy weather it felt a lot safer than her little Silver Bullet.

He had shown her how to programme details into the on-board satnav, so she knew where she was going, and it wasn't exactly difficult. Temptation House actually stood on the Nethergate to St Aldeberge road, with which Libby was very familiar. So she allowed her brain to wander as she drove, all the new information she'd received having been percolating overnight.

Prudence's information first. The odd circumstance of Connie's letter. Why hadn't Pru mentioned it to the police? And how did she know Sergeant Powell had gone? If that meant she knew he was off the case, that is. And why did she mention Connie's cousin? And Fenella. Why had she kept that quiet? Presumably because a problem gambler was rather a blot on the family escutcheon.

Then there were Tony's revelations. That Connie had not only heard of the Raincliffe, but had some kind of titled connection with it. That sounded like Fenella, and did make sense of Trevor Taylor's involvement as a debt collector. But how it all fitted together – who knew?

She pulled in to the gravelled drive of Temptation House at twenty-five past eleven, got out of the car and walked back across the road to peer out at the ill-tempered sea. Within five minutes, another car pulled up behind her.

'Hello, Libby,' said Karen, holding open the passenger door of the vintage Humber that now stood beside the four-by-four. She held out a hand to help her passenger, a small round bundle of black cloth and tired fur.

'Mrs Sarjeant?' asked the bundle, and held out her own hand. 'I'm Dorothy Barton. How d'you do?'

Libby, remembering the manners of the early previous century, shook the hand and repeated the greeting. Dorothy Barton gave her an approving nod.

'Come along in, then,' she said and led the way to the front door, leaving Karen to help Nora out of the back seat of the Humber.

'What a lovely car,' said Libby, as they entered the cold, tiled hall.

'Thank you. It was my father's. I have a very good mechanic who keeps it running despite its age,' said Miss Barton. 'Much as my doctor does for me.' She sent Libby a mischievous smile. Libby decided she liked Miss Barton.

By this time, Nora and Karen had joined them.

'I'll just take off my coat, Dot, then I'll come and make you coffee,' said Nora, scurrying to the imposing staircase.

'Do you need me, Dot?' asked Karen, going to follow her friend.

'No, thank you, Karen. And thank you for driving, as always.'

Libby followed Miss Barton through a door beside the staircase and found herself in the hallway of what appeared to be a small apartment.

'Just bed, bath, living and kitchen,' said Miss Barton, seeing her guest's interest. 'All I need, so it makes sense to let other people use the rest of the house, don't you agree?'

'I do,' said Libby.

'Take your coat off and come and sit down, then.' Miss Barton led the way into a bright sitting room and switched on an imitation log fire. 'Much easier and cleaner than the real thing,' she said, 'but I do like to see the flames.'

They sat either side of the fire, and Libby heard Nora come into the flat and, presumably, go into the kitchen.

'Nora and Karen told me they met you at the Blue Anchor?' Miss Barton looked like a small bird, her head on one side and her eyes bright.

'I did, Miss Barton. Mavis is a friend of mine.'

'A good woman – and, please, call me Dorothy.' She smiled. 'My niece calls me Aunt Dotty, but I feel that has unfortunate connotations. I believe you know Hannah, too, don't you? I'm surprised we haven't met before.'

'So am I,' said Libby. 'I know the vicar at your church, too.'

'Ah, yes.' Dorothy frowned slightly. 'Another good woman, but I'm still coming to terms with that. I'm so very old, you see.' She twinkled at Libby.

'Coming to terms with female clergy, or Patti's lifestyle?' Libby dared to ask.

'Both, in a way. Oh, I'm opposed to neither, it's simply that I was brought up with centuries of male tradition in all the Christian churches, and when I was young, the existence of female homosexuality was never even considered. But of course it went on – think of Radclyffe Hall and *The Well of Loneliness* – although there were those so-called experts who tried to say that both male and female homosexuals were actually a separate species!' Dorothy sat up straighter, looking indignant, while Libby looked on with an appreciative smile. Yes, she did like Dorothy Barton.

'But that is not what I wanted to discuss with you, enjoyable though the discussion would undoubtedly be.' Dorothy looked down at her hands and paused.

'You wanted to tell me about Constance Matthews?' Libby prompted after a moment.

'Indeed.' Dorothy looked up. 'The police have talked to me, of course, a rather unpleasant man first and then, in the last couple of days, a young woman.'

'Sergeant Powell would have been the male officer,' suggested Libby. 'The young woman might have been Acting Inspector Rachel Trent.'

'Exactly right.' Dorothy looked up over Libby's shoulder. 'Ah, here's Nora with the coffee.'

Nora put down a venerable-looking tray with two very modern-looking coffee cups on a small table.

'We like old-fashioned white coffee,' she said. 'I hope you don't mind, Libby?'

'Not at all, thank you, Nora,' said Libby.

Nora smiled, bobbed her head and retreated. This was obviously to be a tête-à-tête.

'I asked to speak to you,' Dorothy continued, 'because I'm not sure how much to say to the police. Or how much they already know.'

'About Ms Matthews? Or about her death?'

'About Ms Matthews, yes, I suppose so. But mainly why I believe she was killed.'

260

Chapter Thirty-Five

'Why . . .?' repeated Libby.

Dorothy picked up her cup and settled back in her chair. 'You knew she approached me hoping to buy this house?'

'Yes, I heard.'

'Stupid, really. She obviously hadn't done her research, or she would have realised that I had already turned this house into – what do they call them? – flatlets, and hardly needed any further income. But of course the man Taylor tried the same thing, assuming I would be green enough to let him sell the house and take most of the profit.' The old lady shook her head. 'Honestly! These people think dementia is an inevitable side effect of ageing.'

'I know a whole group of people in my village who prove that isn't the case,' said Libby, sipping her own coffee. It wasn't bad – for coffee.

Dorothy nodded. 'Be that as it may, neither of them made any headway with me. Constance went on to buy several of the existing holiday homes, as you know, and, unfortunately, several properties with sitting tenants. I believe the cost of living has made second-home owners think twice about their properties, and many were only too glad to sell to Constance. Taylor didn't manage to sell his "homes for the young" project, despite hanging on to her coat-tails.'

'Ah!' said Libby. 'It was that way round, was it? We – and the police – wondered if *he* had introduced *her* to the property business.'

Dorothy sent her a bright, penetrating look. 'Do you know what Taylor's business was?'

'He had a website as an estate agent,' said Libby.

'But before that?'

'He was a debt collector, wasn't he?'

Dorothy looked triumphant. 'He was. And he worked for a company whom Constance employed.'

'Really?' Libby gasped. 'We know she loaned money to places in London . . .'

'And what I'm sure our local police force haven't found out is that she had been doing it for a long time.'

Libby was gobsmacked. 'So it wasn't a new thing? She'd been doing this for – what? Years?'

'She had.' Dorothy sipped more coffee.

'Dorothy, forgive me – but you're referring to Ms Matthews as "Constance". Does that mean you knew her before she arrived here?' Libby almost held her breath.

'Oh, yes, my dear. For many years.' Dorothy allowed a small smile to play on her lips. 'And I'm sorry – I'm allowing myself to enjoy this.'

Libby laughed. 'I'm not surprised! You've stolen a march on all of us.'

'I didn't mean to.' Dorothy shook her head. 'But it has become apparent that the police aren't making headway, and one cannot allow murder to go unpunished, however unpleasant the victim might be.'

'No, of course not,' said Libby, suppressing a smile. 'May I ask how you knew Constance?'

'My parents knew her parents. They were on visiting terms, and Constance used to come with them. Of course, she was younger than I, so we never became friendly. But we mixed in the same circles.'

'I understand you also knew the Howe family?' asked Libby. 'Did the Matthews family know them, too?'

'Well spotted, Libby!' Dorothy put her cup down.

Libby was beginning to see a glimmer of light. 'So Constance knew the Howe Estate before she came to Nethergate?'

'In the same way that she knew Temptation House.' Dorothy nodded. 'She didn't arrive in the area by accident. She had been lending money in theatrical circles for some time, you see. And the company Taylor worked for had been collecting her debts for most of that time. The two instances reported to you and the police were the biggest she had attempted, though. Most of the others were to individuals.'

'What a monster.' Libby shook her head. 'And did she buy rental properties back then, too?'

'I don't know. I believe, sadly, that it was this house that gave her the idea for her holiday business. She wrote to me – oh, long before I told any of my tenants – and told me she was going to buy some property in the town. I believe you know her father owned property in the area?'

'I had heard.'

'She realised she could make money in the holiday market.' Dorothy looked towards the window and blinked. 'And then she thought of Howe.'

'Prudence said she didn't know her,' said Libby. 'She said she didn't know you, either, although her mother-in-law did.'

'You're referring to Lady Howe?' Dorothy looked back at Libby. 'Yes, Prudence.'

Dorothy smiled gently. 'But she isn't, you see, my dear.'

This bombshell completely silenced Libby, who sat stunned.

'If you weren't driving, Libby, I would offer you what we used to call a bracer,' said Dorothy. 'And I believe you have an appointment? You told Karen you had to leave by a quarter past twelve?'

'Er – yes – I have a lunch appointment with my family,' stuttered Libby.

'Well, let me give you a quick outline. I should have just told you straight away.' Dorothy tutted. 'I was enjoying myself, you see. I told you.'

'Yes.' Libby shook herself and cleared her throat. 'I'm rather taken aback. You mean Prudence is not Lady Howe? But the locals remember her coming down with Sir Percy?'

'Yes, my dear. She is – was – that wonderful old-fashioned thing – his mistress. And after Fenella died, she just moved in.' Dorothy sighed. 'I'm not saying she's a bad person, she isn't, and she looked after Percy very well. But she is not his widow. And, as far as I'm aware, she is not entitled to do as she is doing with the estate.'

'Oh, no!' Libby gasped. 'But it's such a *good* thing!'

'Indeed it is.' Dorothy nodded. 'But it strikes me, Libby, that it gave Constance something she could hold over Prudence.'

'She was blackmailing her?' Libby stared, open-mouthed.

'Maybe. I don't know. It also strikes me that Constance may not have known that Prudence wasn't entitled – if you'll pardon the pun – to the estate, and thought it was hers to sell.'

Libby stared into the fire.

'How do you think Constance found the – um – bodyguard who came with her?'

'I don't know, dear. But I'm pretty sure she had a connection to – what did you call him? – Sergeant Powell.'

Libby transferred her gaze to Dorothy. 'And do you think . . .?' she began.

'I don't know, my dear. But I know all is not as it seems, and the police should know what I know. I'm sorry to have burdened you with it, but I'm sure you're far better placed than I to put it before them.'

Libby nodded. 'And I shall.' She sighed and stood up. 'Do Karen and Nora know all of this?'

Dorothy shook her head. 'They know I know something, but not what. I have been loath to put a spoke, as they say, into the plans for the Howe Estate.' She stood up. 'Thank you very much for coming to see me, Libby, and I hope I shall see you again. I believe you said you know many old ladies in your village?'

'I didn't put it quite like that,' said Libby, 'but yes. If you would like to meet them, you would be very welcome.' She picked up her coat. 'Fenella – you knew her?'

'Yes, I did. Poor Fenella.' Dorothy looked solemn. 'She was troubled.'

'She gambled?' suggested Libby tentatively.

Dorothy looked surprised. 'Oh, no. She didn't gamble! That was Prudence.'

Dorothy saw her to the door. There was no sign of Nora or Karen.

'Will you let me know the outcome, please?' Dorothy held out her hand. Libby shook it. One did not kiss Dorothy Barton.

'Of course,' she said, and climbed into the car.

She drove as far as the turning for the Island View caravan park and pulled in.

'Ian?'

'Libby? Are you all right? Are you not at the Manor for lunch?'

'I will be.' Libby swallowed and rubbed her forehead. 'I've got something to tell you.'

And Libby repeated everything Dorothy Barton had told her.

Then she sent a text to Ben apologising for being late for lunch, and drove on. The meeting with Dorothy Barton had been both revealing and shocking, and she needed to rethink practically the whole Constance Matthews scenario.

Prudence Howe was not Prudence Howe. And Connie had obviously known she wasn't. Or at least, that was the inference. And Prudence was the gambler, not the troubled Fenella. And had Connie known that, too? If she had, that would be something else to hold over Prudence's head – but to force her to do what?

Libby turned in to the Steeple Martin road. Of course, no one knew what, exactly, Connie and Prudence had talked about, because Connie died. Would she have forced Prudence to give up the estate? If Dorothy was right, the estate wasn't Prudence's to sell – in which case, whose was it? And – the crucial question – had Prudence killed Connie?

She passed the turning that led to the Tyne Chapel and glanced over to it, half expecting to see Prudence emerging. The Tyne Chapel brought Trevor Taylor to mind, and that led to another question. Why had he been killed? And by whom? Prudence didn't have a connection with him, although –

Libby trod involuntarily on the brake. Had Taylor, in his role as debt collector, been sent after Prudence for gambling debts? Except, of course, that gambling debts were usually enforced by— She swerved. Heavies. Is that how Connie had got hold of her 'accomplice'?

'I don't believe this,' she said out loud. It didn't seem fair that with one fell swoop all her questions had been answered. Was there anything she had heard in the last two weeks that might have given a clue as to what had really happened? Constance herself had given no indication that she even knew the area, let alone anyone in it, although Libby had wondered how she'd known that she herself lived here. Yes, she said to herself, she had wondered that. Even asked Connie. And then the fact that she'd taken herself off to Nethergate – on a whim? Suspicious, surely. Then there was Connie's family connection. Maybe if the police had known at the beginning about Eric Bartlett, they may have been able to piece something together.

Then there was Prudence, who had been almost hysterical when the body had been found, and had wanted Libby to hold her hand. Had she really wanted Libby as protection? She had also not been exactly delighted to see Ian, and had veered away from the mention of Trevor Taylor. Although at the time, that wouldn't have raised any eyebrows.

And lastly, Sergeant Powell. It looked as though he was in somebody's pocket – but whose? Connie? Or Prudence? Of course, he was well placed to divert any penetrating inquiries – and to shield, perhaps, the 'accomplice'. Again, he was in a good position to recruit someone like that. But had he? Libby heaved a great sigh and dropped down to Steeple Martin high street. This was all speculation, and Ian, Rachel and the rest of the local police force now had all the facts, so there was nothing left for her to do. Except go to the Manor for lunch. And only slightly late.

She only took notice of the anonymous white van parked at the end of Allhallow's Lane when she realised that her front door was open. A surge of adrenalin hit her system as she bent to look at the splintered wood, and she found herself fumbling for her phone. Under the pretext of investigating her broken doorframe, she pressed Ben's number and dropped the phone on to the second stair.

She was unsurprised to see Prudence standing in the kitchen doorway, but slightly more surprised – and scared – to see a very large man standing behind her.

'Pru,' she said. 'I suppose Prudence *is* your real name? Even if Howe isn't?'

'You've been to see Dorothy Barton,' said Prudence, her voice shaky. 'Oh, Libby! Why did you have to do that?'

'She asked to see me. She said she didn't think you were a bad person.' Libby nodded at the silent presence in the kitchen. 'Although I don't think she'd say the same about your friend. And was he *your* friend? Or Constance Matthews' employee?'

The accomplice, for Libby had guessed this was he, shifted slightly and grunted.

'Does it matter?' Prudence pushed distractedly at her escaping hair.

'Is he a debt collector?' asked Libby, still striving to sound normal and stay upright, although her legs were threatening to give way any minute.

'Yes!' Prudence shrieked. 'Stop asking questions! You've got to shut up. You're not supposed to be asking questions.'

'I'm supposed to be scared? Are you going to k-kill me?' Libby was beginning to lose the ability to speak normally. 'Or what?'

'*I don't know*!' That was Pru's familiar wail, and Libby realised that she really *didn't* know, and any decisions would be left to the accomplice, which was *not* a good idea. So, keep her talking. That *was* a good idea.

'Why did you do it, Pru? The Howe Estate project was going to be such a wonderful thing for the community. Why spoil it?'

Pru's face crumpled. 'I wanted to do something good! And I thought if I could turn the estate over to people who needed homes, no one would look at me. And then that bloody Matthews woman turns up and threatens to tell everyone I wasn't married to Percy. She'd even got hold of a copy of his will!'

'How?'

'They used the same solicitor. Percy didn't know he was bent – although perhaps he wasn't until Connie and that Taylor person got hold of him.'

'And did the solicitor have Connie's will, too?'

'Yes.' Pru looked triumphant. 'And I've got that now, too.'

'And so you killed her.' Libby shook her head. 'Oh, Pru!'

Prudence's face darkened. 'You see what it's like to be broke and have gorillas like this' – she jerked her head – 'threatening to break your legs.'

'I can see it would focus the mind,' said Libby croakily.

'Stop trying to be funny!' Pru was shrieking again, which was quite a good thing, thought Libby, as it covered the sound of someone coming quietly in through the conservatory. The first Prudence knew about it was when the accomplice uttered a string of profanities and kicked her in the shins.

Then it was all over. Two police constables had hold of the accomplice, and Rachel Trent and Mark Alleyn had moved up beside Prudence, while Ian and Ben arrived through the front door. Libby sank on to a chair at the table.

'Well done with the phone thing again,' said Ian. 'Very quick-thinking.'

'I just wish,' said Ben shakily, 'that she didn't *have* to keep doing it!'

'I didn't know if it would work again,' said Libby, through dry lips. 'Did you phone Ian, Ben?'

'He did – and we were already on the move after your phone call, Lib,' said Ian. 'Especially as former Sergeant Powell had already identified Asa Marten.'

'Is that . . .?'

'The bodyguard, yes,' said Ian. 'Making sure Prudence Holliday didn't say the wrong thing.'

'He wasn't working for her?' Ben was holding Libby's hand so tightly it was beginning to hurt.

'In a way he was. Look – I'll tell you all about it tomorrow. I'll meet you in the Pocket after your celebrations.' Ian bent to give Libby a kiss. 'And someone will come and take a statement, Lib. So relax.'

Epilogue

Libby wisely opted out of accompanying the Steeple Martin Morris to Pucklefield that evening, but refused to allow Ben to stay behind with her. Instead she spent the evening with Peter and Harry, in her favourite saggy chintz chair, being plied with good red wine.

The following day, after she'd given her statement to PC Mark Alleyn, who confided he was about to be made up to detective constable – if he passed the exam – she spent calling everyone she needed to and telling them the surprising outcome of the investigation into Constance Matthews' murder.

'We'll hear the rest from Ian tonight, he says,' she told Fran, 'so you are coming up to watch the Morris, aren't you?'

'Try and keep us away,' said Fran. 'But won't Ben be upset if we all adjourn after the dancing?'

'No, Ian says we'll stay in the Pocket. We'll go down the back end and leave the revellers at the front. The piano's there, anyway.'

Steeple Martin Morris danced through the village that evening, accompanied by the Tolley Hound, played by Colley the dog in his special decorated harness. They finished by dancing outside the Hop Pocket, after which everyone piled inside to where Peter and Harry had supplied an abundance of food. After an interval for food and drink, John Cole, with very little persuasion, sat down at the piano, despite having played his piano accordion for the last hour and a half. Ian, who had appeared at the end of the dancing, moved unobtrusively down to the end of the pub, followed by Libby, Fran, Ben and Guy.

'I don't want to drag you away, Ben,' he said, 'but I do need to fill in the blanks for Libby, particularly.'

'We all want to know, Ian,' said Fran. 'There are lots of unanswered questions.'

'Not any more,' said Ian, grinning at Libby. 'Once Dorothy Barton had unburdened herself to Libby we knew more or less what had happened.'

'Did you?' asked Libby, wide-eyed. 'I was still trying to piece it all together when I found them in my house.'

'From the beginning, then,' said Ian. 'Has everyone got a drink?'

When everyone's drinks had been replenished, courtesy of the management, Ian embarked on his usual Poirot-style round-up.

'First of all, I suppose,' he began, 'we should start with Prudence Holliday. An actress, I guess we should call her, who performed in musicals, mainly in touring productions.'

'I didn't recognise her,' said Libby.

'Neither did I,' said Fran.

'But I believe your friend Judy would have done,' said Ian. 'Prudence was friendly with Fenella, Lady Howe, who also had a theatrical background. She was introduced to Sir Percy and began a relationship. When Fenella died, she moved in.'

'Yes, Dotty Barton told me that,' said Libby.

'Prudence was a gambler. The company who employed Trevor Taylor sent him after her, and, as far as we can tell, he reported to Matthews, who was a client of the debt collection company. She recognised Prudence's name. And so, when she extended her property empire to Nethergate, after having been made aware of its potential through her cousin, Eric, she naturally got in touch and threatened to inform the relevant authorities that Prudence was a fraud.'

'Where do Sergeant Powell and Asa Marten come in?' asked Guy.

'Powell made it his business to make contact with anyone in the area who might be operating under the radar, shall we say. Taylor was one of those, and Powell, for the consideration of keeping him out of prison, set Marten to "look after" him. Constance took Marten over, and when Prudence lost her head – and battered Matthews – Powell, again for a consideration, only this time financial, offered assistance. Marten – who is singing like the proverbial canary – moved Matthews' body. And when Taylor went to see Prudence and threatened to go to the police, Marten killed him, too.'

'Blimey!' said Libby. 'I suppose it does all make sense in a tortured kind of way, but what a pity about the Howe Estate.'

'I wouldn't worry,' said Ian. 'Now we've got hold of the wills, we can trace the legitimate heir to Howe, who turns out to be a second cousin or something, and I have no doubt Prudence's plans will be carried out. Except perhaps for the main house. He – or she – might want to live there.'

'What about Connie's will?' asked Fran.

'No heirs are mentioned, so it becomes property of the Crown,' said Ian.

'Oh, yes – bona something,' said Libby.

Guy choked.

'So that's that,' said Ben. 'All very sad. Prudence wasn't a bad person, really.'

'No – Dorothy Barton said she wasn't.' Libby stared into her glass. 'And it is. Very sad.'

'Murder usually is,' said Ian.

'Even when the victims are unpleasant.' Fran sighed.

'Dorothy Barton said that, too.' Libby nodded.

'I think we must meet this lady,' said Ben.

'I think she's coming to visit Steeple Martin,' said Libby. 'I shall introduce you all.'

'And meanwhile, Libby is going to start on the famous Steeple Martin pantomime and will have no time whatsoever for looking into murders.' Ian stood up and raised his glass. 'Cheers!'

Acknowledgements

Thank you first to Toby Jones of Headline, for continuing to publish Libby and Fran's adventures. To my family for their support, occasional technological expertise, lifts and general encouragement – thank you, Louise, Miles, Phillipa and Leo and of course to The Quayistas: Sophie Weston, Joanna Maitland, Liz Fielding, Sarah Jane Mallory, Louise Allen and Janet Gover, without whose professional friendship and encouragement I doubt I would have written a word. And finally, as always, apologies to the police services of the UK. All mistakes are my own. Mostly.